VICKI KEIRE

ANGEL'S EDGE

GIFTS OF THE BLOOD

CURIOSITY
QUILLS PRESS

A Division of **Whampa, LLC**
P.O. Box 2160
Reston, VA 20195
Tel/Fax: 800-998-2509
http://curiosityquills.com

ISBN 978-1-62007-358-2 (ebook)
ISBN 978-1-62007-359-9 (paperback)
ISBN 978-1-62007-360-5 (hardcover)

TABLE OF CONTENTS

to Emma

my favorite blank page

PROLOGUE

The girl hurried home, her dark hair haphazardly secured at the nape of her neck. Wavy tendrils escaped and framed a softly sweet face. Her gentle prettiness was at odds with the sharp, purposeful way she walked. Her long legs traversed the ground like a person with a low tolerance for nonsense. Although moonlight seeped through the trees and scattered the ground with strips of light and shadow, she paid it no mind. She took this path through the park often; her feet knew the way. Her gray eyes carried the far-away look and pinched narrowness of a chronic worrier.

Liquid silver lurked underneath the gray of those eyes, marking her heritage for any of my kind to see. She wasn't my target, but I was becoming obsessed with her.

I'd been watching her for days. She carried the thick slow scent of death upon her; not her own, but that of someone so close to her it had sunk in soul-deep. And even though she carried on with what passed for a normal life of work, school, bills, and friends, it wouldn't be long now.

Soon, my part in this terrible business would be over, and she would be alone.

I knew she would be in even worse danger then. Her heritage made her a valuable enough commodity, but the fact that she was female, and of gifted blood, made her a rare prize indeed. Others would come for her, and there would be a fight. The question was, what would I do about it after my job here was done? What could I do? My kind wasn't allowed to interfere. I melted back into the shadows, still watching her, more obsessed than ever.

She paused before the entrance to the building where she lived, dropping the key as she juggled two bags of groceries shoved under one arm. She stared at the key on the ground, making no move to retrieve it. I realized her entire upper body was shaking, her head bowed while strands of her long dark hair obscured her face.

I tried to stifle the alarm coursing through me. What was wrong with her? Was she cold? A lot of the humans she had interacted with tonight were wearing light coats or long sleeves, and she wore only jeans and a t shirt. I ran my fingers absently down the front of my leather jacket, wishing for a moment that I could give it to her. But that would be stupid. It would mean revealing myself, and besides, even though the cold didn't bother me, I needed it more than she did.

Or maybe she was hurt, suffering some hidden injury that made it impossible for her to bend over and retrieve the key. She wasn't my target, but suddenly I had to know. If she were hurt… I didn't know what I would do about it, could do about it. But I knew I would do something. No matter what it cost me later.

I moved to the shadows spilling from the alley next to her building. I knew she wouldn't see me; she didn't know creatures like me even existed, let alone were watching her. I'd never seen such a lost look on anyone, not in all my centuries of guarding souls. Her face was slick and wet, but she made no move to stop the tears. And then, after a moment of giving in to her grief, she squared her shoulders, wiped her face with the back of her hand, and retrieved the key. When she straightened, she took a deep breath, collecting herself before a small, labored smile appeared on her face.

I knew it was a look she wore solely for her brother's benefit.

It was also the bravest thing I had seen in centuries. And with that one act of strength, I knew two things at once: I would do anything to protect her from the coming storm, even if it cost me everything. And it would.

I was Falling.

CHAPTER ONE

AN ASSIGNMENT

The weather had just turned from unbearably hot to cool with occasional gusts of frigid as I sat with my sketchbook, trying to capture the change of seasons within its pages. The gathering chill made the sky clearer than the muggy haze of full summer; the warm palette of autumn leaves draped the trees every shade of red from blush to blood. I gripped my chunk of graphite, determined to get the assignment exactly right, and looked out over the St. Clare River.

Autumn was the time of year when my brother Logan and I pulled out long sleeves and boots for the first time and tramped through the woods together, just as we did with our parents before they died four years ago. The woods surrounding Whitfield became our own private, living cathedral. We filled our pockets with its offerings: quartz, oddly shaped pieces of wood, a feather. We linked hands just before sunset and took turns talking to our parents about our lives as we walked. Logan always said he felt them more strongly in the woods than in the graveyard. Then we'd rush home, racing the darkness, and drink hot chocolate and fight over the remote until one of us fell over, dead asleep.

But not this fall. Things were different. Darker. There was no time for long walks through the woods, and no energy even if time could be found. At night, the stars were sharp as paper cut outs in indigo parchment. The crickets and cicadas had a spectacular backdrop against which to sing their last songs of the year. With luck, I could snatch a few minutes to watch night fall over Blind Springs Park as I sprinted between school, work, and home. This fall, I was a freshman at Andreas Academy of Fine Arts with an almost full-time job at the coffee shop two buildings down from our apartment. It didn't cover all the bills, but it did help keep us in health insurance. Things like insurance were actually important to me now. I kept the local bookstore steadily supplied with hand-painted tarot card decks for extra cash, and did all the other things running a household required that Logan couldn't. Which was almost everything.

This fall, Logan had cancer. I watched it leach his brown eyes and his tall, compact carpenter's body of life and vitality as surely as the approaching winter would rob the forest of color and life.

My brother's once strong, sure hands trembled when he did something as simple as open a stubborn jar of pickles. His kind brown eyes were constantly ringed with purplish bruises. Logan, always so active, now had to sit down and rest halfway up the stairs to our third floor apartment. The chemotherapy affected his scent, somehow. I didn't really notice, but our cat Abigail sure did. When Logan came home from a session, she paced the floor and yowled, bewildered as to why he didn't look, smell, or act like her beloved person. That killed him. Abigail was his baby.

Worst of all, there was nothing I could do about any of it. I felt so powerless and angry most of the time. Logan had been eighteen when our parents died. I'd been fifteen. We were barely old enough to live on our own, but we tried. We took care of each other. Now I wasn't yet nineteen, and I was doing my best to take care of everything while inside, I was falling apart.

So when my so-called gift decided this was the perfect time to make its reappearance, I shouldn't have been surprised. Everything else was coming unglued. Why not my head, too?

I was sitting on a wrought iron bench, graphite in hand, overlooking the St. Clare River, when I sketched a piece of my future. I'd been drawing the future for as long as I could hold a crayon.

"It's a gift of your blood, Caspia," my grandmother used to insist. She was the only one to speak to me about it, this "gift of my blood," back before she died. My family knew I had a strange ability, but no one else talked about its origins. "You'll see," she always said, examining the symbols or pictures that seemed to come from nowhere and always frightened me. "You just drew a vision of your future, honey."

She was right. Every single drawing came true.

It's not as dramatic as it sounds. It's not like I draw lottery numbers or predict world disasters. Sometimes, it's as mundane as a really bad grade or a burned roast that sets off the smoke alarm. Sometimes it's good things, like picnic-perfect weather or when I drew a picture of our neighbors, who thought they couldn't have children, with a pair of smiling twins.

But sometimes, I drew very dark things. Like Grandmother's death. Or Logan, thin as a rail and sick in a hospital bed. The fire across the street that killed our neighbor's dogs. The happy family where things got broken and people bruised behind closed doors. Some things I still don't understand. Either they haven't come to pass, or they're just gibberish.

That autumn afternoon, when I drew a strange and furious man less than a dozen feet away from me, I was hoping for gibberish.

I was supposed to be sketching the river. I kept staring at the lines of light and dark across its surface, at the way it seemed to catch on boulders and drag itself around them in great huge ripples like wrinkles in muddy silk. My eyes followed the jagged contours of the distant limestone cliffs. The river below me sheltered fish that leapt, glittering, out of the deep water, and nurtured the lush woodlands that were just now turning the brilliant fiery colors of fall. Every so often, a storm swept through, swelling the St. Clare River and making it angry enough to flood homes or even drown a person.

Powerful. Calm. Sheltering. Beautiful. These were the things I was supposed to be drawing, the things my Drawing II teacher, Dr. Christian, had actually assigned to us. "Go draw the St. Clare River in all its fall splendor," the temperamental Dr. Christian ordered us, shortly after taking roll. A few of the girls actually made quiet sounds of disappointment. That's how drop-dead sexy Dr. Christian was. Even though he'd just given us the day off, probably half the girls would have happily stayed just to look at him.

I wasn't one of them. I loved the weather, and I loved the Riverwalk. I couldn't wait to get started, couldn't wait to lose myself in the sheer joy of creating something out of nothing on the blank page. I was the first one out the door, even though my best friend, Amberlyn, yelled at me to wait. Despite my freakish prophetic ability, or maybe because of it, I lived to draw and paint. And with all that was going on in my life, I was desperate for some physical and mental escape.

And yet I couldn't do it. I couldn't finish a simple assignment like a landscape sketch. I got the basics done quickly enough. Then I started to relax and focus in on the details, like the massive oak on the far bank charred and split by lightening. My fingers moved as if they had tiny minds of their own, drawing the graphite smoothly, fooling my brain into thinking that strange part of me, the part that had been creating prophetic images for as long as I could remember, had gone to sleep or something. But of course it hadn't. It had been months since I'd drawn one of my visions, and it had never happened in public before. Ever. When I looked down at the sketch across my knees, an incomplete but distinct figure that had no business being there stared back at me.

It was male, and I had drawn enough of him to note his protective, even angry stance. He stood with his body squared, his hands loose but steady at waist level, as if he was ready to go for a weapon or block an attack. I'd drawn a dark cloud swirling around him. Soaring planes of light and shapes I couldn't completely make out pierced the dark cloud. The few I could recognize sent my stomach plummeting somewhere south of my ankles: a hand with nails like talons, dripping blood; a shattered knife; a tattered book; a heart-shaped box, smashed to bits. Sleek white lines swirled around the man, whirling with the dark cloud. I squinted. I couldn't tell what they were, if anything. I had only half-drawn his face before I stopped, so he kind of looked like the creepy Twilight Zone character with no mouth. I shivered and zipped my hoodie up all the way.

I had managed to finish his eyes. It was only a charcoal sketch, so I couldn't tell what color they were, but I had done a good job capturing the light in them. His eyes were so light they almost glowed at me out of the charcoal whorls. Narrowed underneath arched brows, his eyes practically sparked with anger. So angry, in fact, that for just a minute I wondered why my drawing didn't catch fire right in my lap.

He stood on the Riverwalk side, a few dozen feet from where I huddled with the rest of my art class against the October breeze. Of course, in reality, there was no one there. No angry mystery man with only half a face glared at me from the banks of the St. Clare River.

Instead, groups of art students, clad in thrift store chic, huddled all along the Riverwalk. Some worked while others goofed off. I had been part of the first group until my freakish ability manifested itself again. After that, I kind of froze in horror. Amberlyn sat with her striped tights pressed up against my knee, bent over her own sketchpad. Like me, she had cut the fingers off a pair of knit gloves to keep her hands warm but still allow her to draw. I had been hoping to finish quickly, with time left over to run home and check on Logan before work. Amberlyn was so into what she was doing that she didn't notice, at first, when I stopped working.

I should have known better. Amberlyn is really, really observant. It's part of what makes her such a good artist. And why she can be such an annoying friend.

"Caspia," she purred, her voice low and throaty like she'd just swallowed honey. "What is that?"

"Well-" I hesitated, not sure what to say. "Um, nothing. No one."

Amberlyn looked at me like I'd insulted her intelligence. I struggled to sound more convincing. "Really. I have no idea who that is. I just made him up." Lame, but true. I tried to cover with a nervous giggle. That was my mistake. I wasn't the giggling type, and Amberlyn knew it.

"Caspia, honey," she drawled, prying the bar of graphite from my fingers. She looked at the crumbling black rod in disgust and threw it in the trashcan the next bench over. I'd snapped it into pieces and ground part of it to dust. "I know you're stressed out. It looks like you just drew a man being eaten by a tornado, or something." She squinted and tilted her head slightly sideways, trying to get a better look. I flipped the drawing facedown so she couldn't see it, trying to look nonchalant about it. She sighed and took my charcoal smeared fingers in her own and massaged them, not caring that I was getting black dust all over her cute pink fingerless gloves. "I just wish you'd tell me if someone's tormenting you so much you need to devour him with an imaginary tornado, instead of doing your homework, no less." She clucked her tongue in mock severity. "I'm trustworthy. I won't even tell Logan," she taunted, emphasizing my brother's name with a wink.

"Oh, God, Amberlyn, shut up!" I squealed. I did not want to think about my best friend and the crush she'd had on my brother since the seventh grade. I jerked my hands away and grabbed the sketchbook from my lap. "It's just… I was just daydreaming, okay? Seriously. There is no one." I started to rip the picture from the book to wad it up, but she stopped me.

"No, wait," she insisted, snatching my sketchbook away. She ignored my squeals. "Daydreaming or not, this is really good, Caspia." She crinkled her perfectly shaped little nose and narrowed her golden-green eyes. "In a Gormenghast meets William Turner kind of way."

"A fantasy-horror landscape painting. That just about sums up my life right now," I moaned, falling back against the bench. My head felt hot and heavy. I let it drop into my hands. "They say there's truth in art." I realized I was near tears.

"Oh, Caspia. Sweetie." She let her golden-brown curls rest against my shoulder. "You know what you need?" Amberlyn snaked an arm around my shoulder. Even in fall, she managed to smell like cocoa butter. "You need a caramel latte with extra caramel. And you need me to buy it for you."

I sat up straight and looked out over the river. School was supposed to be the easy part of my day, and here I was, almost crying. I still had work and chores and homework and Logan. I had better shape up. Then I realized I had just lumped my brother in with chores, and almost started crying again. A sudden chill breeze helped bring me to my senses; I quickly wiped my tears and reached for my knapsack. "I have to check on Logan before I go to work at the place that makes the caramel lattes. Making my own makes it less of a treat," I grumbled.

"Mmm hmm. Just go ahead and be difficult then. Because then I won't have to tell you how much charcoal you just smeared on your face, wiping away your own tears when you had a friend right here to do it for you. And I surely won't have to go buy three extra caramel lattes that someone else made so Logan can have one too and then bring them up to your apartment while you clean yourself up for work."

Amberlyn had already smoothed my incriminating drawing and closed my sketchbook, tying it tightly closed with its black leather cord. She held it with uncharacteristic solemnity. Her golden-brown spiral curls blew all around her café-au-lait skin. In the afternoon light, she looked angelic. I felt suddenly, powerfully alone. We'd been best friends since we both showed up on the first day of junior high with identical cartoon lunch boxes, cementing our eternal torment and instant solidarity all in one day. But my visions were a secret I had never shared. Not even Logan or my parents were comfortable with the subject; Gran had been the only one.

Secrets and pent-up emotions weighed me down. "You don't have to do all that." I started to refuse, but my voice came out in a whine even I was sick of hearing.

"Just promise me two things." I nodded, ready to sign over my first born child for the chance to catch up with Logan, grab a shower, and drink pure sugary sin with my friend before work. Amberlyn slapped me on the forehead with the front of her hand. "Don't be such a martyr. You and Logan are like family." I scowled and rubbed my forehead.

"And the other thing?" I prompted warily, ready to smack her back, if necessary.

She swept her corkscrew curls out of her face with one hand and held my sketchbook out to me with the other. "Don't you dare trash that picture. It's good, Caspia. Really original." I gave her the barest nod before slipping it into my knapsack. A part of me wished it had been my firstborn child after all. She had no idea what that picture represented to me. All my feelings of freakish isolation and impending disaster came bubbling up, threatening to overflow. But then I stopped myself. What if it wasn't bad this time? What if it really was just a picture of some random guy?

I realized then I wasn't afraid of the picture so much as I was of my "gift" reawakening, in public, when everything else was so out of control. But my visions weren't something I could control. Never had been able to. I slung my knapsack across one shoulder and gave Amberlyn a wicked grin. "Try not to get eaten by tornadoes on your way over," I teased. "Logan might actually notice this time."

I tried to dodge the flying object I knew was coming but wasn't quick enough.

CHAPTER TWO

WINTER

I burst through our apartment door, slightly breathless from my sprint up two flights of stairs. We lived two floors above Mr. Moore's tiny hardware store, and one floor above Mr. Moore himself. Jackson Moore had been my father's best friend, and took it upon himself to watch over us after he died. When settling my parents' estate meant selling the turn-of-the-century house Logan and I had been born in, Mr. Moore insisted we take the empty apartment above his. He kept the rent reasonable, and even let Logan and me do some renovations instead of putting down a deposit.

Logan started working odd jobs for him when he was around sixteen. When our parents died, his part-time job grew into a full time job at the hardware store as Mr. Moore's head carpenter. But it had been months since Logan could carry lumber or pound a hammer. So I was learning all kinds of things about insurance, disability, dependants, deductibles, and claims processes until I thought my head might explode. Mr. Moore patiently helped me through all of it. Neither one of us brought up the details with my brother. He had enough to worry about, trying to hang on to his husk of a failing body.

I loved our little apartment. It was just big enough for Logan, Abigail, and me. What it lacked in modern conveniences it made up for in outdated charm, like the oversized claw-footed bathtub, the hand painted kitchen wall tiles, towering ceilings, and ivy-covered patio. It overlooked Whitfield's Old Town Square, with its gorgeous fountain and trees draped with lights year round. I could walk almost anywhere I wanted or needed to be in minutes. Most importantly, it made me feel like I was a part of the city's vibrant beating heart. Whitfield wasn't a big and exciting city. It was definitely Southern and I had lived there all my life, so by rights I should have hated it and been desperate to escape. I didn't. Instead, I felt an intense connection I couldn't exactly put into words. I tried to paint it instead, with varying degrees of success.

"Logan!" I yelled, dropping my knapsack next to the door while I kicked my ratty Chuck Taylors off in two quick, sure movements. "Amberlyn's coming over." My hoodie crumpled onto the gold-varnished wooden floor, missing its hook by inches. I just shrugged and slammed my keys down on top of the bookshelf by the door, knocking several pieces of mail off in the process. "She's bringing delicious beverages," I continued, walking away from the mess I'd made without a second glance. We were both used to my slovenly ways. Logan had given up trying to break me of them long ago. He picked up after my messes, and I did his laundry. "I've got just enough time to grab a shower before work, so if she…"

Logan wasn't listening. He was curled up in a little ball on one side of the sofa, his shoulders rising and falling slowly. Very slowly. A knit navy toboggan covered the tops of his ears and most of his eyes. His bare neck looked pale and graceful in its fragility; I resisted the urge to stroke it. Abigail lay sprawled against as much of him as she could reach, every orange and fluffy inch of her radiating watchful protectiveness. She head-butted me as I leaned over my brother, touching his face, reassuring myself that yes, he was breathing, he was alive.

But he was icy cold to the touch, and the skin under his eyes, even in sleep, looked sunken and hollow. The bones of his face were so sharp, so prominent; it struck me how much weight he'd lost over the last few months. He covered himself in the baggiest clothes these days, so I hadn't really noticed. Or maybe I was just that unobservant. I was failing at this, at taking care of him…

A blurry orange vibration nudged at my hand. I blinked away tears yet again as I petted the purring cat that meowed quietly for my attention. "You're right, Abby," I whispered, pulling an old fleece throw over my sleeping brother. "We'd better not wake him. I'll put a note on the door for Amberlyn, warning her." Abigail flicked her tail in agreement before resuming her position as guardian of Logan's fleece-covered back.

I lingered a moment longer. I knew I had to hurry, that work was waiting, that Amberlyn would come trooping in at any moment like a pack of wild wolves. In the slanted half-light pouring in through our front window blinds, my brother looked like something newborn and delicate, something so vulnerable that the very act of observation might be enough to take him away. I thought of baby rabbits trembling in my hands, of snowflakes melting on coat sleeves, of lightning bugs in mason jars living only until morning. I watched him, hardly daring to breathe, willing myself to memorize this moment when my brother's shoulders brushed too slowly against the fuzzy orange of Abigail the cat.

You're going to lose him soon, a voice whispered deep within my mind. *He's too fragile for this world now. Winter will take him.* I clenched my fists against the truth of it.

"No," I whispered through locked teeth. "I'll fight for him. He's all I have left." I let myself feel the fear, give in to it completely, for the space of several deep, long breaths. Then, because I had no other choice, I let it go.

Under the bay window overlooking Old Town Square stood an antique, mahogany roll top desk that used to belong to my father. We kept our parents' wedding bands, important papers like birth certificates and insurance mumbo jumbo, keepsakes, art, and photographs in it. On the top of its dark surface stood the last picture of the four of us together, surrounded by candles, dried flowers, and whatever odds and ends happened to catch our eye. It was a shrine of sorts, I supposed, although both Logan and I would deny it, if pressed. I went to this picture and lit a half-melted candle.

I wish you could make him better, I thought at the picture, reaching out to touch my parents' smiling faces with two fingers. *I wish… I wish you could help us. There's only me, and I'm not enough.* It was the closest I had come to praying since they died.

I saved my tears for the shower, where they finally took me in great heaving waves, muffled by music and pounding hot water that washed them down the drain.

CHAPTER THREE

A VISITOR

I rinsed off vanilla and brown sugar body scrub as the last bars of "Your Heart to Haunt" faded away. Perfect. I had given myself exactly two songs to shower. No time to soak; I gave the claw-footed tub an apologetic backward glance as I stepped gingerly, dripping wet and naked, into my room. Lost in thoughts of Logan's illness and my long shift at work, I'd forgotten my towel. I started the playlist over as I pawed through my basket of clean but unfolded laundry, relying on the music to keep me moving even if my thoughts wandered. My dark hair was still wet; droplets gathered on the tips below my shoulder blades. Wispy and fine, it would dry on its own before work.

The unimaginatively named Whitfield Coffee Shop had no set uniform. Brown and beige aprons with the company logo emblazoned right across the chest distinguished us from customers. As long as we were clean and relatively covered, we could wear what we wanted. I dug out my second-best pair of jeans and my Feral Fire t-shirt. The weather was turning. Short sleeves wouldn't be an option much longer.

Amberlyn half-sat, half perched in one of the squashy chairs that flanked the sofa when I crept from my bedroom. Thin bright sheets of metal paper rested carefully across one thigh. Eyes narrowed, pink tongue held tightly in place with her teeth, she concentrated on the last folds of a silver origami crane as if the fate of the world depended on its completion. Her school bag and purse sat stacked in a neat pile on the floor, and her black ballet flats flanked them with almost military precision. Logan hadn't moved since I covered him with the blanket. Crane completed, Amberlyn gestured to a plastic-topped cardboard cup on the coffee table without a word. Eyeing Logan, she offered the delicate silver crane to Abigail, who looked at it with interest, but didn't surrender her post.

"Has he moved at all?" I asked as I took a quick gulp. Oh. My. God. Delicious and still so hot it burned my tongue. The extra-caramel latte was one of my own inventions. I invented almost all the drinks at the coffee shop. My boss, Mr. Markov, was Russian and old with the imagination of a turnip. The extra caramel cinnamon spice latte was our flavor of the week, in honor of the changing seasons. It did taste better because I hadn't made it, though. I closed my eyes as I took another sip and tried to guess which one of my twin coworkers, Amelie or Nicolas, had made it. My guess was Nicolas. Amelie always used too much cinnamon. I crossed to Logan's prone form and debated whether to wake him.

Amberlyn shook her head no. She took in my second-best jeans and my freshly scrubbed face with one swift sideways glance. "I'm going to stay with him." She gestured to a lone cup sitting amongst stacks of papers and dishes on the kitchen table. The motion managed to convey elegant disapproval of my slovenliness. "So I guess there's an extra. Take it with you, in case you run into someone who needs a pick-me-up."

"You don't have to do that. You know he hates being fussed over," I protested as vehemently as I could manage without awakening my brother. "Besides, what if he wakes up and wants one then?"

She rolled her golden-green eyes at me. "Then I'll just run two doors down and get you to make me another one." She grinned. "Or two." Amberlyn settled more fully into the chair and made shooing motions at me. "Look, Caspia. I want to stay. The cable's out at my house, and your maid seems to have quit or something." I made a face at her. She ignored me. Her eyes held a hint of desperation I didn't quite understand until she practically growled, "I'm going to cook something and make him eat it if I have to tie him up and force him."

"Oh, sweetie," I said, reaching for her. Amberlyn didn't have the most stable home life. Her mother was long since happily divorced and even happier when she could come and go as she pleased. My best friend had never lacked for anything material, but hadn't seen her father in over a decade and her mother only when it suited her social calendar. Logan was important to her, too. Over the years, I watched as she navigated the lines among secret crush, hero worship, mature friendship and sometimes, some combination of the three. "I've tried, I swear. I've tried all his favorites. One day we ate nothing but ice cream and peanut butter cookies. It's just a part of it, the weight loss. The doctors say he'll gain it back, afterwards."

She shooed me away again, her tiny fingertips darting, quick as hummingbirds, to catch the tears before they collected on her thick dark lashes. "I know, I know. It's entirely a selfish thing. I just want to make him something myself, and try, you know?" I nodded slowly. I did know. God knows I tried it often enough myself. The results were a lot of leftovers and a very fat Abigail. "And don't you think I'm doing this out of the kindness of my heart," she half-whispered, half-hissed.

"Heaven forbid."

"I need your help in Ceramics. I've gotten really behind."

"How far behind?" I asked suspiciously.

"Far. I could really use a second pair of hands at the studio over the weekend."

I groaned. "We're not supposed to 'help' with each other's models." I utterly loathed ceramics, hated using the slimy, dirty water and sloppy clay, and could never scrub the gray stuff out of my nails entirely. I thought fast. "But if we go over the weekend, maybe at night, we should be ok," I assented.

She let out a pent-up sigh. "Thank God. You know I hate that class as much as you do. Maybe, after we get my stuff caught up, we can get some of our other pieces done together, too. Now go! Shoo!"

"Ok, ok," I grouched, giving my apartment one last longing glance before scooting out the door.

Chapter Four

Fairy Lights

The antique iron clock on the corner gave me another twenty minutes before my shift started. I was not known for being early, and I had an extra caramel latte literally burning a hole in my hand. Living right on the square meant I could visit a dozen people in ten minutes or so. The bakery would be open for another few hours. They'd probably already reduced the price of some of the morning's stock, if there was anything left. I licked my lips speculatively. Mr. Peppers might even be willing to trade some of the morning's goodies for my extra beverage.

Or there was J. Roth, Bookseller. The stuffy, half-crazy old man might have some rare new book, fresh from his travels to a place I'd never heard of. If I smiled sweetly enough, he might even let me leaf through it. If he was traveling, there was always his pink-haired punk rock princess of a niece, Calla, who kept the store stocked with magazines and the latest thrillers. Various restaurants and bars dotted Old Town Square; most stayed open late, some until dawn. Life on the square was eclectic and continuous. I sighed happily and sipped. Whom to grace with my brief presence before work?

Twilight was fading into full dark when I hit the sidewalk in front of Moore's Hardware. I stopped, as I always did, to watch the miracle that was

Old Town Square at night. The fountain turned from an impressive, three tiered stone monument to a brightly shining beacon shooting colored streams of water. Graceful Live Oaks spotted the park at the center of the square. Smaller oaks and pines came to life as darkness brought hundreds of tiny white lights to life in their branches. Fairy lights, my mother called them. I never got tired of watching the daily ritual. Only in darkness could the light be so completely, brightly beautiful.

As much as I loved it, I'd spent precious minutes gawking on the sidewalk, so in the end I decided just to run across the street to Mrs. Alice's store to see if any of my hand-painted tarot card sets had sold. Mrs. Alice had been doing business in Whitfield longer than anyone could remember, and adamantly objected to the term "new age" in conjunction with her store. But that was exactly what she ran; her store sold crystals, herbs, books about all kinds of rituals and religions, candles, incense… the works. But Mrs. Alice insisted she ran an apothecary shop, even though she supplied every self-styled Wiccan and pagan in Whitfield. Ironically, her business partner and great-granddaughter, Cassandra, was a veritable poster child of nouveau hippie chic. Her rippling blond hair hung down past her waist; she wore a different hand-dyed caftan or billowy skirt every day. If the wind was right, I could smell her patchouli cloud from across the square.

My cards were a specialty item and unaccountably popular in a town the size of Whitfield. I usually managed to sell a deck or two a month. They were pricey because I put so much detail into the painting. Selling just two was more than enough to pay the electric and cable bills.

A chill wind hit me as I ran. I'd forgotten to grab my hoodie from its spot by the door. I had no one but myself to blame. If I'd spent thirty seconds putting it back on its hook, I might not have forgotten it now. My t-shirt was thin, short-sleeved, with a deep v-neck; the wind sliced straight through it. Oh well, I reassured myself as I crossed my arms protectively, the drink nestled close in one hand. I'll be inside a warm coffee shop for most of the evening anyway.

I practically sprinted through the door, racing the October chill. Wind chimes caught against the edge of the door and announced my arrival in a smashing crescendo of copper and glass. The faint, papery smell of dried herbs mingled with the stronger aroma of scented candles as I practically skidded across the threshold. Cinnamon. Pumpkin. Apple. Clove. The store smelled like autumn. Dried flowers, braided lengths of grasses and herbs, and strings of crystals hung from the front window. Votive candles flickered in neat little lines on glass shelves in the front window, twinkling and welcoming against the deepening darkness. One soft, butter-colored sofa and two sage green love seats faced the counter in a u-formation. Afghans and quilts laid folded across their backs in sharp triangles. Magazines and workbooks laid scattered about the coffee table. Soft, recessed lighting gave the store a drowsy glow- as if it was one giant candle shining steadily in its western corner of Old Town Square, where it had been since before I was born. Other than the noise of my arrival, the store was silent except for the occasional *pop* of wax. That meant Mrs. Alice herself was minding the store. Cassandra always played some nauseating new age track, complete with whales or dolphins or rainforests.

Mrs. Alice popped up from behind her counter with more speed than any sixty-year-old woman had any business possessing and glared at me. She adjusted her purple glasses and looked with disapproval at my heaving chest, wild hair, and wind-blown cheeks. "Caspia Chastain! What's the matter now? Being chased by wolves? Because you almost blew the glass off my door, running in here like that!"

"Sorry… Mrs. Alice." The fact that I had to catch my breath to speak wasn't helping my case. I smiled as angelically as I could and held up my extra caramel latte, which had cooled slightly but was still on the scalding side of warm. The Coffee Shop insulated their beverages like some banks did their vaults. "I forgot my jacket, so I was running to keep warm." She relaxed just a little, so I held up my peace offering. "Besides, I have to get to work in a few minutes and I had an extra coffee, so I wanted to offer it to you before it got cold." Mrs. Alice, being sixty years old, didn't speak barista, so I kept it simple.

"Well, that was thoughtful, child," she smiled, reaching for the cup. "Mmm. Caramel." She sniffed again. "Cinnamon too, I think." Decades of working with herbs gave her a killer sense of smell. Nicolas used only the faintest hint of cinnamon. Mrs. Alice reached under a side cupboard and pulled out a real china cup. "Your fancy coffees deserve a proper vessel, dear." She took a delicate sip, her pinky finger popping out like an aristocratic flag. "Ah, yes. Just as I thought. Perfect thing to knock off the chill. Would you like a cup, dear?"

"No thank you," I said as politely as I could. "I have to work soon, unfortunately."

She nodded in understanding. "Of course, dear. If that boss of yours didn't have you to invent such delicious creations, he'd be serving plain old black coffee in a sterile white room." It was no secret that Mrs. Alice and Mr. Markov didn't exactly get along. Neither one would breathe a word as to why, though. "Well, he might get as inventive as beige. Oh, before you go," she said, reaching under the counter and produced a fat white envelope. "All five of your decks sold today. My entire stock." My jaw dropped. I took a step toward the counter to steady myself. She reached over and gave me a reassuring pat. "To the same person. I didn't know him. From out of town, I suppose. He says he's a collector, and would be interested in a private commission." She slid the heavy envelope toward me, her clear hazel eyes sharp on mine. "He left his number. I wrote it on the envelope. He paid cash."

I fingered the envelope and swallowed hard. It was a very thick envelope. "Cash?" I squeaked out. "All five decks?" Five decks would pay the rent. With plenty left over. Mrs. Alice nodded solemnly. "But who would buy all five of my decks? And what did he mean, private commission?" I mused out loud.

The questions were partly rhetorical. My mind was already racing ahead, trying to juggle my schedule so that I would have time to paint another deck for Mrs. Alice to stock. She liked to keep one or two, and it took so long to paint them. The idea of a private commission sounded out of my league and slightly scary, so I let that idea simmer. Another part of my mind was dividing up the money in the fat white envelope, paying bills and buying groceries, especially the ridiculous things I hadn't bought in months and months. I imagined imported chocolate bars and spicy Red Rock ginger ales and fancy canned cat food with spoiled purebred Persians on the labels. I'd get a real down comforter for Logan. I wouldn't even complain when Abigail got orange fur on it.

Part of my mind was filling up the car with gas. It was still warm enough to take a quick road trip to the ocean. Logan loved the sea. He wasn't supposed to be around a lot of people, but I would get around that. I would pack our food and pump our gas so he wouldn't have to go in restaurants or gas stations. I would personally chase everyone away from our spot by the waves, creating a people-free zone of sand just for Logan where he could lounge under an umbrella while I read to him. I would just go up to people and politely say, "Excuse me, but would you mind moving a bit over there? My brother is sick, and the doctors say being around people might make him sicker, but he loves the beach so much, and I'm afraid that next summer he might… he might not… be here…."

I couldn't see the fat, white envelope full of money anymore. The thick paper was smooth underneath my drumming fingertips, but I couldn't see it. Everything was blurry and light. I was choking and someone was making a strange whimpering sound. The envelope underneath my fingers had torn into ribbons; someone had shredded it. Mrs. Alice was trying to take it from me, but I couldn't see her. Something was wrong with my eyes. Surprisingly strong perfumed arms pulled me down to the sofa. "I know, dear," Mrs. Alice said simply, rubbing the back of my neck in soothing circular motions as I realized the whimpering was coming from my own throat. "I know."

"It's too late," I sobbed. "For money. Too late for it to make a difference. For him." I clung to Mrs. Alice. I don't know why the sight of all that money pushed me over the edge. It was money, after all. It meant, at the very least, that I could take a few days off from work. I could spend some more time with Logan. I could spend some time resting, relaxing. We could get take out and watch bad movies late into the night. But the thought of resting, of not driving myself like a machine, finally clicked the last puzzle piece into place.

I was working myself ragged so I didn't have to face up to how bad things really were.

Nothing on earth would help my brother recover. No matter how hard I worked, no matter how much money or energy or effort I threw into making him better, it was out of my hands. Lilacs engulfed me, blocking out the scent of herbs, and soft cotton grazed my cheek as Mrs. Alice rocked me, making soothing noises. I was beyond embarrassed as the reality of the situation hit me and I cried like a toddler. I was losing him. He was too fragile for this world. All I could do was make my peace with him and try to make him comfortable and content. I should be happy with that. It was more than we had with my parents, who had been taken so suddenly. It was more than most people got. I lost track of how long I let myself rest on Mrs. Alice's lavender colored dress before I pulled away and scrubbed my raw, snotty face with my hands. I opened my mouth to apologize, and she opened hers at the exact same moment, probably to tell me everything was going to be fine or to offer some other kind of grandmotherly comfort.

"Your grief," a soft, wondering voice interrupted. "The depth of it is shocking. I don't know how you can bear it, and live." The voice came from the depths of the store, preceding its owner into the light. The words were low and quiet, but there was steel there too. I thought of smoke and honey, of minerals and snow. It was a voice that beckoned and promised safety, even as it warned away.

Then he stepped into the light and up to Mrs. Alice's counter. The stranger looked down and away, as if not quite daring to study me. His designer clothes marked him as someone who wasn't from Whitfield. His black leather jacket was cut like a blazer, covering a shirt and pants that were soft heather gray. His hair was dark brown shot through with threads of gold, and it stuck up in all kinds of crazy directions like he'd just clutched it in disgust or despair. The stranger's lips were tight and twisted. I wished he would loosen them so I could memorize them, so I could draw him later, this person with warnings on his lips and troubles everywhere else. Thickly fringed lashes rested against smooth skin and high cheekbones. My fingers literally itched for graphite.

And the rest of me tingled as if I had been electrified. I scrambled away from Mrs. Alice, who had gone strangely quiet and still beside me. I was acutely aware of this person's presence, of the way my body reacted to him even before his words registered in my mind. Some force pulled me to him, like a magnet drawn true north or a starving person discovering a food so delicious it satisfied hunger simply by smelling it. I belatedly remembered he had asked me a question. It was a strange question, one that pierced through the emotion swirling inside of me, forcing me to focus to answer him. My throat raw, I managed to croak, "I bear it because there's no one else. We only have each other." My fingers curled around the edges of the butter-colored sofa; I balanced on the very edge, leaning toward this man with my entire body, straining for a closer look. But he kept his head down and away.

Something in me roared and snarled, something primal that I suddenly wanted to put back in its box. I realized I was looking at the only stranger Whitfield had seen in months. The stranger who must have bought all five of my tarot decks. "Is that why you did it?" I prompted when he remained still and silent. "Bought all my cards? Because you heard about the poor girl with the dying brother, and felt sorry for us?" I couldn't keep the anger out of my voice then, although I tried. I worked hard not to be anyone's charity case. The idea that a total stranger had heard about our predicament and felt sorry enough for me to buy all my decks and still want a private commission… whatever that entailed…

His hands formed into fists against the glass counter and he closed his eyes tightly. Whatever heightened senses this man triggered within me flamed and roared. His body was taut, radiating anger; his rage was like cinnamon and sour wine. The air around us became thick with faintly shimmering air and a sweet smell so heavy it was almost unpleasant. I had been shivering only minutes before. Now, I was hot even in my thin t-shirt. He kept his head bowed as he struggled for control. His words, when they finally came, were strangled thunder. "It's true I know of you and your… brother. But I didn't buy your tarot cards, nor do I have need of a private commission," he snarled. He almost choked on the phrase, as if he found the idea obscene. My eyebrows shot up, and Mrs. Alice stirred uneasily beside me. My brain had time to wonder who had bought them, and what scandalous other thing might be wanted from me. I wondered if it paid well. He actually growled then. "I had no idea, when I came, of the grief you carry, the depth of your love. It seems a sick, cruel thing, that your love for him tortures you, as well. I'm not pleased."

Before I could ask him what the hell he was talking about, he finally looked at me. Lifted his head and really looked at me.

His eyes. I recognized them.

I had drawn them just a couple of hours ago.

I couldn't help it; I screamed. Coffee just short of scalding exploded from my hand and pooled on the floor, my crushed cup tumbling after it. I backed slowly away from the sofa, from Mrs. Alice, from the man with the light, glowing eyes. He stood perfectly still, watching me with a mixture of concern and despair. Dimly, through the roar of pounding blood and adrenaline, Mrs. Alice called my name, telling me to be careful, to take my money, but I ignored her. I ignored everything but the stranger's eyes on me as my back hit the door, easing it open, feeling the cold rush in and wrap itself around my body as I inched backward out of the store like frightened prey.

He held out a hand as if he would stop me, but he didn't move. "Caspia. Wait. Please."

My name from his lips was like white lightning straight to my brain. He knew me. I had drawn him, and here he was, in front of me and talking. But as if that wasn't bad enough, now he knew who I was, too? Knew things about me? This had never happened before; it couldn't be happening now. "How the hell do you know my name?" I yelled. "How are you even here?" Air whooshed past me and I realized I was falling. The door had opened behind me; my heel caught the doorframe, dumping me on the cold concrete. My head slammed into the ground but I kept going, kept crawling backward, too shocked to register the pain. "How can you know my name when I only drew you a few hours ago?"

Then he was leaning over me, his warm hand on my forehead, his eyes the same intense light of my sketch. "Caspia," he said again, as if repeating a name he had no business knowing would upset me any less. "I didn't come here to frighten you." He was close, now. He was so close I could see the delicate arch of the eyebrows that had been so angry in my sketch. I could count each individual eyelash, had I wanted to; his eyes, nothing but light and fury in my drawing, were the lightest blue-green, more a tint than a color. I skittered backward, scraping my palms and my side against cold concrete, desperate to get away from him. From this drawing come to life, and what that might mean. It was bad enough I was drawing visions again. But not only had this one come true, it seemed to know my name, my life-all about me. And now he had come for me. In my haste to get away a ripping sound tore through the air, but I kept going.

My terror confused him. His eyebrows drew together tightly. I don't remember seeing him move, but somehow, he knelt right beside me on the concrete. His hand encircled my wrist, a band of steel, and I whimpered at the strength of him. The bones in my hand twisted against each other as he held me. I pulled, but it was like trying to escape solid stone. Skin and tendons pulsed with hot pain against grinding bones, and still I tried to escape him. He looked beyond confused as I whimpered; helplessness lurked as his eyes darted over me, checking me for damage. Fear became the dominant emotion as he realized I was whimpering in pain as much as terror. He looked at my hand in his, swollen, now, and red. He let go abruptly. With a confusion in his light eyes that now echoed mine, he reached out with his other hand and brushed my eyelids with the pad of his thumb, making them heavy, so heavy…

White. Everything was white and heavy and warm. I slept without dreaming.

Chapter Five

In the Shadows

I woke surrounded by feathers.

Warm, soft, and slightly springy, I burrowed deeper into my imitation down comforter. I loved my bed with its rounded oak frame, its sheets with obscenely high thread counts, its piles of pillows and blankets that didn't match. My bed was about comfort, not coordinating. It wasn't even a bed so much as a nest; I sleepily wished I could spend a whole day in it, emerging only to forage for food and make brief treks to the bathroom. How much time did I have left before the alarm went off again and I had to get up or be late for school? Snooze button, I resolved drowsily, burrowing deeper into my cocoon of soft warmth. If it wasn't Dr. Christian's class today, I'd hit snooze. He was so uptight. I didn't understand why all the girls thought he was so… attractive… Next to the curve of my spine, the mattress dipped with someone's body weight. I smelled familiar juniper and cedar aftershave. Logan.

"Mmmph," I objected halfheartedly when cold hands tried to dig me out of my burrow. "Too early for school, Logan. Go 'way."

The hands paused before withdrawing entirely. I still smelled the aftershave I had given him last Christmas, so I knew he hadn't left. Despite my best efforts, I was slowly waking up anyway. Some part of me suspected I really didn't want to do that. "Caspia," he finally said, patting where he thought my head would be underneath the comforter. He managed to bang my nose. "Hey. What time do you think it is right now?"

The question was strange. Didn't he know? Wasn't there a clock? "Um. I'm not sure. Early?" The voice he used alarmed me even more than the question itself. He spoke with the careful, even cadences of someone addressing a child, or a crazy person. With a sinking feeling, I scrambled to get out of my self-inflicted wrappings, sitting straight up to stare at him in the pitch dark. I couldn't see the clock. Logan looked deathly pale in the wash of moonlight through my big bay window. It was the only light in the room.

His dark eyes glittered in deepest shadow under his baseball cap, making it difficult to see his exact expression. Only the slant of his mouth told me he was worried. He reached out long, pale fingers and skimmed my hair back from my eyes. His touch on my cheek was slow, almost languid, like all his movements these days. His fingers were cold, but the gesture warmed me anyway. Even his smallest touches spoke volumes. Little gestures were really all he had left. "You don't remember, then? What happened?" He lay back against the headboard with a sigh of frustration. The glitter under his baseball cap disappeared. He must have closed his eyes. "How about your hand? How does it feel now?"

"My hand?" I echoed into the quiet air, trying to pull my thoughts together without success. I looked down at myself in the moonlight. The blankets had fallen away to my waist. My skin, pale and abraded in the dimness, peeked through a gap in my t-shirt where the side had ripped from hem to waist. A bandage encased my wrist from knuckle to forearm. I tried to bend it, experimentally, and a sharp pain shot through my arm as my wrist met the resistance of bandages and a splint. I yelped. "Ow! Holy hells, Logan!" The entire evening came flooding back to me as I stared at my injury. Caramel latte; Mrs. Alice; selling all five tarot decks; total stranger; me, screaming my head off, crawling backward, trying to get away from…

…from a total stranger with inhuman strength who knew my name and approached me in Mrs. Alice's store who had come from a sketch I'd drawn earlier this afternoon. I exhaled like someone punched me in the stomach, and then grabbed my brother with my good arm.

"Caspia?" he asked, alarm plain in his voice now. "Are you all right? Should I get someone? Amberlyn?"

"No! Logan! Listen. This is very important." I pulled him close, trying to keep my voice level and low. After the way I acted earlier, the entire town probably thought I was insane, but it was vital Logan take me seriously. "I was at the Riverwalk today, and I—

"I thought you were supposed to be in class," he interrupted. I heard the reprimand, barely suppressed by his concern.

"Dr. Christian told us to go draw the St. Clare River. So we did. Except I didn't. I mean, I did. I tried. At first. And then, it happened. You know. It." I gave him a gentle poke in the ribs, expecting him to understand me. We didn't talk much about how I sometimes drew the future. He knew it happened, but Grandmother had been the only person who seemed really comfortable discussing it with me. Since her death, I almost never spoke of it, and I was at a loss as to how to do so now. Logan shifted uncomfortably.

"It?" he echoed.

"Yes! It!" I finally exploded. I poked him again. He flinched away and I pulled back, angry that I might have caused him pain. "I drew someone," I finally admitted, reluctant, afraid he wouldn't believe me. I needed him to believe me. There was no one else.

"You're not making any sense," he snapped back.

"It's not supposed to make any sense! It never does!" I flopped back down on my bed, frustrated that I couldn't communicate with him. I couldn't make him understand the significance of something I didn't fully understand myself. I just knew it was important, and I had a bad feeling about it. I sat up, ignoring the scrape where my shirt had torn, and tried again. "Only it wasn't an 'it' this time. It was a person, a guy, the very same guy from Mrs. Alice's store, so when he walked up to us and started talking, naturally I freaked out."

When I tried explaining things from the safety of my bedroom, however, the incident didn't sound quite so desperate. I had freaked out because a stranger had tried to talk to me. I had severely overreacted and was being childish, Logan probably thought. That, or he was convinced I was having a break down. I had to make Logan understand the truth: that one of my visions had not only come true, but was now actively stalking me.

Logan was silent for several long breaths. His slim pale fingers drummed impatiently against his jeans. It meant he was thinking, trying to digest. It meant he was trying to phrase his words carefully, using the good communications skills our dad, a therapist, had drilled into us. "I'm hearing you say…" he started. I gritted my teeth in annoyance. Logan threw up his hands. "Oh, to hell with it. I'm still confused. You freaked out because some guy started talking to you? And what does Amberlyn and the Riverwalk and skipping school have to do with it?"

I leapt out of bed, infuriated. I was wearing the same outfit I'd left the house in, minus my socks. "I was not skipping school!" I yelled as my bare feet hit the carpet. "I was supposed to be drawing the river, but I drew…" Too late, I realized how wobbly I was. I felt as if I had been given a sedative of some kind to make me sleep so deeply, at the wrong time of day. What had the stranger done to me, and what other abilities might he have? My legs buckled underneath me, pitching me into my closet on my side. I silently blessed my slovenly ways as a pile of clothes on the floor cushioned my fall. I followed this almost instantly with a scream of pain when I instinctively tried to push myself up with my injured right hand. Logan's arms reached for me, pulling me up in the darkness, but I pushed him away. I didn't want to strain him any more than I already had. Plus, I was mad at him.

"Caspia," he said, a note of pleading creeping in. "I'm worried about you. You went hysterical and passed out right on the square. You're hurt and not making sense. You scared the hell out of me."

A familiar soft sigh floated into the room over his shoulder. "Me too, Caspia," Amberlyn seconded. "No one could get any sense out of you. Mrs. Alice said you went from crying to hysterical in less than a minute, and after you got nothing but good news, too. Thank goodness she was there to dress your arm; you burned it when you crushed your coffee cup. And if that nice guy hadn't been there to help carry you back here, I don't know what we would have done."

I sputtered in my closet. I absolutely ached to tell Logan I had drawn a stranger standing in a storm of talons, blood and planes of light by the St. Clare River earlier today, but doing so would mean letting Amberlyn know all about my freakish ability. I didn't need her to think insanity was a permanent condition of mine; bad enough she thought it a temporary one. I kicked a pile of clothes in frustration and tried another route. "What nice man? The one who just came up out of nowhere and knew all about me in Mrs. Alice's store? That nice young man? He's the one who upset me in the first place! He did this to my arm! Logan, I've been trying to tell you!" I fumed. Logan went rigid. Something in his face, his stance, even in the deep shadows of my darkened room, made my insides freeze and my body still. Logan looked more than just shocked; he was hiding something. Years of silent communication between siblings warned me he had a secret. Well, I had one, too. I desperately needed to get him alone. I began to pace.

"Oh," Amberlyn said softly from over Logan's shoulder. "Mrs. Alice didn't say anything about that, Caspia." She twisted a huge rose quartz ring on her delicate finger. "Are you sure? You were really upset, you know. Nobody blames you; we even kind of expected it, actually." She and my brother exchanged quick, guilty looks. I suppressed a surge of annoyance. They'd been talking about me, then. Behind my back. "You've been pushing yourself so hard, and been under so much strain," she began, her voice softening as she retreated underneath her curtain of spiral curls. "We were worried about you."

Logan's stance had gone from confused to protective in the space of a breath. "Amberlyn's right. We thought maybe you were just over-stressed or something. Mrs. Alice told us about selling all your cards, and how much it upset you." He gave me a reassuring squeeze. "It just didn't make sense, that a big sale would upset you so much."

"It wasn't the sale," I insisted, drawing on reserves of patience I didn't know I possessed. My mind raced ahead, planning ways to get Amberlyn out of the apartment as fast as possible so I could tell Logan about the vision and show him my sketch. Then he'd have to believe me. "It was…" I took a deep breath. "Look, you're just going to have to trust me on this. That guy scared me, ok? You have a point about me being over-stressed and all of that, but if you're looking for a catalyst, he's it."

That guilty, furtive look traveled quickly between my brother and my best friend again. They didn't believe me. I groaned. My hands curled automatically into fists. I shrieked when my right wrist twisted in pain; I had forgotten about my injury. I sagged against the doorframe, feeling the impact of my day fully hit me. It didn't matter what I did or said; they didn't believe me, and they wouldn't, unless I showed them. I needed a bath and fresh clothes. I wanted food and ibuprofen. Eventually, Amberlyn would finish plotting with my brother behind my back and leave so I could show him my drawing and explain that I wasn't crazy. I didn't care what the whole town thought of me, as long as Logan knew I was all right. I tried to push past them, but Amberlyn blocked my way.

"You're not going to like this, Caspia," she said, her voice low and serious, her hand against my shoulder firm.

"What?" I growled suspiciously.

She sighed. "Well, see, we needed help."

"So?"

"So. He brought you here."

"You said that already." I tried to push past her again. Her other arm shot out. She was smaller than me. I thought about shoving past her anyway, but something in her golden-green eyes stopped me. Logan stepped between us.

"He's still here," my brother said. "The man from Mrs. Alice's shop."

I froze. "What?" I ground out.

"He clearly had medical training," Logan rationalized. "It seemed like a real blessing, actually. It was him or the paramedics. And please don't take this the wrong way, but we didn't want to make any more of a scene than we already had. It just seemed like the easiest thing." Logan eyed me anxiously, as if waiting for another explosion.

Part of it didn't matter; half the town had seen or heard me yelling, and the other half would hear about it soon enough. I could look forward to a new life as Crazy Caspia, Whitfield's newest freak. But then Logan had said… "He's here?" I croaked, hugging myself as my brother's words fully registered. "Right now? In this apartment?" I looked wildly at the two doors leading out of my bedroom, and wondered which one he lurked behind.

"Frightening Caspia was the last thing I wanted to do," said a voice like smoke and honey. It came from the shadows between my wingback reading chair and my sagging, overstuffed bookshelf. I stopped breathing. He must have slipped in through the hallway door. I hadn't heard a sound. Warmth radiated from the shadows; my brother and my best friend angled their bodies toward it. Even I caught myself straining forward, and I was terrified. "She was so upset when I first saw her," he said as the lightest pair of blue-green eyes I'd ever seen came closer. "I walked right up to her as if she already knew me. I just wanted to help." He turned the full force of his presence on me while I tried to both shrink into the closet and remember to breathe. "But I only made things worse. I pushed her to talk to me. Add that to the shock of her biggest sale ever, on top of all the other strain she has been under, and of course she lashed out at me. Rightly so." He bowed slightly at the waist, keeping his eyes locked on mine the entire time. "I'm grateful I have the chance to apologize. Again."

I kept my eyes locked on his, but fought the urge to retreat further into the closet. His explanation sounded good. Too good. My eyes narrowed. Probably because, like most lies and evasions, it was grounded in truth; he had done all those things. Except he was leaving out one huge, important part: he'd walked out of a drawing knowing too much about me to be a mere stranger. He was hiding who, or what, he really was. Ooh, I needed Logan to myself for just a minute or two.

"Oh, you've done more than enough," I said through clenched teeth. "No apologies needed."

"Very well, Caspia," he exhaled. Ice and green leaves. Effervescence and wind. Logan didn't move. Why wasn't anyone else reacting as I was? Couldn't anyone else sense his strangeness? An automatic, primal protectiveness flared deep within as Logan stood, an unwitting barrier between this stranger and myself. I prowled closer, my stomach against my brother's back, my injured arm resting on his shoulder. I hid my exposed side against his bulky dark sweatshirt. Eyes the color of a secluded spring-fed pool watched Logan and I steadily. "The burns are superficial," the interloper said calmly. "The herbalist treated them well. Your wrist is most likely sprained, but you might want to get it x-rayed if it doesn't improve after a couple of days. Keep it elevated."

I snorted.

"That means a sling," Logan lectured. I rolled my eyes. A sling. Yeah, right. But then the rest of the conversation penetrated.

"A couple of days?" I repeated. "How am I supposed to make left-handed lattes?" My thoughts skittered sideways, away from the strangeness in front of me, latching on to the mundane reality of things like bills and food. "I have to work," I murmured, clinging more tightly to Logan. "And what about school? I can't draw left-handed, and something tells me Dr. Christian won't care."

"Relax. I called Markov. The twins both said they'd cover for you," my brother told me. He leaned backward. He wanted to shield me, and for just a moment, I was tired enough to let him. "Everybody's been concerned and supportive, Cas. Your job's not going anywhere. When Amberlyn got the call, we ran across the square. Mrs. Alice had something for your burn, and he was evaluating your wrist. Between the two of them, they got it salved, splinted, and wrapped. He carried you all the way here. I'm not strong enough anymore; believe me, I wish…"

"Shh," I cut him off softly. His weight against me was slight, so slight. I thought of him running in the cold wind, my brother who had to rest midway up the stairs to our apartment. I imagined him seeing me, motionless on the ground, trying unsuccessfully to lift me, seeing what hell that must have been. Blue-green eyes glowed steadily at me from the dark of my room, peering into me; forcing me, in turn, to see. Not strong enough. The winter will take him, a tiny voice whispered in the back of my mind. "No," I whispered to the stranger across the room. "No, Logan, you're fine." Twin blue-green glowing orbs stared back at me, unblinking and unconvinced.

"Of course I'm fine," Logan agreed, turning to pull me close in a tight hug. He was more sweatshirt than muscle, but he put his entire body into the hug. I leaned into him gratefully. "Everything's fine, Caspia," he murmured, petting my hair like he'd done since we were kids. "You should get some rest."

"I have to talk to you," I murmured into his chest. "Alone," I added sharply.

"I have to talk to Amberlyn, and help her get her stuff together," Logan promised, easing back with a smile. "But I'm not going anywhere. I live here, remember?"

"I'd like to speak with you as well, Caspia Chastain," said the voice like smoke and honey. "Alone."

Inwardly, I groaned. Of course he would. "I don't even know your name," I said, flinging up the first protest I could think of.

Amberlyn laughed, a quick and light melodious trill. "Ethan told you his name four or five times already, Caspia. You really must have hit your head hard."

"Perhaps I'd better look at it again," the unsettling man allegedly named Ethan said with a frown. Was there anything he hadn't thought of? I stepped backward in alarm, looking wildly at my brother. Logan sighed.

"I'd appreciate that, Ethan. If she'll let you. And thanks again." He paused with his hand on the doorknob and pinned me with a half-accusing, half-exasperated frown. "I'll be just on the other side of the wall if he tries to bandage you to death, Cas." With a shake of his head, he shuffled after my best friend.

Leaving me alone with him.

CHAPTER SIX

INVOLVED

The stranger sighed, running his fingers through his hair, in the darkness while he stared at me. I eyed both exits, calculated his proximity to both of them, and judged my chances of getting past him to be zero. I was acutely conscious of the huge rip in the side of my t-shirt, baring my side to the open air, and to him. I tried to tug the edges of the rip together with my bandaged wrist and winced when it twisted unexpectedly.

He grimaced when I did. "Don't do that! You'll hurt yourself more."

"I figured that out," I snapped. "Why are you still here? I don't care what you have to say to me." I frowned and bit my lower lip because that wasn't exactly true. I was almost as curious as I was alarmed by my drawing come to life. "You pretty much lied to them, letting them think you were just some helpful bystander, and now they think I'm crazy. I don't need that. My brother doesn't need that." I formed each word with careful, angry precision, pacing sideways until I stood in the middle of my room.

He considered my words. "I'm still here because I'm sorry. I want to make sure you're okay. I insist on it, actually. And because I want to know why you're so afraid of me." He raised his hands slightly and spread them open as if to show he wasn't hiding anything. The shadows of my darkened room rippled at his back.

Something strange was definitely going on here. Something stranger than just a drawing come to life. My desire to know overpowered my fear and apprehension.

I took tiny, careful steps backward until I bumped against my refinished thrift store dresser. I grazed my fingers gingerly along its sanded, whitewashed surface until I found my tiny beaded lamp among piles of jewelry, books, candles, and art supplies. He didn't move as I flipped the switch and suffused the room with low light. I tilted my head and looked at him, slowly, trying not to be afraid this time, rationalizing that both Logan and Mr. Mason would come running if I screamed hard enough. I narrowed my eyes and tried to see him as if I might draw him with care and attention, instead of conjuring him wildly from some unknown place in my head. He stood motionless, receptive to my gaze but not relaxed.

My little lamp illuminated only one side of him, casting the other half in shadow. The effect was startling. One half of him practically shone with life and color, while the other seemed stark and cold. Light fighting shadow, darkness threatening order; he was a creature at war with himself. His blue-green eyes were the color of oceans; streaks of gold flecked his brown hair. Even his skin looked faintly golden. The lines of his features demanded pencil rather than coarse graphite or charcoal. His lips called for a series of soft, feathery curves to capture the lines properly. His cheekbones and jaw needed firm straight angles to convey their strength. A bit of shading over the cheeks and chin would soften the features and show the hint of vulnerability, of confusion hidden there. In the shadowy half-light of my bedroom, I saw that my earlier sketch had gotten everything wrong, given only a hint of his appearance. No wonder Amberlyn didn't recognize him.

"I don't know what you are, other than a sign I don't understand yet," I finally admitted. "But what's more important, I don't know what you mean." He merely raised an eyebrow at me. I raised a finger to silence him before he could interrupt me. "Look, I'm really bad at articulating this, so just bear with me." I took a deep breath. "Sometimes, I draw the future."

I waited for the explosion, for the laughter, but he merely stood there, nodding, waiting for me to finish. Like I'd announced the time, or that I wanted waffles for breakfast. I waited another minute to see if the explosion was going to be delayed, but he just stood there, watching me serenely with those blue-green eyes of his.

"Ok, then," I continued doubtfully. "So, earlier today, instead of drawing my art assignment, I drew you."

Still no explosion, only expectant waiting.

"In a storm of darkness and these huge planes of light and some really creepy symbols like bloody talons and a broken knife and a smashed heart." I thought back, trying to remember. "Oh, and you were angry. Thermonuclear angry. You looked ready to fight. Or maybe defend. Or both."

That got a reaction, but not the one I was expecting. I blinked, and suddenly he was in my face. I mean, one second he was over by my door, and the next, he was right in front of me. I didn't see him move. His warm hands gripped me around the waist, their heat and texture against my bare skin enough to chase away any thoughts not of him and us and now. My injured side, scraped against concrete when I struggled against him, flared with pulsing heat where my raw skin met his. His touch was surface-soft, but I could sense the bruising strength underneath, like granite wrapped in velvet. I was breakable, and in that instant we both knew it. His hold on me was so precise and careful the rest of him seemed a mere extension of the contact between us. Taut with the effort of holding me without hurting, his eyes locked on mine as the universe narrowed to his voice alone.

"I didn't mean to hurt you." Soft and layered like whispered echoes through mist, his words wrapped around me like a warm cocoon. "I wasn't supposed to get involved." His entire face twisted in confusion, and I saw, again, a being cast half in shadow, half in light. "When I touched you… it was without thought, or preparation. I hurt you through my carelessness. There will be… repercussions." The desperation of an unreleased apology hid in his eyes; it lurked there like an unfamiliar and unwelcome weight. He studied me, warmth pulsing from his hands at my sides. Then he let me go. The heat, the welcome quiet in my mind—all of it vanished when he released his careful hold. A single soft brush of fingertips up my exposed side ended with my bandaged hand cradled between his cupped palms.

Everyday reality came crashing back in: Logan speaking in a low voice in the other room over medium-loud music, traffic on the street, Abigail twining herself through my legs and Ethan's, purring and butting her head against us. I stumbled backward at the change in atmosphere. My head spun more from the abrupt lack of contact with him rather than the sudden swarm of a normal evening at home. Fire lingered on my skin where his hands held me; the rest of me felt bathed in goosebumps. I stumbled, falling to the ground as Abigail meowed in dismay. I twisted, trying not to land on my bandaged arm or my brother's cat.

Fingers like fired clay slid over my forearm while a heavy warm palm settled, briefly, against the small of my back, steadying me. By the time I finished blinking, I found myself several feet away on the edge of my bed. Ethan sat next to me, leaving half a foot between us. He stared steadily at me in the soft glow of my tiny, beaded lamp, still the only light in the room besides moonlight. The dizzying speed with which I'd been moved hit me suddenly and I doubled over, my good arm wrapped tightly across my churning stomach. Abigail jumped up between us, nudging Ethan impatiently and purring. I groaned.

"I'm sorry," he apologized again. "I didn't want you to fall. You're wobbly, even for a human." Abigail purred her agreement as he rubbed under her chin. I spared her a sharp glare. Traitor.

"You're inhumanly fast," I snapped back without thinking. My head spun; Abigail purred louder and louder, twining herself around Ethan as if he had catnip stashed somewhere on his person. Two phrases replayed themselves in my head as my brother's usually reserved orange cat crouched down in Ethan's lap and rolled right onto her back.

Him: "You're wobbly, even for a human."

Me: "You're inhumanly fast."

Ethan's warm fingers moved in lazy figure eights across Abigail's white and star-shaped belly. I stared. Cats rarely expose their bellies; it's a sign of extreme trust. Abby only did it with Logan, and only once or twice, when she'd fallen asleep. He'd had her since she was a kitten. With others, she rarely got past the hissing and hiding phase. But there she was, fully awake and playful, stretched out belly-up across a total stranger's lap.

Human. Inhuman.

My nausea morphed into the cold ache of fear. Maybe I had hit my head harder than I realized. Maybe I was crazy after all.

Abigail's purr increased in volume before doubling and deepening until it sounded like there were two cats next to me. Ethan stared down at her, his fingers still moving across her belly, his light eyes half-lidded and his mouth slightly open, the edges curled as if discovering a smile. I realized the other half of the double purr was coming from the back of his throat.

"You speak cat." I think I meant to be funny, but my voice came out flat and strange. His mouth snapped shut and his fingers quit moving, to

Abigail's indignation. She yowled, but he ignored her, his blue-green eyes trained on my gray ones.

"Caspia," he said evenly. "You said you drew me." I nodded carefully. "Does anyone else know of this drawing?"

I blinked. He was so matter-of-fact, so accepting. Even my own brother had trouble accepting what I could do. Ethan's unconditional acceptance unnerved me almost more than his inhuman speed, his ability to win total strangers' trust, his strength, his appearance in my sketch, or the fact that he spoke cat. "Aren't you going to tell me I'm crazy? Aren't you going to tell me it's impossible? That no one can draw the future?"

"I know you're not crazy," he said patiently, but his tone didn't match his eyes. They looked stormy, exactly like gathering lightening. He flexed his hands against his thighs, the heather gray fabric of his pants mysteriously free of cat hair.

"Amberlyn," I blurted out. "She saw the sketch, but she doesn't know what it means, and she didn't seem to recognize you. And I tried to tell Logan, but you see how well that went."

He nodded once, and then dropped his head as if in prayer or deep thought. He put a hand on one elbow, as if to guide me or keep me from running. "Can you show me this drawing that frightened you so badly you screamed the first time you saw me?"

I shrugged, trying to act like I didn't care, but truthfully, suddenly I didn't want to. I didn't want to produce the frightening, damning drawing that would prove to him I was crazy and strange. I pointed at my knapsack, leaning up against my dresser, mere feet from where we sat. "It's over there," I said in a hoarse whisper, unaccountably afraid of something I'd been eager to show Logan earlier. He looked at me once, sharply, before kneeling to retrieve my black, ribbon-bound sketchbook in one easy motion. He held it out to me.

When I took it from him, our fingertips brushed.

His skin was like hot porous metal, radiating up my arm in electric spirals. I sucked in a breath and held it. My fingers trembled as I unbound the book. I tried, unsuccessfully, to still my shaking hands. I had to settle for going slowly so as not to damage my work. I flipped past still life drawings in charcoal and pencil of fruit, flowers, and classmates. Pastel drawings of the historic district, Old Town Square, and our ivy-draped patio followed. Finally, I came to the landscapes: Eddington Forest, the St.

Clare and Navau Rivers, and the final sketch from today of the Riverwalk. I took a deep breath as I came to the last one, meeting his intense, flickering eyes over the edges of the page.

I let go of the breath I'd forgotten I was holding and didn't take another one. The picture was gone. Smooth cut edges hugged the spine where my drawing had been excised clean away.

Someone had taken my drawing. As my gray eyes locked with Ethan's narrowing river-colored ones, I felt a sensation like drowning. Something important was happening, something I didn't fully understand. If the drawing had been "a gift of the blood," as my Gran used to say, then its theft whispered to the same long buried instincts, awakening them, urging them to watchful protectiveness.

If someone could steal the products of my strange ability, what else could they take?

The winter will take him.

Logan.

CHAPTER SEVEN

STUBBORN

My entire body shook violently as I smoothed out the last drawing I'd completed before I'd sketched Ethan earlier this afternoon. It was one of my better ones, really. Our cat, Abigail, slept underneath a wooden shelf that held a dying plant on our ivy-screened patio. The drawing was done in pastel crayon. I'd spent a lot of time getting the exact hue correct; orange is tricky, after all. Also, Abby is really fluffy, so I'd put in a lot of detail. The warm weight of Ethan pressed next to me on the edge of my bed. I kept shaking as I flipped the page, searching for some clue besides a cut edge to prove my Riverwalk sketch had once existed, but there was nothing. A big, fat tear pooled onto the page and sank into the paper, blurring a patch of Abby's fur. He lifted the sketchbook from my hands. "There you have it," I gasped, almost too shocked to breathe. "The horrifying drawing of the future. A fluffy orange cat." More tears followed the first.

"You're a talented artist," he began, and I burst into more tears. He jumped up, agitated, and tried to give the book back to me. "What?" he demanded anxiously. "I mean it! You are! Orange is tricky!" At his almost exact echo of my thoughts, I crumpled sideways onto my bed and curled up into a ball, my shoulders shaking so violently with muffled sobs I could feel the bed tremble. It was too much. It had been a long day of too much, and now my drawing was gone. He stared at me, incredulous.

"I was trying to make you feel better, and I upset you, again." He fisted his hands in his hair. "I'm terrible at this. I tried to make you feel better earlier today, and I upset you so much you started yelling, and then, when I tried to calm you, I almost broke your wrist. There's obviously a reason my kind is not supposed to get involved." I gaped at him, crying silently, wishing he would start making sense because I couldn't handle two dubiously sane people at the same time. He grabbed a t-shirt from the floor and shoved it at me. "Here. Take this. Or is it supposed to be tissues? I don't see any, and I'm afraid if I leave you'll start crying again." He paced, his fist against his mouth, occasionally stealing covert glances at me. I held the t-shirt in one hand, the closed sketchbook in the other, and let silent tears roll down my face unchecked while I let my brain lockdown and refuse to process any further information.

"You believe me?" I finally asked, after what seemed like miles of watching him pace.

"Of course," he said matter-of-factly. "Which part, exactly?"

I cleared my throat. It felt like swallowing sand. "About the drawing?"

He nodded to the bed. "May I?" he asked, as if afraid. I nodded. He carefully put at least a foot between us as he sat. "I believe you about the drawing," he said heavily. He smiled a little. "In fact, I much prefer it as an explanation for your reaction to me earlier today than to think you felt that way on your own."

"Oh." I turned my head so he couldn't see my blush. I hadn't thought about how insulting my first reaction to him must have been. But then, until just a little while ago, until his matter-of-fact acceptance of my ability, I hadn't cared. "Oh! I meant do you believe that someone took it?"

He shook his head, exasperated. "Obviously. The edges were cleanly cut."

"But… why? Why would someone do that? And how would they know?"

He was silent a long time, staring off at the patches of moonlight that crept in through the big bay window that took up most of my bedroom's front wall. His eyes were a little unfocused, his head tilted as if listening intently. I studied his profile, thinking of him as lines and angles, of mysteries and secrets. Logan must have fallen asleep; the apartment was silent. The only noise was the faint sound of people and traffic from the square. "I don't know," he finally murmured, as if the silence had given him an answer. "I wish I did. But I don't like it." My scraped-up side pressed into the sheets beneath me. It throbbed dully, reminding me of other aches. Full-body tiredness crept across me like steam from a hot scented bath I suddenly wanted. I felt pleasantly foggy and slow. Unusually foggy and slow. Almost like I'd been drugged, like the feeling I had when he brushed his fingers across my eyelids outside Mrs. Alice's shop. Suddenly, I didn't want to fight anything or anyone anymore. Only drowsy acceptance seeped through me.

"Ethan," I murmured into my forearm. I wondered where he would go. Did drawings come to life have places to sleep? I imagined him picking random paintings from his imagination and stepping into them. "If I was a drawing come to life," I began, swinging my legs over the side of my bed even though it felt like moving through syrup. "I would pick a different famous painting every night to sneak into." He had moved, again without me noticing, to the very center of my bay window. He stared at the sky as if looking for something specific. I joined him there, leaning my forehead against the cold glass. "Starry Starry Night," I sighed. "I'd like to sleep under a sky like that." The full chill of October after dark hit me, seeping through my thin ripped t-shirt and chilling me all the way down to my toes. I shivered violently, but it didn't break my dreamy lassitude. "Do you have a place to stay, Ethan?" I asked. I knew I should be horrified, giving a stranger-than-stranger the option to stay, but I wasn't. I just shivered some more and looked at the sky, trying to see what Ethan found so fascinating up there. Only a few pinpricks of white, meant to be stars, pierced the light pollution haze.

Warm fingers draped a soft leather jacket around my shoulders. Behind me, he lifted my tangled dark brown hair from beneath the collar and smoothed it so it hung across my shoulder blades. I leaned backward into his touch as Abigail had nudged him for petting. Later, I would wonder at this, and would be angry at myself for relaxing so completely and unwisely with someone who'd scared me senseless earlier that very day. But for now, I was conscious only of Ethan's fingers untangling my hair and a growing sense of peace, stronger than anything I'd felt since before Logan's diagnosis.

"What else, Caspia?" he almost whispered, warmth and the scent of new growing things all around me. "What other paintings would you visit, if you could?" His arms wrapped around me, tight with nervous care. Sleep pulled against me like waterlogged socks.

"I want to live in that Escher drawing," I murmured. My eyes fluttered closed. "The house with all the crazy stairs." Movement carried me and warmth followed.

"Relativity." He supplied the name absently, as if his thoughts were far away. I opened my eyes to find we were no longer by the window, but back on my bed. I lay stretched out on my uninjured side, covered with his jacket. He knelt by my side, his tinted eyes clear again and even with mine. I reached out for him, but my hand felt weighted, even manacled, so I pulled it back under his jacket. I remembered feeling sedated when I first woke up, after meeting him for the first time in Mrs. Alice's shop and panicking like hell.

"Hey," I tried to demand, but the word slurred as if I'd been drinking. "Did you do something to me earlier? Outside Mrs. Alice's shop?"

"Other than scare the hell out of you, you mean?" He snorted. "I sincerely hope so."

"You are so not answering my questions," I accused through half-closed eyes.

"You are so resistant to… routine persuasion," he sighed. He traced my half-closed eyes with his fingers. The gesture seemed familiar, but I couldn't place it. "I think you might be in danger," he said.

"Is that why I drew you? Why you came?" I asked.

He looked absolutely, positively grief-stricken. "I'm not here for you at all." He visibly sagged after the words left his mouth like he'd just admitted to the darkest sin of all. "But it didn't make a difference, did it?" He laughed bitterly. "I… interfered. Like my half-cursed brothers. I'm no better." He moved so quickly I couldn't track him. One second he was staring at me by my bed, and the next, he was at the window, palms flat against the glass as if in supplication.

I tried to sit up, but sleep threatened to drag me under like a drug. "How do you do that? Move so fast?" I complained. "And what do you mean, I'm in danger? Or that you interfered? With what?"

"How is it," he countered, turning to me, his voice low and dangerous now, "that you're still awake and asking questions?"

"I'm stubborn like that." I tried to sound fierce, but I wasn't very convincing. I could barely keep my eyes open and my vision was starting to fuzz. "And don't forget your jacket when you get the hell out of my…"

"Keep it." My eyes were mere slits, struggling to stay open against a sudden vivid light. "You might need it. It offers some protection against… cold, and… other things." He ground out his words, sounding frustrated, and the light flared painfully. Still I tried to keep my eyes open, desperately curious about the light, about Ethan, about…

Sleep, Caspia. I'll see you again. Sleep.

The voice came from inside my head. I fell into the same warm, white blankness from before when I'd hit my head outside Mrs. Alice's store. Soft, white warmth enveloped me, but this time it had Ethan's voice, his scent, and his strength. For the second time in one day, I relaxed into deep, calming sleep. But unlike before, this time I dreamed.

Light. Sheltering light softer than thought wrapped around me while storms gathered and lightening lashed the ground as far as I could see.

Chapter Eight

Neighborly

From underwater, I watched as two huge clear globes of air fought their way drunkenly to the surface. They exploded on contact, sending ripples and waves in outward spreading circles while smaller silver bubbles of air followed them up. I hugged my knees to my chest, ignoring my burning lungs and blinking rapidly as the hot water stung my eyes. Long strands of reddish-brown hair floated lazily past my face like aimless seaweed. I ignored them, determined to shut out the world as completely as I could for as long as my lungs would let me.

The scrapes along my side stung, but not as badly as the burns along my right hand and forearm. I'd purposely left the water plain, even though I had enough bath additives to stock a small store. No gardenia or jasmine salts to agitate eyes and injuries. I craved peace and quiet and didn't want to be interrupted by added pain. The huge claw foot tub was my refuge, my equivalent of a meditation room or chapel. After last night, I desperately needed some time to get my head together before I started another whirlwind day. Cocooned in hot, silent water, I tried to set my thoughts into something resembling order.

Point one: I'd drawn one of my visions yesterday, and events began unfolding in the same day. I frowned underneath the water. I'd never drawn a person before, especially a strange one who seemed intent on becoming involved in my life. I blew more bubbles as I realized the error in my thinking. I did draw people. I'd been doing it all my life. I drew Grandmother's accident, and the Everly's surprise twins. The difference, I realized, was that these were all people I knew well before I drew them, and that my drawings weren't so much of them, but of events surrounding them. That was what was so shocking about Ethan's sudden appearance in my sketchbook and then again in real life. I didn't know him, and I had no way of knowing if my drawing foresaw his arrival in my life or pointed to some event involving him that hadn't happened yet.

This was a good segue into point two: the strange symbols surrounding Ethan in my drawing and his ominous appearance in general. He'd been surrounded by a storm of darkness and frightening objects. He'd been furious. So if my drawing represented a forthcoming event, it was bound to be bad. For at least the fiftieth time since waking, I wished for my missing drawing so I could study it again. I ran through what I remembered, lightning fast: soaring light like doors in darkness, bloody talons, broken knife, ragged book, smashed heart. Remember it, I told myself. Be ready.

Point three: My drawing was missing. Someone had sliced it neatly free from my sketchbook. Someone had stolen my property and my proof. My hands curled into fists, the injured one throbbing mildly in protest as my burning, oxygen-deprived chest matched my suddenly blazing anger. Someone had been in my house and stolen my property. I wasn't sure which upset me more: the drawing and all it represented, or its theft and the violation of my home. I couldn't think of a motive or a suspect. Logan hadn't known the drawing existed, Amberlyn didn't understand its significance, and Ethan had been with me the entire time.

Lack of oxygen finally drove me to the surface in an explosion of droplets. I flipped my hair backward, out of my eyes, and gripped the edge of the tub. Ethan. Point four, and by far the most unsettling. I thought about the black leather jacket folded neatly across the back of my winged-back reading chair. I awoke slightly before the alarm, nestled underneath it with all my clothes on. He'd covered me with it and tucked me in. That much I remembered, along with his light piercing eyes and his promise that he'd see me again.

That, and the dreams.

I squirmed in the tub, letting the hot water swish around me in mild waves as I remembered the Ethan dreams. Storms swept across my dreamscape; I remembered a world of mist and wind, pierced occasionally by lightening. I drew with my fingers in the thick mist, shadows streaming from my fingertips in thick jagged lines. I stood on tiptoe and carved great dark rips in an otherwise hazy white world. "This is dangerous, Caspia," someone said from far away. Ethan. "It's not allowed. You'll draw their attention." But I didn't want to stop. In the dream he moved as quickly as he did in real life, and suddenly he was embracing me, running his hands up my arms, trying to stop me. His river-colored eyes flared slightly as he grappled with me. In my dream he held me close, around my waist.

I blushed, quite a feat when I was flushed from the hot water anyway. I had no business dreaming about a man I barely knew who had an as-yet undefined role in my life and could do things like move faster than my eyes could follow. And speak cat.

As if on cue, Abigail nudged her way into the bathroom through the connecting door to my room. She looked at me with queenly impatience. “Oh, okay already,” I grumbled, climbing out and toweling vigorously. “Breakfast in five, your highness. You have to wait like everyone else.” She flicked her tail to show her displeasure and stalked back out the door.

The black leather jacket tugged at the edges of my thoughts as I rifled quickly through my closet. I held two long-sleeved shirts up in front of my full-length, freestanding mirror. My long hair was starting to dry around the edges, framing my face with wild wispy strands. I was tall for a woman. At five foot nine, I towered over most of my female classmates, including the petite Amberlyn. I would never qualify as thin or tiny, but my tall frame and the fact that I walked almost everywhere, carrying all my belongings and purchases, kept me reasonably fit. Former boyfriends had gone so far as to describe me as "energetic" and "graceful." I twisted at the waist, my eyes lingering on the small of my back, remembering Ethan’s steadying hands on me last night. I'd been anything but graceful with him around. He’d kept me from falling. And his jacket… what was it? “For protection,” I murmured, remembering.

As I slipped on underwear and the warmer of the two shirts, I knew that, contrary to good sense and even some compelling evidence, at some point last night I’d decided to trust Ethan. It had been my own senseless, mad dash across the concrete outside Mrs. Alice’s shop that had gotten me injured. Ethan had let go immediately when he realized I was hurt. I remembered his look of horror, like he didn’t realize how fragile I was. I remembered the way he held me around the waist, as if I was breakable, and the way he'd moved me around my own room.

Because I was wobbly, for a human. And he was inhumanly fast. I sank onto the edge of my bed with a groan. "Christ, Ethan, what are you, and what are you doing here?" I asked his jacket. "Do I even want to know?"

"Know what?" Amberlyn's springy curls were confined in a ponytail, but they still managed to bounce in time with her cheerful walk straight to my closet. "What to wear? Because it can't be that hard, and breakfast is getting cold." She turned and started rummaging. "I, for one, like my coffee hot."

"Jesus, Amberlyn!" I shouted, grabbing the first pair of semi-clean jeans I could find on the floor. "Don't you believe in knocking?"

She turned back, arms loaded with clothes, and frowned at my wrinkled jeans. "I brought double-chocolate banana bread. Mr. Peppers just took it out of the pan. It's still hot." She handed me my favorite hoodie and two socks that didn't match. "I think that qualifies as grounds for a home invasion."

I held up my as-yet unbandaged hand. "It's a two woman job. Help me?"

"It looks better," she finally said after snapping the last clip in place.

"It is." In the kitchen, I reached for a stack of plates with my left hand, but Logan's long arm shot up and restrained me. Clad in his dark green Adidas tracksuit, he pinned me to the sink.

"Hey, Amberlyn." The deep rumble of his voice reverberated against my back. "You giving Cas a ride?"

"You've got your oncologist's appointment today," I said, dodging neatly around him to put the juice out. "You're going to need the car."

He nodded. His baseball cap matched his tracksuit, pulled down low enough to hide both his hollow eyes and his completely bald head. "You just always walk everywhere. Andreas is pretty close."

"It's finally turned cold enough that she's consented to ride in the hippie car," Amberlyn smirked, carving neat slices of breakfast bread so dark and moist it was more like cake.

I actually growled. "You wish it was a hippie car. I hate to break it to you, but anything built this millennia doesn't qualify. And if you keep calling it that, I will walk, no matter how cold it is."

Logan just shook his head. He was used to our bickering. He nodded at my hand. "How are you going to manage today with that?"

"School's easy, actually." I popped the corner of Mr. Pepper's best-selling bread in my mouth and stifled a moan of ecstasy. "Art history is straight lecture. Then we have ceramics, and I'm so terrible in there being left-handed might actually be an improvement." I ate more bread. "How did you get this fresh, Amberlyn? He usually sells out at dawn, or something."

She fiddled with her coffee cup. "He held one back for you."

I choked. "What?"

"That's what I said." Logan sat motionless, watching me intently. Amberlyn's golden-green eyes pleaded with me to understand. "I think he was worried about you after last night. It's sweet, really," she tried to reassure me, but I exploded out of my chair.

I mentally filled in her unspoken commentary: He's worried because the whole town heard you had a screaming nervous breakdown and had to be carried off the square, unconscious and hurt.

"What? How the hell did Mr. Peppers know about that? Who else knows?" When Logan didn't meet my eyes, I sat back down with a defeated plop. "Maybe I better rephrase that. Who else doesn't know?"

"Mr. Markov called while you were in the bath," my brother said carefully. I noticed he hadn't touched his breakfast. Not good. I should be used to his lack of appetite by now, but I wasn't. I kept hoping something, somewhere would tempt him to eat. If Mr. Pepper's famous double chocolate banana bread couldn't do it… I shut down the thought and refocused on my brother's words.

"He said to call if you needed more time," Logan said softly.

"Oh. My. God." I let my head flop forward into my waiting arms. "This is horrible. I'm supposed to work this afternoon. I need my job. I even like my job. Most of the time."

"He didn't fire you, Caspia." Cold fingers brushed my hair back from my forehead. "He just wondered if… well." The fingers withdrew. I sat up and stared at Logan, who looked at Amberlyn. "We were talking and we think you've been pushing yourself too hard. We think… I think you should slow down."

"This is about last night," I accused. No one contradicted me. I thought fast and hard. They were partially right. I had, after all, come to the same conclusion before Ethan approached me and scared the hell out of me. Yes, I had been working myself a bit too hard. So I could admit that much. But the rest of it? No way. If they already thought I was unbalanced, I could only imagine what would happen if I tried to tell them about prophetic drawings and the man who'd helped me last night who could do impossible things and had stepped out of one. I looked at their worried faces, at my brother who only toyed with a slice of something he would have eaten a whole loaf of this time last year, and made a decision.

"You're absolutely right," I announced, scooting back up to the table and helping myself to another slice of bread. I ignored their shocked expressions with satisfaction. "I thought about it myself. I've been pushing myself so hard so I won't have time to think about… unpleasant… things." I looked at Logan. "And that has to stop. It's not going to change anything. It just means we have less time together." He nodded at me in grim shock. "So I'll talk to Markov. I don't want to make any radical changes. It's not a crisis situation, or anything. I'd like to finish out my schedule for the week, since it's already made and I don't want to mess up anyone else's. But I will see about reducing my hours so that we can have more time together. Since I made some extra money this month, I can afford to take some time before the holidays." I couldn't help myself. I threw my arms around Logan's neck and squeezed. He squeezed back.

"We could go to the orchard together," he said into my hair. "The Parsons opened up about a month ago."

"And buy apples and cider, and come back here and watch scary movies all night long," Amberlyn added, her voice tight.

"Like we do every year." I squeezed Logan once more, tightly, before I reluctantly let him go. I tried to ignore the sensation that time was running out as we hurried through breakfast and I gathered my things for school. I was halfway down the stairs when I turned on my heel, not quite looking Amberlyn in the eye. "Hey. I forgot something. Go on ahead; I won't be a minute."

Logan sat on the couch, a purring Abigail in his lap. I balanced uneasily on the edge of the coffee table, facing him. "I will skip all my classes and work too if you want me to go to that appointment with you," I said. He smiled into Abigail's satisfied face.

"You hate doctors'offices," he said. "You've had a rough twenty four hours, Cas. You've been right beside me for this whole thing. Missing one doctor's visit isn't going to hurt." He gave a startled little laugh when Abigail put her paws on his chest and started to give him a bath, cat style, starting with the tip of his nose. "I know you'd go, and I appreciate it. But I'd rather you have a normal day. You help me that way, by being steady and reminding me there's a normal world that isn't centered on me being sick." He deflected further bathing maneuvers with one hand and took my fingers with his other. "I don't know if I've ever thanked you for that, Caspia. For being steady and keeping me anchored to reality. Without you, I don't know where I'd be."

I swallowed hard. He was counting on me to keep him anchored to reality? Oh, hell. "It's what sisters do," I told him solemnly. "Or at least, we try," I amended. Below us, Amberlyn honked her late-model VW Bug. "I'll see you right after Ceramics, aka Slime-a-ramics, before work, ok?"

I left him laughing on the couch, Ethan's jacket draped over one of my arms. "It offers some protection against the cold and… other things…" he'd said. The shiver that took me when I slipped it on had nothing to do with the chill October wind that welcomed me when my feet hit the sidewalk. Instead, I shivered as I wondered what those "other things" might be, in anticipation and fear of finding out, and in stubborn rejection of that tiny voice that hadn't left me, the one still reminding me that my brother was too fragile. The winter will take him, the winter will take him.

"Like hell," I announced as I sprinted to Amberlyn's car, pulling Ethan's jacket closer.

Chapter Nine

Silver

"What are you, like, my shadow now?"

I balanced a pile of fabric, including a heavier than it looked leather jacket, an extra sweater my landlord Mr. Moore had just shoved at me, and my work apron on one forearm while I made a fist with my other hand and jammed it against my hip. I tried to look fierce as a tall, dark-clad figure uncoiled itself from the alley wall that ran perpendicular to my apartment.

"I told you I would see you again." In the full afternoon light, he looked almost disappointingly normal. I remembered just a flash of the dreams he'd starred in last night and ducked my head to hide a blush. Today, his blue-green eyes sparkled with amusement rather than some strange inner light. His mouth twisted slightly at one corner as if holding back his full smile. He was dressed for the weather like any other citizen of Whitfield; jeans this time, paired with a thick black sweater. "You've been busy all day. I thought I might walk you to work."

"Oh." My mouth stayed in that perfect round formation longer than it needed to as his words sunk in. He knew my schedule. He knew the shape of my days. I turned to him, the opening of the alley dappled with wavering patterns of sunlight and shade. "Do I dare ask how you know that?" I finally ventured.

He slipped up beside me, taking my bandaged hand in his own. "It doesn't matter," he said, flipping my hand so it lay palm up in his own. He wouldn't meet my eyes. "I'm involved now. I'm not supposed to be, but I am." His thumb rubbed against my exposed palm in a slow circular motion. That one single piece of skin seemed to grow and expand until it took up a disproportionate amount of my attention, focusing my brain in like a laser on the sole point of contact between us. It made it hard to think. I might have protested if it didn't feel so good.

A chill wind barreled down the alley opening at the same time that a cloud hid all sunlight. A violent, full body shiver brought me back to myself, and I wrenched my hand away from his. "What's that supposed to mean?" I demanded while I still had the chance to think straight.

He sighed. "Different things." Somehow, when he was rubbing my palm, he'd managed to take my extra clothes from me. He held them neatly stacked underneath one arm. "Right now, it means getting you to work safely, and on time." His fingers curled around my upper arm, propelling me down the sidewalk.

I had about a million questions for him. I sorted through them, trying to pick the ones I thought he might actually answer in the short time it took to walk two stores over to The Whitfield Coffee Shop. There was nothing. My questions were all too huge and crazy for the sidewalk in front of work. "I brought your jacket," I finally said, after several false starts. "It's cold. You should wear your jacket."

He laughed. "I'm warm enough." We had stopped walking again. People moved around us like currents of water flowing around rocks. I dimly registered that we were right in front of the window of my job. Rows of tea lights stood sentinel along the windowsill, waiting for me to come in and light them. Ethan's leather jacket hung from my shoulders, warm and scented like soft cotton sheets pulled straight from the dryer. Impossible, I wanted to protest. Leather didn't smell like warm cotton. Firm fingers forced my chin up, level with his.

"Your eyes are more silver than gray," he said solemnly like he was imparting important information. "Did you know?"

"I know what color they are," I told him, although no one had ever called them silver before. I wanted to break eye contact. I wondered how many of my co-workers and customers were watching, and how badly they were going to tease me for this.

"The jacket is yours," he said, his fingers sliding under my chin to cup the side of my jaw. "I meant what I said, about protection. Please wear it."

"You said you thought I was in danger." The words came out in a hoarse whisper. I leaned into him as I spoke, so closely that the thickly knit cabled texture of his sweater pressed through my thermal long-sleeved shirt. A few more inches, and our faces would touch. "Is that why you're here? Is my brother in danger, too?"

Both of his hands cradled my face in a grip at once both so fierce and careful his entire body vibrated from the force of it. My injured arm dangled uselessly; the other held my extra sweater and apron. Once again, I hadn't seen him move. Once again, his eyes promised a gathering storm, lightening flickering in their depths, tightly leashed. "I hope to keep you both from harm, Caspia Chastain. As much as I am able." He released me abruptly and I staggered back almost hitting the glass. His hand on the small of my back steadied me.

"Oh. Wow. Okay, then." I closed my eyes and focused on breathing. It wouldn't do to walk into work hyperventilating at the start of my shift.

"You will manage? With your injury?" he asked, his voice gone cold and formal. I looked up to see he had moved several feet back on the sidewalk. The sudden distance twisted something inside me.

"I always manage," I said with as much dignity as I could gather. Behind the glass, Mr. Markov stared, sightless and moody, at his eternal game of chess. Nicolas put out new dessert trays while sneaking covert glances my way. His twin sister Amelie had no such pretenses. She outright stared at Ethan and me, a neatly folded towel in one hand as she leaned against the counter. "Look, thanks for the walk and the jacket and all. Don't worry about me. I only live two stores away. I'll be fine," I said tiredly. I was supposed to close and take the deposit to the bank tonight, but there was no way I was telling him that. I could look after myself just fine. I'd been doing it for years now.

Ethan looked far from pleased. He stuffed his hands into his jeans pocket and kicked at the sidewalk. "I don't doubt your competence. Nevertheless, I'll be here to escort you to the bank, should you wish for company." My jaw dropped. How did he know? I hastily snapped it shut again as he continued. "Should you not wish for company, I understand. I'll stay several feet behind you. Either way, if you have questions, I'll do my best to answer them." He glared at a staring Amelie, who paled and began frantically wiping the counter. "After work."

"After work," I agreed, slipping into the warm, strongly scented air of my job. I looked at the clock. It was going to be a long six-hour shift.

Chapter Ten

The Lighter Spectrum

I watched as Amelie took her third sip of my cinnamon-dusted, whipped cream topped coffee confection. Her silvered eyelids pulsed against the urge to fly open, but she repressed it; that would be cheating. Her perfect mouth twisted slightly in her pale face, amused, even as her nostrils flared over her steaming cup. Amelie was so pale, with snow-blond hair and ice-gray eyes, that she could only wear pale or sheer shades of make-up. But her features were frozen perfection and she knew it, and used it to her advantage. Her skin glowed with some kind of outrageously expensive cream imported from her native France. If I looked closely enough, I could see tiny sparkles as she moved in the light. Her eyes and mouth were the only features she could highlight without looking like a circus clown. Today she'd chosen a deep red lipstick, the color of pomegranates, which left generous circles on the white coffee cup as she played her part of our nightly game.

"Vanilla and brown sugar?" she guessed, a flash of pink tongue lapping at her top lip as she waited.

"Oh, come on," I huffed, a little insulted. "You are so off. Those are summer flavors, Amelie, and you know it. Give me some credit."

When she smiled in triumph, her deep red lips an almost cruel, curling beauty in her snow queen face, I bit my lip in annoyance. Damn her. "Why, thank you, Caspia, for that vital clue. So it's seasonal, hmm?" I didn't answer. "How many guesses do I have left?"

"Just one," I ground out, crossing my fingers and wishing hard. "You just used your second." We played this game whenever we closed together. The loser had to wash the dishes. Since Mr. Markov never invested in a dishwasher, someone had to wash everything by hand. It was the least popular chore. The dishwasher was almost always the last one out and the closer by default. Tonight I really hoped to go early; I'd tried to devise an unusual drink, hoping to stump Amelie and win my early freedom.

"Mmm." Amelie sipped again, her pink tongue licking up whipped cream. "I'll have to go with…" I held my breath. I so did not want to be the last one out and then have to go to the bank too. Plus there was the tiny little matter of Ethan and his slightly puzzling comment about keeping me company, my even more puzzling anticipation that he might actually show, and the extremely high creepiness factor that he knew things he shouldn't and appeared to be stalking me…

Amelie snapped her perfectly manicured fingers in my face. "Hello? Pretending to be in a coma won't save you. It has to be pumpkin." She gave me a wintry smile that matched the growing unease in the pit of my stomach and cradled her drink. "Admit it, Caspia, so I can finish up and go home."

"Pumpkin spice, actually," I told her, slumping back against a bare expanse of green marble countertop in defeat. "But close enough."

She finished off what was left in her cup in one quick, unladylike gulp. "It really is quite good. What are you going to call it?"

"Pumpkin spice?" I said dully, feeling about as imaginative as Mr. Markov. My entire body went limp as the weight of my day pressed down on me. I looked out the storefront windows, every one of them lit up with tea lights across the sill, at the darkness lurking just beyond and tried to imagine what waited for me out there. Take the deposit to the bank in the dark, possibly accompanied by a strangely attractive stalker person heralding impending doom, then home to a dying brother and a bedroom that had been secretly robbed of a worthless, but prophetic homework assignment. I shook violently with cold and stress before I could stop myself. Was I forgetting anything?

Dying. Brother.

The winter will take him.

Amelie was beside me almost instantly, her slim, cool, garnet-tipped fingers stroking my hair, pulling it loose from the clip it had half-escaped anyway. "Hey there," she said softly, her nails gently raking my scalp before working their way down the tangled mass of my fine dark hair like a makeshift comb. I stared down at her, into eyes that seemed pale, jeweled versions of my own: diamond against steel. She moved to take my hands in hers, in some kind of comforting gesture, but touched my bandaged hand and flinched. "Oh, Caspia, I forgot," she exhaled. Pity flashed in her diamond, ice queen eyes. She wrapped herself around me in a tight hug. I was so surprised I froze. Amelie and her twin, Nicolas, were famously aloof when it came to personal space. The strength of her hold surprised me, as did her cool skin and faint, cloying perfume, like dying roses. She murmured to me in French, her native language, and even though I didn't understand the meaning of her words, they comforted me nonetheless. "Je suis un idiot. Vous souffrez en douleur. Vous ne me laissez pas vous aider, bien que je sois votre ami. Que est-ce que je pense?"

"Um," I said brilliantly. "Sure?"

She stepped smoothly back from me. She looked me up and down, her snow-blonde hair rippling like silver tinsel under the light, before shaking her head slowly. "Forget it, Caspia. Tonight I will wash the dishes."

"But," I sputtered. "You guessed. You won. I wash. It's what we do," I protested. Amelie merely arched one perfect silver eyebrow at me and threw me a damp towel. To her credit, she knew me well enough not to mention or even look at my bandaged hand. She knew how stubborn I could be when my pride was damaged, and she also knew I was smarting from the sympathetic glances and not-so-subtle comments so many of our customers had flung my way tonight. Early into our shift, she elbowed me away from the front counter and the cash register after yet another customer sweetly inquired how I was feeling after my "nasty fall." I sputtered every single time one of our customers referenced the events of the night before. It shouldn't have surprised how fast the news of my public humiliation had spread, but it did. Amelie interrupted one particularly gossipy inquiry after my health by "accidentally" spilling a café au lait on a customer, and then banished me to clean up duty. When I finished, she had smoothly inserted herself into my old post by the counter and refused to budge. I spent the rest of the night frothing milk and lining up espresso shots, stepping back and forth between the dessert displays, lining up steaming lines of ceramic mugs, or bringing Mr. Markov and Erik—the guitar player—a plain black cup of coffee when things were slow.

"You have to take the deposit anyway," she reasoned. "If you wipe down the tables, we'll be even." When I opened my mouth to protest further, she stomped one black-booted foot and fisted her hands on her hips. "Mon Dieu! I will wash the damn dishes, you stubborn creature, and that is all I have to say!" She spun on one heel and flounced away in her designer jeans and perfect silver hair. I stared after her, my mouth drooping open in shock. Amelie, sweet Amelie, never shouted and stormed off. She was more the glaring coldly and gliding away type; quiet anger suited her pale beauty more than passionate outbursts. I shook my head and slipped the daily deposit into my messenger bag. It was heavy. We must have had a good night. Behind the tall, steel espresso machines, where I had spent the majority of my evening hiding from nosy neighbors, it had been hard to tell. I wondered darkly just how many customers had come to gawk at Crazy Caspia, Whitfield's newest mental case, and then shrugged. If they had, at least Mr. Markov had made some money off me.

I looked around the store as I methodically wiped the tables down. Erik's tall stool was empty next to the rough gray stone fireplace. He'd taken the microphone and amp with him; he probably had another gig tomorrow somewhere. Usually, he just left his equipment neatly in the corner. I put down my towel and stacked the board games together on the large glass-topped table, which was hemmed in by four mismatched sofas. I straightened their cushions and collected stray books and magazines, depositing them on the shelves that dotted the room randomly. By the time I got back to my tables, the fire had almost completely died, and Mr. Markov was awake again. But instead of staring at his chessboard, as usual, he stared straight at me.

Since Mr. Markov was blind, I found his direct gaze especially unnerving.

His heavily lined face looked almost cruel in the banked glow of the dying fire. My boss was heavily scarred and wrinkled. His fingers rested in permanent curves, perfect, he told me, for holding a cane or a chess piece. I knew that his hands had been broken decades ago before he escaped to Whitfield from his native Russia, from what he would only call his "life before." He wouldn't elaborate further, but my overactive imagination could fill in the blanks. His bent, scarred body bore witness to the secrets he wouldn't speak, and his sightless eyes were eerily observant. They raked over me now, seeing through me, reminding me to count my blessings and take nothing for granted. No one would ever call him gentle, but he would do anything for those he trusted. He had a soft spot for orphans and immigrants, like the twins and me. I think we reminded him of some parts of himself: alone in a strange country.

Wind battered against the windows, rattling the door and snuffing out a few tea lights. The winter will take him, it seemed to echo. I had to talk to Mr. Markov. I'd promised Logan. We were going to spend more time together. We were going to pick apples and drink cider, then watch horror movies all night long. We were going to have a normal autumn together, and that could only happen if I didn't work myself into oblivion and exhaustion. The dying fire cast a flickering perimeter of a dark scarlet glow, enveloping Markov and his eternal chessboard. I stood just outside the bright arc of dying light, unsure of how to ask for something I needed, but didn't want.

He kicked out the chair opposite him with his boot and nodded at it sharply. I sighed and went to him, taking my towel with me. I ignored the chair, hoping that maybe I could go back to my toweling and be on my way, avoiding the whole subject for another day. "Yes, Mr. Markov?" I asked, my voice wavering a little. I couldn't meet his dark, hooded eyes even though logic told me he couldn't see me. "Do you want more coffee? I can see if there's any left."

"Sit down, Caspia," he said, in the grim intonations of a man who was about to foretell an accident or predict a storm. My stomach twisted. I sat.

He held a clear glass knight in his hands, passing it back and forth between his fingers. Mr. Markov wore a heavy gold ring with a carved red stone on his left hand. The red stone gleamed in the firelight and refracted off the glass chess piece until it seemed as if he cradled actual fire in his scarred, cupped palms. As neatly as if he were flipping a coin, he snapped the knight back between two fingers and used it to capture an opaque glass bishop. Although he looked at the chessboard, his smile felt aimed at me as he offered me the captured piece. I held the milky white bishop up to the firelight and wondered if Mr. Markov could somehow sense my answering smile. "Don't you ever get tired of beating yourself?" I asked, placing the captured bishop in a neat line with his fallen comrades.

"Of course." He had the low, gravelly voice of a chronic smoker. "But this is balanced by the joy of winning against myself." I snorted as he moved another piece. "Tell me what kind of candy drink you have invented today, my dear," he invited, his rough fingers brushing lightly over the tops of the remaining pieces.

"Pumpkin spice latte," I said with a sigh. "It's been popular. Amelie wants to make it the flavor of the week. And espresso drinks aren't candy. They're Italian."

"That is just as bad."

"Whatever," I said, trying not to laugh. The man had no imagination at all. Beige aprons, boring business name, plus he drank nothing but plain black coffee. "You'd be lost without us." I propped my head on my arms and watched him demolish the board in three quick moves. I shook my head in admiration; there was a reason he played himself most of the time. No one in Whitfield was much competition. "Aren't they supposed to be black and white?" I asked as he packed the pieces away. "Your pieces, and even your board, are glass. All white swirls, or clear glass."

"Ah, that is because I do not see things in black and white, dear Caspia. In my world, it does not exist." He tapped his head and smiled. "Everything exists in shades of gray. Personally, I try to stick with the lighter spectrum."

"Because you're… because of your eyes?"

"Because I am blind, you mean? Perhaps." He leaned toward the fireplace, where the last dying embers glowed underneath a pile of darkening ash. "But I like to think of life in those terms, too. That there are no absolutes, and that even the deepest darknesses have shades of light in them." His rough, permanently curved hand settled on my forearm. "Do you understand me, Caspia?"

The winter will take him. "I'm going to Parson's Orchard with Logan," I heard myself say through clenched teeth. Tears and words got twisted, somehow. They came out of me at the same time and I made no move to stop them. "I'm getting him a real down comforter for Christmas. Don't tell him. It's a secret." The dying embers heaped along the bottom of the fireplace looked a bit like a bleeding wound through the tears I refused to wipe away. Wiping them away would mean acknowledging they were there.

"…more time with your brother," Mr. Markov was saying kindly when my ears started working again. The back of my throat felt numb as I nodded. "An extra day or two a week, just through the holidays. Of course, if you need money, you must tell me," he said, squeezing my forearm gently. I wanted to tell him I was grateful for knowing what I needed without me even having to ask, but I settled for nodding. I thought of the extra money I'd made from my tarot card sales, and of how Mr. Mason had cornered me on the stairs before work and told me he wouldn't let us pay December rent, that it was to be his Christmas present to us.

"No, we should be okay for money," I said, covering my boss' hands with both of my own. "So don't worry about us. I'll still be here, and one of my buyers offered me a private commission if I need extra cash." If I haven't lost the stupid number forever, I thought with a frown, wondering what I had done with it. Maybe Mrs. Alice had kept a copy, or would remember it.

That was the last thought I had before things changed.

Mr. Markov jerked his hands out from under mine with lightening speed and grabbed his cane. He held it in both palms and stood in one fluid movement in front of me, silhouetted by a faint halo of dying fire. I never in a million years dreamed a blind, old man could move so fast. "Who's there?" he barked out in a voice thick with authority. I was so startled I spun sideways in my chair, knocking the closed and latched box that held the chess pieces off the table.

Thank god it's latched, I thought as I tried to catch it. I imagined all those beautiful pieces, so lovingly handled, all smashed to bits because of me. I lunged from my chair, knowing I was going to be too late, sickened because it was one of the few things Mr. Markov had managed to smuggle out of Russia.

A familiar hand settled in the curve of my spine, steadying me, pulling me upright against a dark cable knit sweater. I looked into unblinking eyes. No storm flickered behind them tonight; instead, they pinned me with the steady intensity of twin searchlights. "Still wobbly," he said, and smiled. I held the box of chess pieces securely in my left hand, cradled between us. He'd put it there, and I hadn't noticed. I leaned back a little, testing him, and the hand in the curve of my spine pulled me closer, tighter. I smiled.

"Still…" I inhaled. He smelled of sunshine and pine tonight. "Fast," I finished softly, silently adding the words I dared not say out loud.

Wobbly, for a human.

Inhumanly fast.

Ethan.

"And who the hell are you?" Mr. Markov demanded loudly. Inwardly, I groaned, suddenly conscious of my coffee-stained apron and my belligerent boss. I fought a sudden urge to hide behind Ethan's shoulder.

"I'm sorry about your chess set," I told Mr. Markov, replacing it on the table. "Ethan startled me." I stripped off my apron as fast as I could. "But no harm done."

"Indeed," Markov snorted, sounding personally offended.

"Caspia," Ethan said softly, but when I looked up at him, he stared intently at my boss. "Have you decided if you want my company? For your walk?"

"Um, yes?" I half-answered, half-questioned. Both men completely ignored me, focused on each other instead. I found Ethan unsettling enough under the best of circumstances, but to see him engaged in some silent contest of wills with a blind man did funny things to my heart rate. Even stranger, Mr. Markov stared at Ethan just as intently, his sightless eyes moving in jerky slips up and down his form as if he could see him. I slipped my messenger bag, heavy with the night's deposit, across my chest. "And I'm ready to go. Right. Now."

"You should get your jacket," Ethan reminded me, gaze still locked on Markov, another meaning not meant for me hidden under his words.

They stared at each other, showing no intention of moving. "Ok, then," I sighed. "I'll, uh, be right back." Hopefully, they wouldn't kill each other in the interim. What was going on? Did Mr. Markov feel threatened for some reason, like he had to defend his territory or something? Men, I huffed, as I dodged the couches. I would never understand them, young or old. I practically sprinted to the front coat rack. Amelie sung something in French over the sound of running water from the depths of the kitchen. I snagged the jacket, guiltily grateful she would miss meeting Ethan. She would ask a million questions I didn't have answers for, and my boss' reaction had been strange enough.

Mr. Markov acted exactly as if he could see Ethan. And he hadn't liked what he'd seen, whatever it had been. My hand froze over the leather. Warm fingers took the jacket from me, slipping it over my shoulders. I jumped. In that moment, I hated the silent way Ethan moved. "Ready?" he asked, holding the door open for me. I hesitated for just a second. Mr. Markov sat by the cold, dead fireplace, his sightless eyes trained directly on me. Just what did the blind man see when he looked at the not-quite-human drawing come to life? Did I want to find out?

Streetlights touched off strands of gold in Ethan's hair. He held the door for me, waiting. Of course I wanted to know.

"Goodnight!" I called out. "And thank you!" I stood on the threshold until I saw my boss nod in acknowledgement, then I let myself be pulled out into the night. "What was that about?" I asked as Ethan spun me toward him on the sidewalk. He straightened the jacket over my shoulders, buttoning the top button so it hung off me like a cloak.

"He cares about you," he said simply.

"Was he sizing you up?"

"Something like that."

I groaned. "Oh, god. I'm sorry. He means well."

Ethan smiled, a quick, tiny flash of a gesture, dismissing the incident. "What would you like to do?"

"Mmm." I looked at him sideways. "Bank first, to get rid of this deposit. That means a walk through the park. And then, after that, what plans do you have?"

He frowned, puzzled. "Am I expected to have any?"

I paused for a second and decided he wasn't joking. "Right, then. No plans." I put my hand lightly, shyly, on top of his arm. "I'd like to show you Old Town Square."

Another boy might have laughed. Another boy might have looked at the four streets lined with small, brightly lit shops and restaurants boxing in a haphazard scattering of light-laden trees and seen boredom and decay instead of a vibrant beating box-shaped heart. Most people my age were desperate to escape to bigger cities and faster lives. Instead, I loved my strange little town with its eclectic businesses open at all kinds of odd hours and its even odder citizens who stuck their noses into everybody else's lives. I couldn't imagine living any other way. But not everyone understood; boys had laughed at me before, and gone home to play their Xboxes and get wasted instead. I kept my head down and my expectations in check, waiting.

Warm rough fingers lifted my chin until I could look nowhere else but his bright eyes. "Yes, please," he said simply. "And then we'll go home."

"Yes," I echoed, the word one long exhalation that tasted like a long-held promise. "Home."

He tucked my arm underneath his and walked with me into patches of flowing dark spaces and trees flecked with steady white lights.

Chapter Eleven

Light and Promises

The night air was chillier than normal for early fall in the South; my breath made faint skeletal wreaths of mist that faded quickly in the wind. On a normal night, I would have taken the straightest path through the park to get to the bank, then back to my brother and a long soak to banish the last stubborn scents of coffee. But tonight, I had Ethan. I wanted privacy and enough time alone with him to force him to answer my questions. Neither of us spoke as we crossed the street and headed into the park. I had so many questions that I barely registered the silence between us, trying to sort through and prioritize the things I most wanted to know. I intentionally steered us onto one of the footpaths that was little more than a trail thinly covered with leaves winding through patches of darkness and dimly lit trees. The bright lights of the gurgling triple tiered fountain with its marble gargoyles, nymphs, and chimeras faded as I led us deeper into the deserted wooded part of the park.

Funny how little details like what path I chose through the park that night or in what order I did my errands or even what kind of bag I carried altered the shape of so many people's lives.

I probably shouldn't have trusted him. I didn't know him, this almost stranger who unbalanced me and freely augured danger. I knew better than to walk in the woods after dark with strangers, even if we were only in

Blind Springs Park and within walking proximity to my home. But I felt no alarm, no fear at all as I pulled my hand free of his arm, sliding it down the length of his dark sweater until I found his warm strange hand and took it in mine. I kept my eyes locked on the toes of my brown hiking boots as I laced my fingers through his. His skin against mine was so rough it was almost abrasive. I rubbed my thumb against his and thought of porous stone, of statues worn away by time. My muscles stretched and tightened as he became a weight I pulled behind me, not unwilling to follow but a little resistant, as if he was uncertain of my purpose. It was enough to slow and annoy me.

"Caspia." His voice was tight with warning and regret, almost strangling my name. My fingers curled defiantly around his at the tension in his voice. He was a solid presence at my back. Tonight I would have answers, I promised myself. I thought of my brother and of how little time we had left. I remembered the first time I saw Ethan, in Mrs. Alice's shop, and the way my entire being had reacted to his presence.

There was too much at stake not to have answers.

"What?" I replied. It was barely a whisper, fainter than the mist from my breath on the wind. I wouldn't let him turn me, confusing me with his impossible presence and the feeling that as long as he was near, everything was safe. It wasn't; nothing was safe, and he was all the more dangerous for making me forget that.

"You have tasks to fulfill, and a home waiting for you." He leaned into me, his words whispered into my hair. "We shouldn't linger here, in the dark and off the path. Come and show me your town square."

It was tempting. My god, it was tempting. How could someone feel like spring in the middle of its opposite season? Being near him was like being wrapped in a dry warm mist, like feathers, or sugar-white sand. "Blind Springs Park is safe as can be," I told him, angling to face him at last. His eyes were luminous slants of worry. "I've been playing here alone since I could walk. And besides," I used my bandaged hand to try to smooth his brow. He only frowned more, seeing it. I sighed. "Nothing ever happens in Whitfield."

He gave me a strange look of regret as his lips curved down and he slightly shook his head. I chose to ignore it.

Our fingers laced tight together, the wind and cold a thin barrier between us. I was afraid if I let him speak he would banish the fear, loss and darkness I'd kept bottled inside since my parents' death and again after Logan's diagnosis. The attraction in me that burned for him was too powerful, too primal. I realized then, under sky and shadow, that he had the power to exorcise everything within me that had kept me functioning for so many countless months. He could take away my anger, my rage, my fear, and if they were gone I'd be forced to feel things and acknowledge my powerlessness yet again and I didn't want to, couldn't, even; I needed my darkness like warriors needed armor. I couldn't face every single day watching my world fall apart without my armor.

He stood there, with eyes like light and promises, and I realized for the first time what kind of danger I was really in. He would make me feel things again. He already had. He would again.

If I could feel, I could hurt.

When he exhaled his breath didn't wreath the wind with mist as mine had, but I didn't pause to wonder at it. "Caspia," he said again, with new urgency. "I promise you don't want the answers to some of the things I can tell you. Can we not allow some things between us to simply just… be?"

"No," I insisted, suddenly panicked, digging the fingers of both my hands into his forearms so hard it hurt. I wanted answers as badly as I was afraid of them. I walked backward quickly, pulling him with me into the quiet part of the park where it gradually melts into the Historic District. "No," I repeated. There were no borders, no lines of demarcation, but I knew when I saw the distant lights of Whitfield's oldest church that we were close to the edge of the park. Ethan wanted to resist me, I could tell, and it made me suddenly, powerfully angry. I pulled on the front of his sweater. "I don't want anything from you but answers to my questions." I shoved at him, intending to push him against a tree trunk, but it was like trying to move a heavy statue. I strangled a cry of frustration and got even madder when he voluntarily moved against the tree I'd tried to shove him against. Never had the differences between us been so stark: I was no match for his inhuman strength. He was here because he wanted to be. His eyes narrowed.

"Calm down." His voice had a soothing quality that worked almost instantly. He adjusted my jacket to better keep the wind off. Dimly I noticed the weight of my shoulder bag, heavy with money and coins, gone. He'd taken it from me somehow. I was sure of it. He did little things like that, carrying things, making sure I was warm, keeping me from falling, chasing away fear. I hadn't invited him to do these things; he just did, until without even realizing, I had come to like it. My body leaned toward his without me even realizing it. Ethan affected me as no one ever had. He was trying to calm me, but I refused to let him. I shoved into his shoulders, hard.

"No," I hissed. "I need to be angry. I need to be cold and tired and too busy to notice things like the stars tonight or how much people care or how bright your eyes are because if I don't… when I stop…"

"What?" he demanded, pinning my arms to my sides. "What happens when you stop, Caspia? When you let people help you? Love you?" His whisper sliced through my ragged breathing, clear and precise as a surgeon's scalpel. "What happens when you stop and let yourself feel?"

Something hard and inhuman tore its way from my throat. I didn't want to process his words; they cut through me, through the wall of isolation and hard work I'd built around myself. A pair of birds abandoned the tree above us as I hit my knees, swaying. An endless whimpering tumbled from my lip when I found myself on the ground, cradled against the curve of Ethan's neck. "Shh, it's ok," he whispered desperately, his eyes huge and sad. "Shh, Caspia," he murmured, as if to an infant. My face was wet and my throat was raw, but as he half-held, half-pinned me, the awful sound coming from the back of my own throat subsided into quiet normal sobbing. "I'm so sorry," he said, pressing his forehead against mine. I think he'd been trying to stroke my hair, but his fingers had gotten all tangled in it instead. He trembled against me. I silently willed him to hold me harder, and told him the thing I kept locked deep inside.

"My brother is going to die," I said out loud at last. "And then I'll be alone."

"I know," he answered. His hands cupped my face. They still trembled.

I thought I might feel better, admitting it to another person, but I didn't. A hollowness ripped through me, tearing at my heart. "Ethan, why are you here? The real reason why." He loomed over me, a shadowy outline against swaying branches and the occasional glimpse of stars. "I can handle anything but lies, no matter how outrageous," I promised, and hoped I meant it.

"Because I'm not human, and your brother is dying." He wouldn't meet my eyes, and I knew it pained him to admit it. Just hearing my deepest fear verified out loud hurt, eclipsing his pronouncement of inhumanity. I suppose I had known that, too. "At first, I came for him, to guard his soul until his passing. But there were… complications. I found the both of you hunted by darkness. And then—" he looked up at the stars—"I saw a girl with liquid silver eyes, and everything changed." He watched me intently, as if memorizing me. He brushed my cheek, traced my lower lip. He looked both fascinated and angry as his fingers trembled against my face. "You. You changed everything, and now I have no words for this… this feeling boiling inside me, and no way to answer the expectations I see every minute in your eyes." He gestured to the space between us as if it disgusted him. As if it was impenetrable.

"Oh." It was all I could think of to say. My fingers fluttered toward him as if they, too, would trace his lips, his face, but it struck me how ridiculously fragile, how mismatched we were as I watched my hand shake with nothing stronger than cold and nerves. I snatched my hand back, making it into a fist instead and ground it against my heart. "This feeling?" I asked after a long moment during which I sifted through the things he'd said. Not human. Hunted by darkness. Everything changed. I decided they might make more sense if I tried to bridge the gap between us.

My fingers crept up around the curve of his neck, resting against the taut hollow where his shoulder bent toward me. They were a knot of bunched nerves and muscles that relaxed slightly under my touch. He was always so warm; I traced small, slow circles at the base of his neck, and he leaned in toward me even more in response. I slid my fingers up through his hair and pulled his head down toward mine, touching my lips to his.

I'd expected hesitance, perhaps even resistance. But my whole world narrowed into the feeling of his mouth just barely grazing mine, warm and rough. It was just barely enough, like getting a sprinkler instead of a pool on a really hot summer day and it left me aching and arching up against him. His body was warm all around me and he kissed me, a slow and wondering exploration, his arms a tight arc around us, protecting me, melding me to him. I slid my cheek against his, registering hot dim abrasion of skin. Blood throbbed in my head and heart. I hooked one of my legs across the back of his knees and tried to pull him closer only to have him whisper, "Shh. The weight of me. Too much." He was under me in one fluid movement, his blue-green eyes wide and luminous and startled, and I had time to think *yes this* before his fingers locked themselves around my waist and pulled me flat on top of him.

His lips were hesitant on mine at first, as if asking permission, but I couldn't respond fast enough or hard enough. I rested my weight on my elbows and forearms, framing his face with them as we kissed. My upper body pressed against his, letting him take most of the weight of me. He reached up with his strong hands and pulled my arms down to my sides, which were heaving with adrenaline and the sheer wonder of having him underneath me. He pinned me to him with one arm around my waist while he slowly, shyly explored the side of my face with his fingers. I stopped kissing him long enough to let him run his rough thumb across my upper lip, and then I had his mouth again.

We lay locked together like that until I thought my lungs would explode. I pulled back slightly, my breathing deep and ragged. He stared at me with wonder and alarm. My lips stung in the cold night air, rubbed raw on his strangely rough skin, my face raw as well. I had a brief mental picture of how I must look, red-faced and wild haired and struggling for breath, backlit by falling dead leaves and patchy darkness. I wanted to tell him I was fine, he hadn't hurt me, but I would have been lying. He moved me before I completed the thought. I found myself on the ground next to him before I could speak.

"Hey!" I protested, and tried to climb into his lap.

"You weren't breathing right," he said, pulling me firmly against him. "It scared me."

"I don't want to breathe right," I said, trying to wiggle out from under his arms. "Really, it's okay."

"I'm not human," he said darkly. "I don't want to injure you again."

"Oh." That was a really hard objection to overcome. "Right. That."

"Yes. That."

Long moments passed while I tried to get myself under control. The shock of such close, passionate contact being suddenly withdrawn left me cold and aching. I leaned into his side, seeking the warmth and reassurance that he was still there for me, was still mine if I wanted him. And I did want him. I ached with it. And although his breathing didn't match my almost-panting, he held himself so rigidly careful I knew he was struggling for control, as I was.

Instead I looked at the wild beauty of the park around us. Wind moved tree branches. Ethan was a warm solid presence beside me. "I guess I already knew," I admitted, watching his profile. He looked up at the stars as if connected to them by an invisible string. He vibrated a kind of tense, quiet energy. It reminded me of the way Abigail got during thunderstorms. I found myself stroking his neck and speaking in low, soothing tones. "It's ok. I'm not afraid. You said you were here to protect my brother. You won't hurt us." He recoiled as if I'd struck him. "Ethan? Hey. Shh." I wrapped my own arms around him. "I'm the girl who draws the future, remember? I'm not exactly normal, either. You can trust me."

He sagged against me. The warm, unexpected weight of him almost knocked me over. He checked himself in time. "Caspia, what do you know about your gift for prophecy? Is it common in your family?"

"No," I said, a little unbalanced by his abrupt change in conversation. But if hearing about my ability would help him trust me, so be it. "Only my grandmother could do something similar. She was the only person who knew what the drawings meant. She helped me not be afraid when it happened." I wrapped my arms around my knees, sad as always when I thought of my grandmother. I missed her.

"Tell me about her," he commanded.

"Well," I said slowly, gathering my thoughts in the face of this odd and abrupt request I was beginning to resent just a little. I wiggled closer for warmth. The strange tension in him hadn't eased. "She was born right here in Whitfield. All my family has been, on my mother's side, anyway, all the way back to my grandmother's grandmother. She came though Ellis Island in the late nineteenth century. She's the real family mystery. She was sixteen years old, completely alone, didn't speak a word of English, and pregnant. We don't know anything else about Gran's side of the family before her. It's like she didn't exist before Ellis Island. No birth certificate, no baptismal certificate, no papers or identification of any kind." I smiled into the darkness. "It was a shameful thing, back then, to be pregnant out of wedlock. But I've always been proud of my great-great-grandmother. She must have been very brave. I'm named for her. Supposedly, she came from the Caspian Sea."

"And this is also the bloodline that bears your gift of prophecy." His voice was flat and cold. I wanted his hands on my waist again, his fierce eyes on mine, not this detached creature sitting next to me. I butted against him, frustrated.

"Ethan, what are you trying to tell me? Why don't you just come out and say it? What do you know about my 'bloodline'? What does it have to do with you being here?"

"I think I Fell the moment I saw you," he told me with the dark fervor of a man taking a deadly oath. I could hear the capital letter roll off his tongue. I wanted to tell him to stop. I wanted to go back to kissing him, but his words became a torrent unleashed so fast I had to struggle to comprehend. "I didn't know it then. I just saw a girl whose silver eyes had turned steel with pain, and I didn't know how you could bear it and live. But then I saw how this pain couldn't exist if you didn't love your brother more than anything. It seemed wrong, that love should cause such suffering. So I interfered." He smiled at me in the darkness, an expression full of grace and bitterness and a touch of fear. "And thus it began. Others of my kind have Fallen since the beginning of time but it was most often Rebellion or Darkness. Never me, I thought. I have ever loved the Light, Caspia. I will never join the Fallen, I thought. Some few of my brothers had walked among humans and dared to love human women. These Fallen loved fiercely and deeply. It seemed to me they had been struck with a sickness, or taken prisoner, and I dared to pity them. How sad, I thought, to Fall because of love. Until it happened to me."

The Fallen.

Fallen angels.

My blood felt like it had little shards of ice in it. My throat had trouble working. I choked the words out anyway. "What are you… are you saying… Ethan?" I slipped a cautious hand over his taut fist, smashed against the earth. "That you're Fallen? As in, an angel? A Fallen one?"

"In Latin, angelus," he corrected sharply. "In Greek, aggelos. To the Babylonians, we were sukkalin; in West Africa, malaika. Time passes, kingdoms fall, people die and with them, their names for us, but what we do stays the same."

"And what is that?"

"Whatever we're told," he said softly, and still he wouldn't look at me. "I cannot fathom how many of your lifetimes I have done what I've been told. A messenger of the Light; an intermediary. Until now." His fist spasmed under my hand. "Until you."

I shook my head, desperate to calm him almost as much as I was to calm myself. "It'll be all right. That you're…" I gulped. "An angel. It will, you'll see," I promised, making my words as convincing as I could. "But what does any of this have to do with my bloodline?"

A strange new voice, darkly taunting with a ribbon of ice running through it, reached us through the trees. "What are you telling her, E'than'i'el? Surely not the truth. She wouldn't like you if you did that."

I have never seen such an instant and frightening change come over a person as I did watching Ethan as he knelt in front of me. At the sound of the strange new voice, with its low, rolling sneer, his back arched and his hands curled from fists underneath mine into claws hooked into the earth. His eyes had flashed like tightly leashed storms before. Now they looked as if they harbored full force hurricanes.

"This is neutral territory," Ethan growled, nostrils flaring as he tilted his head to the side in the speaker's direction. "She cannot be touched."

"Neutral only for mortals and innocents," said a new voice directly behind me. I froze. At least two, then. Well. There were two of us. The odds were still good. I squared my shoulders against a slowly building anger. I didn't know these voices, these strangers in my park. They were oddly double-layered voices, hiding a skin-crawling sibilance. I eased slightly forward from a sitting position into a crouch, trying to remember everything Logan had taught me about fighting dirty and male anatomy. Ethan looked desperately at me.

"She is neither mortal nor innocent," chimed in a third person from my right. Great. Now we were officially outnumbered, and the victims of lame insults. I growled. "So she's fair game." At this pronouncement, Ethan exploded upward from his crouch, pulling me with him. I found my back against the same tree I'd tried to push him into earlier, my view of these newcomers completely obscured by Ethan's stubborn and immovable back.

One of the voices started laughing. "Is this her, E'than'i'el? This girl? This breakable, fragile girl?" Ethan pushed so hard against me all the air rushed out of me. The muscles of his back moved as he shifted his balance, his arms held at waist level, and I remembered my drawing. I wondered what his face looked like. I wondered if it matched my missing sketch. I wondered if I was going to pass out from lack of air. Ethan shifted his weight forward and I drank down oxygen. The sneering voice kept taunting. "The Great One himself. Fallen, and for such a vulnerable, little thing. You have no idea how much trouble she's going to be. It will all be for nothing."

"You may as well give her up now," said another one. "She'll give you up as soon as she finds out."

"Finds out what?" I managed to gasp, tired of pushing against a back that wouldn't move.

"Ethan'i'el is here to kill your brother," said the one in the middle. "And if he doesn't, one of us will."

It couldn't be. I didn't believe it. And yet, some tiny, traitorous part of me couldn't help whispering, "Ethan, is that true?"

"No," he snapped tersely. The tendons in his neck stretched as his head snapped back and forth between the three men who advanced on us in a slowly closing arc, just visible in the shadows. They dressed similarly, much like Ethan had the night I'd met him, in dark colors and leather jackets. Their features blended together in similar expressions of feral delight; narrowed eyes betrayed no individual colors, and their lips curled in almost identical sneers. Only their leather jackets showed individuality. The one on my right wore a subtle snakeskin pattern that gathered the dim light to it like a living thing, while his companion to my left wore dull brown leather studded with rivets and patches I couldn't identify.

My breath caught in my throat when the one in the middle stepped into the light. He wore an exact copy of the jacket now snugly buttoned over my messenger's bag full of money, except his was blood red. I looked down at myself, confused. When had I buttoned myself into my jacket? Ethan must have done it when he moved me. Why would he take the time to button my jacket up in a fight? I looked intently at its blood red leather twin. Its owner saw me looking at him and smiled, a quick burning look filled with sharp promises and dark knowledge.

"Well, technically he's not going to kill your brother," the one in red leather corrected carefully, as if every word he managed to slip to me past Ethan was indescribably lovely to him. "He's just going to wait until the cancer finishes him off and then he's going to take his soul." He smiled at me again, enjoying Ethan's low growl as he did it. "But we're going to get him first. And you too, darling."

"Like hell," I hissed.

"That's the general idea," he said, and when he rushed us I couldn't help it. I screamed.

Something huge and dark rippled across his back. Something like wings.

All three of them had them.

As Ethan tensed to meet them, suddenly he did, too.

CHAPTER TWELVE

A DARK AND TERRIBLE BEAUTY

Angels. Fallen ones.

In Whitfield.

Nothing ever happens in Whitfield, I'd told Ethan before dragging him into the darkest part of the park. I'd been so sure of my world, so secure of my place in it when I left work with the night's deposit over one shoulder and Ethan's arm under mine. Before tonight, things were simple. I made coffee. I went to art school. I did the laundry and Logan did the dishes, and the strangest things in my world were the occasional odd prophetic drawing and my brother's illness.

Now there were angels. Fallen messengers of the Light.

I watched with my back plastered against the rough bark of a tree as three men with rippling waves of wing-shaped darkness tried to get past Ethan's guard. Their wings weren't so much distinct shapes as they were an absence of light, as if the three men who bore them carried black holes with them wherever they went. The darkness was heavy and hungry. Staring into it made me feel as if I was simultaneously drowning and falling. The edges fluttered more like torn curtains dragging in the wind than feathers. I ripped my gaze away; even a quick glance left me disoriented, as if I'd been fighting against a current.

Ethan stood with his back to me, practically trembling with rage. I think he growled at me not to move, but the sudden appearance of pulsing, vibrating light at his back wiped away all capacity for independent thought. I don't know how long I stood there, transfixed by the sheer wall of light in front of me. I knew only that it seemed a living thing, rippling with heat and sentience and power, and I was every bit as afraid of it as I was of the powerful, hungry, wing-shaped darkness. The edges of this wing-shaped wall of light were sharp, jagged like sparks or broken glass, and they throbbed with barely restrained power.

I understood a fundamental difference, then. Whatever else these Dark attacking creatures were, they were creatures of absence. Theirs was an emptying destruction, freezing and hollowing their enemies. Ethan would pulse and push, letting the Light that rode him burn and level anything in his way.

"Angels," I choked, and clung even harder to my tree.

What Renaissance idiot first painted angels as chubby, diaper-wearing infants with bundles of feathers on their backs? What idiot ever painted wings as feathers at all? As if angels were human-bird hybrids? As Ethan slammed into one of them with his shoulder, sending him sprawling on his back, a detached part of my mind studied these creatures and their wings as hard as I could. It seemed to me that what the human mind interpreted as wings was more like a glimpse into some place I could only think of as Other. They weren't wings at all, but more like openings into the places they came from. These angels carried one world on their back while they walked in yet another. Was I the only person who saw them this way? Did other people truly see feathers and babies in diapers? What made me different?

Ethan used his fists and a knee on the one wearing snakeskin. He dropped, but was back up in a minute, advancing on us again, slightly behind the one in blood red. Ethan rushed them again, and they became a tangled blur, moving too fast for my eyes to track. All I saw were flashes of light and even more flashes of darkness. The tangled roiling mass of light and dark broke apart suddenly. The Fallen angel in the snakeskin jacket lay several feet away on his back. His chest was open in one long, diagonal slash seeping dark liquid. He didn't appear to be moving. The remaining two circled Ethan, the one in brown leather making quick feints inside his guard. The one in the blood red jacket merely circled, watching. He was pale in the moonlight, his thick black hair a shocking contrast to the diamond-bright eyes he suddenly turned on me as he circled Ethan. He was so beautiful my fingers twitched in spite of myself, as if they held a phantom pencil I could capture his image with before I died. He smiled at me with full cruel lips. Pastel crayon, I thought stupidly before Ethan's howl of pain shattered the night.

Ethan's jeans seeped blood in long gashes down one thigh. The Fallen one in the brown leather jacket had shredded his sweater from shoulder to forearm. Deep bloody gouges snaked down his arm. "Ethan!" As I broke and ran for him, I realized his name had come from my own throat. It cut off abruptly as something blunt and hard hit me in the stomach, stealing all my breath. I had time to see Ethan look at me in pure horror before the Fallen angel in brown leather came at him again and my vision started going gray around the edges.

"Run, Caspia," I heard him call. There was fighting again, too fast for me to follow. "You have to…"

"Oh no you don't," whispered a voice as calm and cruel as dull knives. A blood red arm held me around the waist, squeezing me against him. The blur that was Ethan and the other Dark angel slowed again. Ethan had him pinned, forearm on throat, as he opened a deep gash across his chest using nothing more than his hand. Ethan drew back for another strike, but the creature under him twisted just a little to the side. Ethan's hand would have hit the brown leather jacket. He muttered something and fisted his hand at the last second. The Fallen under him grimaced as something audibly cracked.

They fought bare handed? They'd done that much damage to each other with their bare hands? What chance did I have against that?

The arm under me hauled me backward, deeper into the trees. It loosened enough to let a thin trickle of air down my lungs. Cold, cold terror swamped me as I realized I was going to die. I was going die before Logan. Who would look after him, then? I was supposed be the strong one, there for him no matter what. I wouldn't let these Dark creatures take that from him. I would not. For no good reason at all, my fingers tightened on my messenger bag, full of the night's deposit.

"You must be very embarrassed," I said, surprising even myself by speaking. It hurt to talk. My lower ribs ached as if smashed, and I was glad I'd been too busy at work to eat dinner. I would have thrown it up by now.

Birds moved restlessly in the trees around us. I couldn' see the sky through the branches. I didn't know where we were in the park, or even if we were still in the park at all. Given how fast Ethan could move, we could have been on the outskirts of town for all I knew.

"Pardon me?" Just like Ethan, the beautiful black-haired angel moved without me seeing. One second he had a death grip around my waist, dragging me backward, and the next he stood facing me. He held my forearm between us, gripped painfully between his fingers. I narrowed my eyes when I noticed his fingernails, long like talons and dripping blood.

"You hurt Ethan," I said, but I remembered my drawing. Here was one of the symbols, right in front of me. I tried to quell the brief flare of hope that if one symbol had come true, I might live to see them all come true.

He snorted and tightened his grip. "I hardly find slicing E'than'i'el open embarrassing. And you have other things to worry about. Like the fact that, over the long years of my exile, I have developed a taste for human hearts."

"Right. Of course." I took a deep, steadying breath. "I only meant that I would die of shame if I had thousands of years of pictures of me in a diaper with feather dusters on my back."

For a moment his grip on my arm got tighter, his nails digging so deep I was sure I had puncture wounds down to the bone. I whimpered and his diamond-bright eyes locked on mine. Then he did a terrible, unexpected thing: he threw back his head and laughed. His laugh deepened and echoed, disturbing the birds in the trees around us. Worst of all, the wing shaped void at his back rippled and bulged, exactly as if it was laughing, too.

I kept my face perfectly still as he pulled me very close. He was cold where Ethan had been warm. He gripped me tightly around the waist. "I think I like you, Caspia Chastain," he hissed right into my face. "I think I'll let you live a little bit longer. Just long enough to paint me as I really am." He smirked, and I hated his dark and terrible beauty.

I hated the artist part of me that wanted to capture it even more.

"How do you know I can see you as you really are? What if you get dimples and feathers again instead?" I challenged.

"Because, sweet Caspia, it's a gift of your blood," he crooned into my ear, his breath sending ice shards through my racing heart. "Your Nephilim blood, passed down through your great-grandmother's line. Even thinned with mortal taint, it gives you gifts, which you will use in my service unless you crave a long and painful death for your brother and yourself." He bit my earlobe. I yelped.

"Ink," I gasped out as cold fingers curled around the base of my neck, tightening painfully, making it hard to think. "Ink as black as the voids on your back."

"Good girl," he crooned again, as if to a pet, right before he punched me and everything went black and cold.

Chapter Thirteen

A Demonstration

I woke with my face pressed flat against a frozen obsidian lake of fire. My temple throbbed and my eyes wouldn't stay open and if I wasn't actually in hell, no one had bothered to tell my headache yet.

I focused on breathing, slow and even. When my vision cleared a little, I realized the frozen obsidian was the black marble top of a really long, highly polished table. The fire came from numerous candelabras scattered about its surface, reflected back to me and multiplied until the surface of the table looked like a bonfire-ringed mirror. I lay half sprawled over it, the bottom half of me resting quite comfortably in a cushy chair of indeterminate fabric.

Unfortunately, the table's highly reflective surface meant that I could see my own appearance in the candlelight. If I had any doubts about what had happened to me, they vanished when I tried to lift my throbbing head. A darkly blooming red mark throbbed just above my temple. The beautiful deadly kidnapper had, indeed, punched me in the face. I eased back from the table gradually, clinging to the edge tightly as I studied myself for more damage.

There was none. Wherever I was, however he had brought me here, I was wearing exactly what I had on in Blind Springs Park, down to Ethan's jacket and my messenger bag with the deposit in it, slung sideways across my chest. Not even my hair was messier than usual. I leaned closer into the table and studied the mark again. It was a skilled hit, designed to knock me out. With luck, it wouldn't spread enough to blacken my eye. Whoever he was, he had tremendous control over his inhuman strength. I remembered Ethan ripping through the Fallen one's chest with his bare hands.

Whoever he was, the angel in the dark red leather really wanted me alive.

I groaned, resisting the urge to flop back down against the table and sleep. Instead, I pulled my knees up against my chest and wrapped my arms around them. Ethan's jacket clung to me like a second skin, amazingly enough, and I nuzzled into its contradictory scents of black leather and cotton. I tried not to think about my last vision of him, covered in blood and fighting for both our lives.

Icy fingers wrapped themselves around my neck, pinning my cheek against my arms. "You should take that off. You must be uncomfortable."

I held myself perfectly still, letting only my lips move. Even my teeth stayed locked together. "My discomfort has nothing to do with what I'm wearing."

"Pity." His fingers wound their way up through my hair. I registered their disappearance at the same moment a long, wicked looking knife appeared in his other hand, hovering inches over my heart. "Are you sure you don't want to take it off?" he asked again.

"I think I'll keep my clothes on, thanks," I repeated. I couldn't look away from the knife.

He made no other response before driving the knife down, hard and fast. I watched in helpless horror as the blade bent and shattered against Ethan's black leather. His pale hands held the handle against my jacket, as if he'd managed to stab me anyway, while he slowly, deliberately picked up the broken bits of blade from my lap. I remembered my drawing. A broken knife had been one of the symbols.

Oh, and the darkly beautiful Fallen angel had tried to kill me. I choked. "What… happened?"

"It's armor. The modern version. We'd look a bit odd, walking around in a breastplate or chain mail. He gave you his armor with his own two hands, and no one can take it from you. Not even him."

It offers protection, from the cold and… other things. He'd buttoned me into it as soon as the fighting started. "Why did you tell me? Why not keep it secret?" I asked warily, when my voice finally returned.

He shrugged elaborately, a human gesture probably performed solely for my benefit. It looked like an alien caricature on him. "For reasons of my own. And also so you would know exactly what your protection cost him."

I struggled for breath. "So… when you fought. He didn't have armor, and you did?"

"You didn't see me or my associates without our jackets on, did you?" I closed my eyes and leaned into my hands, sick and dizzy. I remembered Ethan's howl of pain, the blood and slashes through his jeans and sweater. I remembered how he'd punched instead of clawed when he'd encountered brown leather. He'd fought, unarmored, for me. I groaned.

My cruel pale host stood just inside the warm line of candlelight, watching, several feet from my chair. I hadn't seen him move. His wings had disappeared. Perhaps they were only for special occasions. I stared at him blankly. He arched one dark slash of an eyebrow toward me. "I feel sick," I said softly.

Cold fingers ghosted across my hand. I held a plastic tumbler of ice water. "Drink it." He stood inside the arc of candlelight once again, watching me. The plastic tumbler matched one I had in my kitchen. Logan could be drinking juice from it right now, petting Abigail and calling my friends to find out where the hell I was. This insanely mundane detail shocked me out of paralysis. I pushed back from the table and tried to run. My pathetic escape attempt had barely begun when my black-haired captor already held my forearms in his hands. He pulled me tightly back against him, leather sliding against leather, his cold careful strength an echo of how Ethan steadied me. The pressure of his hold increased gradually until it hurt me. I forced myself to perfect stillness like a rabbit in a wolf's embrace. "Okay?" He drew the word out, making it both question and threat. I didn't even nod.

"Okay."

"Good girl." Again we moved. Another room this time, dark and bare except for a low sofa and tall windows completely covered with heavy velvet drapes. I sat. He looked down at me. Apparently he didn't like to sit. I pulled Ethan's jacket tighter.

"Who are you and what do you want and what happened to Ethan?" It came out of me in one long monotonous breath. When I was through, I clung to the edge of the cushion and looked anywhere but at his terrible, beautiful face.

He didn't like that. "Look at me," he thundered, dangerous and angry and low. I looked. His pale skin and soot black hair were too young, too soft for a creature spun from nightmares. His diamond eyes were sharp and cold in a face so delicate it was almost pretty. He was beautiful and terrifying and would hurt me until I did anything he said. "I am Asheroth. Look at me and tell me what you see. What would you paint, Caspia with the gift of Nephilim blood?"

I inhaled sharply through my teeth, remembering my grandmother's words. Gifts of my blood, she had told me. My paintings, the sketches, they were gifts of my blood. Nephilim blood? And what if he was right, this nightmare creature in front of me? They were still Gran's words coming out of his beautiful cruel mouth, and he was twisting them, and he had no right.

"I don't know Nephilim, or the ways of angels," I snapped. I shook with the effort of sitting still. A strange cold rage burned through me, and I knew then I didn't care if I died for my honesty. "I know that Ethan was kind, and you are cruel. I know that I saw wings, where now I see none, but I have an artist's memory. Ethan's were light and warmth and something, and yours were ragged black holes of nothingness. Here is what I see: You are blackest ink on plain white canvas, and I will paint your lips and jacket red with real blood for there's no paint on earth to capture their cruelty."

Sharp nails raked their way down my jaw line and traced the outline of my lips. I jerked my face away, outraged. "Your eyes are liquid silver now, Caspia." His voice was mild for someone who was about to kill me. "Like mercury. Did you know?"

I raised my chin. "Ethan told me. So?"

"Did he happen to tell you why this is important, even dangerous, for you and your brother?" He sat next to me on the sofa, my chin still in his hand. Cold radiated off him in waves, invading the barrier of my clothing. I couldn't suppress my shiver at his touch, his nearness, but if he took offense, he didn't show it. I couldn't turn away from his hot white eyes.

"We were quite rudely attacked," I hissed. The angrier I got, the more it pleased him. "I'm sure he would have, had he not been interrupted and assaulted."

"Ethan'i'el is currently unharmed, unfortunately."

"Glad to hear it," I snapped.

"Are you really? You won't be for long. Your brother is dying, Caspia, and the death of a Nephilim, even one with blood as thinned as yours, is a rare treat. It is enough to gather every being with a trace of angelic blood to the both of you like a flock of vultures waiting for rotting road kill. Your brother lacks the tell-tale Nephilim eyes that you possess because he has displayed no gifts, unlike you. But it makes him no less valuable. And when he dies…" Furious, I pushed against Asheroth, my palms white and fingers splayed with the effort, but he only pulled me closer to his beautiful burning face. "When he dies, there will be a fight such as you have never dreamed for the dying light of his soul. Ethan's only purpose here is to watch your brother die and take him from you, Caspia. He will take him for the Light, but he will take him nonetheless. You will be alone."

He echoed the exact word I'd whispered to Ethan, underneath him in the park. My mind skittered sideways as it did sometimes when I didn't want to think about something truly unpleasant. I filed cruel Asheroth's words away to take out later, when things were calm and I was safe again. "You lie." It was a statement, flat and cold. He smiled to hear it and stroked my cheek.

"What will happen to you, sweet Caspia, when your brother is dead?" I tried to jump off the couch. I landed flat on my back on the cold hard floor, his alabaster face and black hair inches above me. His hands manacled my wrists, his ice cold skin almost burning mine at point of contact. His body crouched over mine, caging me, trapping me. "When your brother is dead and the disappointed vultures see you standing there with your silver crying eyes and watered down Nephilim blood and no protector? Tell me, Caspia. Do you know how rare women with Nephilim blood are?" I stared at him, expressionless. I dared not show fear. I didn't even move. He was a predator, but I wasn't prey. "How long do you think you'll last after your brother dies?" he purred.

"Maybe," I told him, shocked to realize I spoke the truth even as it rolled off my tongue, "I don't care."

Chapter Fourteen

A Reason It's Called Falling

Asheroth didn't like apathy. He preferred terror or fury.

His beautiful lips twisted bitterly. "Then it is fortunate," he snarled, so close his black hair blinded me and his cold inhuman cheek rested against mine, "that I got to you first." He pulled me up from the floor. I think he meant to be gentle as he deposited me back on the sofa in one single jerky movement. It was as if he had forgotten how to handle someone as fragile as a human. I watched him stalk from me to one of the windows with a fluid, leonine prowl. "You love him," he said, as if to himself. "How unexpected. How dangerous." It was a brief respite, though; Asheroth was back in my face, his eyes blazing anger and hate, as if I had done something unforgivable. "Love is the most dangerous thing there is!" Perfect lips curled back from sharp white teeth. Icy fingers pulsed against the back of my neck, alternating between vise and caress.

He's crazy. How long before he hurts me? Really hurts me? I said the first thing that popped into my head. "Ethan said he had Fallen." I tried to think, to clear my head and plan. "What did he mean?"

Asheroth's diamond eyes brightened even more. My own eyes burned, staring into them, but I wouldn't twist or wiggle. I wouldn't make myself look vulnerable, turning myself into his prey. "When angels Fall, they don't get choices." He released me. I stood by the low sofa again, gripping its back as the room spun. I hated how fast they could move. Asheroth stood with his back to me, his hand toying with the edge of a drape. "We don't get second chances, either."

"That makes no sense at all." *Keep him talking. Say anything.*

"It's simple. You have free will. We do not. You can choose whom to love. We cannot. When we love a human, it is with total and complete devotion, and utterly beyond our control. It means exile and the chance to love one single human soul."

I remembered Ethan, under the trees, his smile bitter and graceful. "It sounds more like slavery."

Asheroth turned to me then, and my artist's mind said yes, this. His beautiful face was twisted with grief as well as cruelty and madness. His body bowed backward as if there was a hollow place somewhere inside and he couldn't find it, but he would spend all his long cruel eternity trying to fill it anyway. "That's why it's called Falling," he said flatly.

Yes, this. I would paint him this way, lost and murderous and hurt and stunning, in blood red leather and shadows.

If I lived.

"She left you," I finally said as the last puzzle piece clicked into place. "Who was she? Your human?"

Dozens of studio-quality track lights blazed into life. Momentarily blinded, I gripped the sofa for balance. "She didn't leave me," he said from behind me. I wisely closed my eyes the second cold fingers touched my waist, moving me. "She just didn't love me back. Not enough. Not as I loved her. She let another human debase and defile her." His voice dropped into a low, dangerous growl. "And then she died, as humans always do."

A life-size painting of a young woman dominated the wall in front of me. Honey blonde hair framed a soft, pretty face with gray eyes. She sat on a crumbling stone wall with a book in her lap, tattered around the edges and obviously well loved. Her bare hair rippled slightly in an invisible wind that lifted her skirts enough to show equally bare feet. A discarded hat and ribboned slippers laid tossed aside in a heap. She looked defiant and proud. Her clothes and the book, even worn, spoke of wealth, as did the quality of the oil painting itself. "Nineteenth century. European." I looked for a signature and found none.

He kept his hands on my waist and turned me slowly around the room. I noticed other paintings, from other times. A piano. A bookshelf lined neatly with leather-bound volumes and small items. The edge of a drawing peeking out, done in charcoal, with the side cut unevenly but cleanly, as if with a knife. A hand-painted deck of tarot cards.

A sketch, done in charcoal?

Was it my missing drawing?

But the tarot cards. Hand-painted.

Definitely mine.

"I've kept track of her descendants," he said softly—so softly, that I might have mistaken his tone for gentleness if not for the darkness it stirred in my blood.

"Those are my cards." I tried to keep my voice light, conversational, because if I didn't I might start screaming and never stop.

"Her eyes were silver, too. You can't really tell in the painting, but the artist didn't have your skill."

"Did you buy the rest of them, too? Of my cards? Are you the collector who wanted a private commission from me because if you are you don't have to do this…" I babbled.

"Shh," he cut me off, drawing a single finger across my lips in a disturbingly knife-like gesture. "No, I'm not your collector. I try not to get too involved where her descendants are concerned. I find it hard to maintain objectivity. But when I saw you with him… with one of us." He was going to start hurting me really, really soon. I couldn't help it; I tried to break free. He crushed me against him so tightly I stopped breathing. "She had Nephilim blood. You have to understand. She chose to let a human have her, a human, and you are the result, you and your brother and your mother and grandmother before you, but you have her eyes and I will not let E'than'i'el have what I couldn't."

"You never even knew her, not really," I said, desperately. "If you did, you'd know I'm not her."

It was the wrong thing to say.

"*She* is who made me what I am," Asheroth raged against my ear. His cold fingers curled around the base of my neck. My heart sped. We faced the painting together again. I could feel the twin voids of darkness unfurling on his back, as if their darkness called to the cursed angel's blood that throbbed within my veins. I thrashed against him and he let me, secure in the knowledge that he had me by the neck. My vision was gray around the edges. Nothing but the painting filled my sight. The proud, defiant girl looked right at me. I saw the book in her lap again. Tattered, worn, obviously read many times. I wondered what it was that this ancestress of mine loved to read. And then I bit the soft inside of my lip to keep from crying out because I recognized it, the book; I had drawn it, it was one of the symbols, they were all coming true. There was only one more.

My fingers curled around my messenger bag, slung sideways across me underneath Ethan's jacket. It was sturdy canvas, a trendy cranberry color. I'd picked it out in a moment of insanity on a rare trip to a mega mall last summer. It had heart-shaped buckles. Remembering my drawing, I knew what I had to do. I unsnapped one buckle of the messenger bag, readying it to drop.

"Her name was Caspia," Asheroth said. With every word he spoke, he tightened his grip on my neck like a vise. *He's going to break my neck.* "Just. Like. You."

Armor, from his own two hands, I thought, and let Ethan's jacket fall open over buttons loosened while I'd been thrashing. I caught the armor-wrapped bag full of money and coins by its long, loose strap and slammed it in a fast arc against Asheroth's unguarded knee. The buckle snapped on impact. His fingers loosened. I didn't know if I succeeded in hurting him or if he was just sickly amused, playing with me.

I don't know what I was thinking. Angels were fast, but I had to try.

I managed to take Ethan's jacket with me as I ran.

Straight into Asheroth's blood red chest.

It hurt. Worse than the time I wrecked my bike flat against the brick walls of Blind Springs Park, worse than the time Pansy Holt beat me up in junior high. I lay flat on my back thinking, this is it, I'll never see them again, waiting for Asheroth to finish me.

Except he didn't.

Sounds like boxed thunder and statues growling, full of emotions so fierce they had no human names, echoed through the room behind me, followed by crashing and breaking. Flat on my back, I watched as lines cracked and webbed across the plaster ceiling. The sounds were more terrible than fighting. They promised more than winning and losing; they promised the end of someone's existence. I wanted to pull Ethan's jacket over my face and hide, but I couldn't. I was a part of this conflict until the last bestial snarl.

"I think she's in shock," said a soft, familiar voice. Worried brown eyes shaded by a baseball cap, pulled low over a thin face, leaned over me. "She's awake, but she's not moving." Light touches at my neck, my wrist. He brushed my hair back from my face. "Cas, honey? Can you hear me?"

I didn't want to believe and have it yanked away from me again, not while the inhuman growling rose and fell in pitch around us. Were we both dead? Had vulture angels eaten his soul and gotten mine as well, as Asheroth promised?

"You're wearing a Yankees cap," I said after several good long squints. "Either you're not Logan, or we're both dead and in hell."

My favorite pair of brown eyes in the entire world almost disappeared into the shadows and lines of his face while he shook with silent laughter. When had the shadows gotten so deep? But his hand squeezed mine with the barest echo of its familiar strength, and his smile was all I wanted from the universe right then. "I had to raid a blind Russian's closet," he explained, still laughing. "So you can't blame either one of us."

"Of course she's in shock. She probably won't be fit to face the public for weeks," a heavily accented smoker's growl agreed. Mr. Markov? Something sharp rapped my ankle, right on the bone. I jerked. "But at least she can move. She doesn't need her brain to wash dishes."

"Don't listen to him, Cas," my brother soothed. He hadn't moved from his crouch next to me. "He's been worried out of his mind. He's just grouchy. It's how Russians show they care."

I propped myself up on my elbows slowly. Mr. Markov stood at my feet. His sightless eyes looked through me. The head of his cane, always a plain glass ball before, now glowed bright gold. I had no idea what it meant and I didn't care because they were here and alive and wouldn't hurt me.

I threw myself into my brother's lap, locking my arms around his thin shoulders, not caring for once how fragile he might be. In that moment, he was my strong big brother, and I needed him. I let him rock me as I cried and told him truths crazier than any lies I had ever spoken. "I was going to die, Logan. More than once. He wanted our souls, and… he was beautiful. We have Nephilim blood. Both of us. And Ethan… Oh, Logan. He gave me his jacket and he wants your soul and I don't know what to believe."

He rocked me steadily, like he'd done for as long as we'd been alive, rubbing the small of my back. "Hush, Cas. It's all right, Cas. It'll all make sense soon."

I decided to pretend I believed him.

"How did you find me?" I'd made my brother's shoulder a snotty wet mess.

Mr. Markov cleared his throat. His cane had stopped glowing. "There are a few things you need to know about Whitfield, Caspia. When you're feeling better."

His words nudged ominously against the precarious safety of my brother's encircling arms. I waved them away as if warding off evil. Bad enough my world was suddenly populated with angels and Nephilim and that my brother and I both shared one as a long-ago ancestor. I rested my cheek in the hollow underneath Logan's knife-sharp collarbone and closed my eyes tight. I was grateful to Mr. Markov for helping with the rescue efforts, and I was curious about why his cane had glowed gold, but I failed to see why my boring, peaceful little hometown had any relevance. Whitfield had no secrets; I'd lived there all my life.

I realized the sounds of fighting had stopped just as Ethan appeared in the doorway. He wore the same clothes as he had in the park. They were shredded in places, and stiff with dried blood. Fresh gouges seeped dark crimson on his cheek and chest. His breathing was even, though, and he walked without stumbling. I tried to rise, but he put his hand on my shoulder and dropped gently beside me. Luminous blue-green eyes steady as searchlights fixed directly on me. His face was nearly expressionless as he looked me over. He saw the bruise over my temple and narrowed his eyes.

"I'm not going to ask if you're alright," he said evenly, but his voice was hard. Only then did I notice how tightly clenched his fists were. "I know that you aren't. For now, I just need"—he closed his eyes and swallowed hard—"I just need to know that you'll tell me what happened. When you can."

I made myself ask, flat and merciless. "Is he dead?"

Ethan shook his head. "We're hard to kill. But he's injured and gone to a place it's rather hard to come back from."

I nodded sharply and touched his fist. "You're hurt. You should take your jacket. Asheroth told me what it meant." I thought of the knife, shattering over my heart. "Actually, he showed me."

"Did he now?" I didn't know voices could have temperatures, but his did, and it dropped. "Keep it." Black leather that smelled impossibly of cotton settled over my shoulders like a cape. "It was a gift."

"He said a lot," I whispered. I tried to keep the terror out, but it clawed its way up my throat. "Asheroth. He said Logan and I… that we're…" I stopped. I couldn't find a way to say what I meant. "I'm scared," I finally admitted. I couldn't make my voice rise above a shaky whisper. "I want to go home." I took maybe the deepest breath of my life and carefully did not look him in the eyes. Instead, I studied the subtly shifting lines of light and shadow just beneath his cheekbones. "Come with us."

Ethan nodded once, sharply. "I was going to, even if only to haunt your hall." He smiled his graceful, bitter smile. "I have nowhere else to go, now." He looked to Logan, who nodded easily in invitation, then back to me. "There's a reason it's called Falling."

I risked a look at his eyes then, but for once, I couldn't read them. They were as carefully blank as new canvas or an un-walked path.

CHAPTER FIFTEEN

WARDED

Logan was petting my hair. He leaned against me as I sat at our table, my body limp against its polished wooden surface. My arms splayed out amongst scattered potted plants and candles. His long, thin fingers moved carefully through the tangled mess of my hair, pausing now and again to work loose a knot or remove a bit of forest floor. He spoke to me of our sleepy, little hometown, and of how it was a sanctuary for the strange and unexplained, that it had always been this way, but he hadn't known it until Mr. Markov burst in on him earlier, waving his glowing cane, exclaiming that he knew I was in trouble because he'd put a tracking spell on the night's deposit.

"Guess I'm not the only freak in town," I said dully into the table, feeling cold and strangely betrayed. I didn't know how many more revelations I could handle before I snapped. "We should have a coming out party."

"Cas," Logan said patiently. "Mr. Markov was talking about spells, and others like him. In Whitfield. He talked to me while we tracked you to the park." He stiffened, his voice distant. "That's when we found Ethan. Fighting. They had… not wings, exactly; more like planes of light and darkness on their backs, and there was all this blood, and you were gone…"

"I know, Logan," I murmured, closing my eyes. "I was there. I don't want to think about it right now." His fingers were as light and soothing as my mother's had been. It would have been easy to pretend we were younger and our parents were alive, except for one or two things. For one, Logan handled me a bit too carefully as if I was made of glass and might shatter at any moment under his hands. For another, I could faintly hear Mr. Markov as he laid hands on every single door and window in our apartment, speaking identical phrases of coaxing, languid sibilance every time. As Logan's fingers, light as vapor, traveled through my hair, I wondered what language this man I thought I knew spoke. It was beautiful and terrifying all at once, and it certainly wasn't Russian. I'd heard him curse and demand, shout and threaten, and more rarely, praise in his native tongue, and what came from his mouth now as he moved from threshold to windowpane was like nothing I'd ever heard before.

"Stupid, blind Russian wizard," I swore softly. "I'm getting a raise out of this somehow."

"What was that, sweetheart?" Logan asked softly in the carefully measured tones he reserved for extremely stressful situations. I ignored him and closed my eyes even tighter, wanting to hang onto the illusion of safety and familiarity for as long as I could.

Ethan interrupted Mr. Markov's repetitious chanting. "This will work as you intend? You're sure?"

My boss sighed. "It's the best I can do." He sounded very tired. "We don't want to keep out all supernaturals, mind you. That would bar half the town, ourselves included. I only set wards specifically against the darker forces."

"It's not perfect," Ethan agreed. I heard cabinets open, water running. Only seconds before, he'd been standing beside Mr. Markov at the front window. Asheroth had moved that quickly too. I shuddered. "But even the best defenses rarely are." Fresh coffee and the *clang* of mugs; Ethan sat, radiating warmth from the chair next to me.

"Bah." It was a uniquely Russian sound of dismissal. I sat up slowly as gnarled fingers reached for a mug and familiar, sightless eyes looked right over my head. "Think of my wards as a home security system. They are only part of the solution. The wise home owner should also have a good guard dog, and a firearm or two, to guard his gold."

Logan's hand had dropped to my shoulder as if he sensed how shaky I still was. He gave it a reassuring squeeze. "So which one are you, Ethan?" he tried to joke. "Guard dog or firearm?"

"Depends on the intruder," he said, grinning. Logan and Mr. Markov laughed. Ethan joined them. It occurred to me that I had never seen him laugh before; lines appeared at the corners of eyes and lips, making him look softer, more vulnerable. More human. His eyes locked with mine and I could read the plea buried there: laugh with me, Caspia, but I couldn't. Everyone in the room was laughing but me. It wasn't a very good joke, but that wasn't why. Underneath those eyes the color of oceans, eyes that were older than breath, he wanted to be human with me, for just a moment.

Be human with me, Caspia.

For a minute I could see it, us together, not laughing yet, but I could let myself lie down against the warmth of his skin through his borrowed clothes and find safety there. The slightest of movements on my part would take me there, into arms like eternal summer carved just for me.

For the span of one fragile mortal lifetime, and then, for Ethan, an eternity alone. How long before he went insane, before the beautiful planes of light across his back turned into dark sucking abscesses, before he hated humans and tried to hurt them?

Asheroth had loved a human named Caspia once.

My hands gripped the edge of the table carefully as if I sat at the keys of a grand piano and might, at any moment, launch into a Nocturne. I realized I was shaking very, very slightly, tiny tremors of fear and rage and shock traveling up and down my body in waves. I opened my mouth, but no sound came out. Blind Mr. Markov slapped a mug down in front of me as surely as if declaring checkmate. It quickly filled with coffee, black and strong. It must have been Ethan again, because no one moved to get the pot from the kitchen. It was just there. They stared at me, waiting.

I was waiting too. I was waiting for answers. I was waiting to know what was safe to tell and what had to be kept secret, and from whom. I was waiting for my brother to die and for my brother to get better. I was waiting for Ethan to stay and for him to go. I was waiting for Asheroth and his minions to come back and to wake up and find out it had all been a dream.

I was sick of waiting.

I don't remember how I got there. Perhaps my Nephilim blood suddenly boiled over, gifting me with impossible speed at last, or perhaps I forgot everything else in the grip of enraged shock. I know even Ethan wasn't fast enough to stop me as I grabbed our final family photograph from my father's roll top desk. "I want to know why." My fingers curled around the edges of the frame. To me, my slow prowl back toward the table seemed calm and reasonable, but everyone else looked at me as if I had picked up a deadly weapon. "Why?" I shook the picture, the four of us smiling, frozen forever behind glass. "Why couldn't they tell us who we are? Why couldn't she," I smashed the frame, glass down, against the back edge of my chair. It made a satisfying crunching sound. "Tell me I had the same blood," I whacked the picture harder, sending glass flying. "As Asheroth?" I used both hands this time. The frame snapped in half. "That Dark angels," I ripped the picture free, "want to kidnap me and steal my brother's soul when he's dead?" I compressed the picture into the tightest ball I could as my voice climbed to a shriek even I recognized as hysterical.

Hands like stone caught mine and held them. I recognized the warm, maddening, calming presence against my back. I leaned into him in spite of myself. "I won't let them," Ethan promised. There was nothing soft or soothing to this vow. There was nothing soft about him at all as he held me motionless. "They won't take your brother and I won't let you hurt yourself, either."

Logan appeared in front of me, hollowed from the night's revelations, to pry the remains of our family photo from my fist. "I'm not dead yet, Caspia." He sounded almost angry.

It burned in me, this last dark secret between us. I felt as if I was disgorging snakes when I let it out, at last. "But you will be." I jerked again against Ethan's hold. "He wouldn't be here, if you weren't. You realize that, don't you?"

Logan leaned in really close and wiped the tears from my eyes. I got the sense it wasn't out of tenderness. Rather, he wanted me to have a good look at his face. "How much of our time together have you wasted acting like I'm already dead, little sister?" He poked me in the stomach, hard. "Don't blame him. At least he doesn't treat me like a walking corpse."

Then Logan was gone from my field of vision. Mr. Markov had gone at some point, too. Ethan's hands slipped from mine and I stood alone in our living room. I thought about going after Logan, about crawling up next to him in his bed. I wanted to apologize and promise to do better and cry and have him hold me, but something held me back. "He's right," I told the empty living room. "I'm a terrible person, and he doesn't need me."

"You're an idiot," Ethan said into my ear, gathering me close. "Do you think that was any easier for him than it was for you?" One hand molded itself against the curve at the base of my spine, and I felt him smile against my cheek. "You were brave, the both of you. Truth is hard when you love someone." He set me down in a room full of hot steam and the sound of running water. The tiles were slick beneath my feet. We had moved together with the speed of angels, from living room to the sanctuary of my bathroom, and I had been too wrapped up in myself to notice.

"B… bath?" I confronted the half-filled tub, surprised. My body trembled, completely independent of what I commanded it to do. I scrabbled at the last two buttons of my jacket, my fingers shaking too much to do anything but get them halfway undone. "I'm so cold."

"I know," he said softly. The jacket came off easily in his hands. "One of the symptoms of shock. The bath will warm you. Do you want me to get your brother to help you?"

"G… god no!" I perched on the edge of the tub. "I can manage." He nodded. "Where will you be?" I asked, fear crashing back over me again. I suddenly very much did not want to be alone.

"Just outside the door. If you need me." The water cut off almost exactly at the same time his warm hands lifted my face to his. "I won't let him hurt you, Caspia. Ever again."

I let my fingers trail along the surface of the hot water. I didn't want Ethan to leave. If he left, I'd be alone for the first time since I encountered him in the alley next to work. Since before I had been taken, before I knew about angels and Nephilim and that exciting things do indeed happen in Whitfield. So I stalled.

"Tell me a hard truth," I whispered straight into his softly glowing eyes.

He knelt on one knee until he rested level with me. He laced his fingers together across my thighs, the warmth of them pleasantly abrasive against my skin. "A trade then, Caspia Chastain. My truth for yours." His eyes narrowed and held. "The hard kind."

"Okay." I took a deep breath and asked one of my fears out loud. "Asheroth said your kind doesn't't get choices when they…. when you …." My voice turned shy as I danced around the word, looking for ways to not risk saying it outright. But Ethan wanted plain truth, so I just averted my eyes and said it anyway. "When you love a human. Are you going to turn into Asheroth, then? Without me?"

His fingers spasmed across my thighs. My muscles tensed in response. "I'd like to think not," he answered at last. "I cannot see the future, you know. But I'm pretty sure the answer is no." I nodded, exhaling slowly, relieved.

"My turn." Ethan rubbed my thigh with his thumb for a moment before snapping his eyes to mine. The intensity was shocking, at once intimate and fiercely angry. "Tell me what happened. What he said to you, what he did." He smiled a very little. "What you did to him."

I found my smile a bit more easily than I had in many long hours. "Did he have knee trouble?" I guessed.

"To put it mildly," he affirmed.

"Ok then." I trailed my fingers through bubbles, not wanting to look at him, not knowing what I'd do if he rejected me. "Wait for me. After my bath."

"That bad?"

"I don't know," I answered honestly. "He left marks. I don't know how badly. That's why I need the mirror. And then I'm going to crawl in my bed and have a small nervous breakdown." My voice was very muted, almost childlike, when I added, as if it was an afterthought, "I'd feel much safer if you were there."

Bathe fast, I heard, and he was gone.

I might have imagined it, though.

CHAPTER SIXTEEN

DECLARATION

I lost track of time in the steamy heaven of my bath. I refused to let myself dwell on what had just happened. It was like I'd created a door through which I could shove anything unpleasant. Anytime the door threatened to open, disgorging the events of the previous few hours, I would sink all the way under the water, watching the bubbles of my breath shoot upwards. I knew my temporary haven wouldn't last. Ethan was demanding answers, and I couldn't put him off forever. All I could do was avoid thinking about things for as long as possible. But I must have taken too long because Ethan was waiting for me when I surfaced for the fourth time.

"You're going to need a shower after your bath, just to get all that stuff off you," Ethan said, leaning against the door adjoining my bedroom. I gaped at him from the depths of my bathwater, covered from neck to toes by steamy scented bubbles. I felt horribly exposed, as if he could see through the foam, through my skin, even, to my too-rapidly beating heart. I hugged my knees to my chest, but it did little to dispel the feelings of vulnerability.

All traces of blood and fighting were gone from him. Ethan's face was whole again without even the shadow of a bruise or scrape. Logan had found some clothes for him. A long-sleeved brown t-shirt and jeans fit him as well as they once had my brother, before he'd lost so much weight. His light eyes narrowed and he seemed tense, blocking the door to my bedroom as if guarding me was all he knew how to do. He stood there with bare feet and both hands clenched in his pockets, watching me with careful patience as if trying to decide if it was safe to approach me and if not, then what to do instead.

He seemed to want some kind of guidance.

He wasn't the only one. I had no idea where we were supposed to go from here. I wanted him here, desperately; he'd protected me and fought for me. His presence was the one thing making me feel safe at the moment. But at what cost? If I understood him correctly, he had already Fallen. Because of me. How would that change things between us? I flicked forlornly at a nearby bubble. I had no idea what to think, let alone say.

I was just crying and having a bath, I tried to explain. I looked at the sheet of bubbles and wondered if he felt as lost and empty as I did. I wanted to tell him I was frightened and aching and I'd never had a boy in my bathroom before, angelic or not, who wasn't my brother, and that I had no idea what to do. What came out instead was, "I think my world looks good on you."

I realized as soon as the words left my mouth that they were probably the stupidest things I'd ever said. I wondered if I had time to drown myself.

But he smiled and he had never looked more human.

He must have heard something he needed in my voice. Permission, maybe. When I looked up, my bedroom door was empty. Fingers softly touched my neck, just resting there. I stiffened. Ethan's hands felt like warm pumice, lying lightly against my skin. But Asheroth…

He must have felt me stiffen. "Am I hurting you?" he asked, as if he feared the answer.

"No." The single syllable swelled in my throat. I breathed through it. "It's just that… Asheroth held me there. Hard."

His hands vanished instantly. I missed his touch just as quickly, but then he lifted the damp mass of my hair, exposing the back of my neck to the light. "Bruising," he said tightly, letting my hair fall. He knelt by the side of the claw-footed tub, a look of concern locked on his face. "Have you looked yourself over yet? I just assumed…"

"I'm perfectly fine," I growled, low and fierce. I didn't want to remember the attack, let alone discuss it.

Ethan's eyes widened in surprise that darkened quickly into anger. I blinked to find him several feet away. He stood flat against the wall next to the closet where we kept medical supplies and towels, his face a cold stone mask around eyes that burned much too brightly. He assessed me, his face calm and dangerous. Once again, I didn't see him move. Lightning-fast, I found myself standing in the tub like a landed fish, bathwater running off me in sheets, Ethan's hands on my slick bare skin pulling me right against him. His fingers dug into my shoulders, holding me so that the front of our bodies were one long point of contact, and every breath I took pressed me closer up against him. "You just lied to me," he said flatly. "You are very obviously not fine."

Note to self: Do not lie to Ethan. Especially when wet and naked.

"It's a figure of speech," I said defensively. "That I'm fine. Sort of." Highly conscious that I wore nothing but water, each breath against Ethan's borrowed shirt drove home the discovery that wet skin was more sensitive than dry skin. His fingers kneaded my shoulders, infusing them with pressure and warmth rather than pain. The fire from his skin seeped through his borrowed clothes, heating my own skin where we touched and reminding me that he wasn't quite human. His still furious eyes locked onto mine, and I found I could look nowhere else. "I'd like a towel, please," I said in a voice that sounded too high-pitched and trembling to belong to me.

He let go and I swayed in the tub. Before I had time to feel too horribly exposed, a huge brown bath towel enveloped me, its bottom soaking up bathwater. As quickly as he'd hauled me out of my bath, I was alone again.

I didn't want to be.

I dressed quickly and peeked out the bathroom door. Ethan paced my bedroom like a caged jungle cat, agitation evident in every line of his muscles. I cleared my throat and he was there in front of me instantly, worry warring with anger as he touched the tips of my fingers.

"I'm sorry," I squeaked.

"You've got nothing to be sorry for," he soothed, tugging gently on our joined hands. "I am… unaccustomed… to such strong emotions, especially the negative ones. I assure you, my anger is aimed elsewhere." His face darkened. "At the one who marked you." He pulled me gently forward.

And so I found myself in the middle of my bedroom, in front of my full-length mahogany frame mirror, wearing an oversized t-shirt I often slept in and loose cotton shorts while Ethan prowled around me in a slow, tight circle, stopping periodically to look closely at some part of my body. He got more agitated as he paced. Every light I owned blazed. I kept my eyes fixed on piles of laundry and stacks of books, my mind on the song playing softly from the playlist I'd started when I walked in. I did not want to look at my reflection. I did not want to see what had been done to me.

"Where else are you hurt?" He traced patterns on my skin, his fingers like fire. "What did he do to you?" His touch, his tone, everything about him was coaxing, inviting, but with an edge. Tell me. Trust me. So I can break his neck.

I couldn't. The words wouldn't come.

Ethan stopped suddenly behind me. He kissed the back of my neck. I shivered. He traced one warm rough finger down my upper arms and made feather-light circles there. "Slight bruising here. Finger marks," he said, not unkindly, although I could hear the strain there, what it cost him to stay calm. He held out one forearm. Despite myself, I looked at our reflections in my mirror. I looked so pale against him, his arm supporting mine. With every light blazing, crescent shaped marks throbbed red in the glass. "Cuts. From his nails," he whispered. Light kisses over each mark. And then he held me against his chest, tucking me close with his arms tight around me. His lips brushed the place on my temple where Asheroth had hit me. "And here." He kissed me there again, a little longer. "What happened here?"

"He knocked me out. So he could take me… wherever he took me."

Ethan went perfectly still. "It could have killed you. A blow like that."

Something a little too hysterical and high-pitched to be called a laugh escaped me. "No, he wanted me very much alive. It was more fun that way."

"Why?" The word grated and scraped, like he'd had to drag it out from the depths of himself.

I finally began to shake, wearing nothing but damp skin and sleep clothes and Ethan's arms. "He… said things. About you. About why you were here, and Logan and my blood…" My body shook so much in his arms I bit my own tongue.

"Shh," he soothed, drawing me close. He was as warm as I remembered. "Where else, Caspia?" he asked again, dredging up patience and gentleness from somewhere. "Can you show me, if you can't tell me?"

I inched up my t-shirt, baring my stomach to the mirror. Asheroth had first caught me there, dragging me away from Ethan, and I'd fought him before I knew it was useless to struggle. Still, the bruising wasn't as bad as I'd thought. At first it felt like I'd broken ribs. But now, in the safety of my bedroom and the dark anger of Ethan's watchful presence, a faint tracing of red and purplish bruises crept across my stomach like lace.

He could have hurt me so much more. As he'd hurt Ethan. I'd expected him to, at any moment. Why hadn't he?

"I don't know," Ethan said. I realized I'd spoken out loud. Warm fingers skimmed just over my bruises, charging the air between his skin and mine. I inhaled sharply at the quick unexpected slap of electricity. "It almost worries me more. Like he was saving you for something especially sinister. Did he say or do anything else, Caspia? Anything at all?"

How did we wind up on my bed? Soft, but mismatched sheets tangled at my back, pillows scattered all around. Maybe because my legs gave out in sheer terror at the thought of Asheroth saving me for "something especially sinister." I clung to Ethan's shoulders as he leaned over me. How to explain the twisted and beautiful, but utterly mad creature that was Asheroth? Asheroth, who had loved a human with eyes like mine and my name and my blood? Would Ethan wind up mad and beautiful and cruel centuries from now, too? But at this moment, in the light and shadows of my dimly lit bedroom, I wanted there to no one and nothing else but him. I clung to him so tightly my muscles hurt.

"Asheroth said I had… Nephilim blood. Nephilim gifts. And that women with my blood were especially rare." I almost choked on the words, but I got them out. "I won't pretend I know what all that means or that it doesn't scare the hell out of me." I strained toward him, not wanting to let go. "He was… torn, I think. Twisted. He loved a human once." I closed my eyes to say it, the hardest thing of all. "My great-great grandmother. He's been watching us, all of us, my whole family, since she left him. However long ago that was."

Over me, Ethan froze. No breathing, no movement. Then slowly, as if by inches, he pulled me up and into his lap, wrapping us both in a soft chenille blanket. "He told you this?" Ethan asked, incredulous, stroking my damp hair.

"He tries not to interfere, he said. With her descendants." Me. I was her descendent. My voice cracked. "He has trouble remaining objective. But he saw you with me, and he couldn't… let us…"

"Shh," he whispered, but he kept on stroking my hair. I relaxed into him, together under our blanket. "Brave Caspia. What else? Can you tell me?"

"You saw the portrait?" I felt, rather than saw, his nod. "He said I have her eyes. She had Nephilim blood, and she turned him down. And he's been alone ever since. He said… humans have a choice about whom they love. He didn't. Do you, Ethan? Do you have a choice?"

"Perhaps," he said, after a long moment. "But I always have a choice in my actions, Caspia. Everyone does."

I burrowed against the rough warm skin of his arms. "I'm not sure Asheroth does anymore. I think that's one of the definitions of madness." I forced myself not to look away from him, to purge the worst of Asheroth's poisonous accusations before they festered any deeper. "He said you only came for Ethan's soul, and that when he was d… dead, you would leave me for the Dark Nephilim to fight over. Like vultures over road kill."

He didn't look away either, but rage simmered like a slow-burning fuse. "Do you believe him?"

"No." I felt warmer, stronger, now that the worst was out.

"And trust?" His face was deadly serious. "Do you trust me? After what he told you?"

"Of course," I whispered, realizing it was true as the words left my mouth. "Who else would I trust with this?"

He smiled briefly at that. But only briefly. "I have an idea," he said hesitantly. I tilted my head, listening. "You tell me one thing that happened, and I'll tell you any one thing you want to know."

I narrowed my eyes suspiciously. "Anything?"

He smiled a little. "If it's within my power to tell, yes. I don't, for instance, know lottery numbers or what Abigail is thinking at any given moment."

I pulled his hand to my face for no other reason than that I wanted to nuzzle it. "I think I can get through that," I agreed. I remembered being on top of him in the park, kissing him until I couldn't breathe, my skin rubbed raw against his. I scraped my cheek against the palm of his hand. "But not tonight." I kissed the dead center of his palm. "Oh, Ethan. No more pain and madness tonight."

"Caspia." He sounded a little winded, but he didn't pull back. He spread his fingers wider, opening his palm to another, deeper kiss. I looked to find him leaning closer, his blue-green eyes very wide. "It's been a long, trying day." His voice was rough, labored. "You need rest. Where do you want me to sleep?"

"Stay with me," I said, as calmly and matter-of-factly as I could. "Please."

I stared at him very hard, willing him not to look away from me. "Oh," he said, and he didn't. His eyes began to glow with the ferocity of gathering storms. He held himself very, very still. "I suppose I meant, where would you like me to go? I don't need to sleep right now. I'm too keyed up, and I'd prefer to be awake anyway, to guard against…"

My fingers tightened their hold on his shirt without any further directions from me. "With. Me." I realized I was shaking again. It shocked me, how frightened I still was. I wondered if it was because of Asheroth, or because Ethan might get up and walk away. "Just until I fall asleep." I lowered my voice to a hoarse whisper, trying to disguise the desperation I couldn't keep out.

Lightning flashed in his eyes before he closed them. "Just let me get the lights."

My fingers were claws in his t-shirt. "That's what blankets are for." He pulled more up around us, but they did little to stop my shaking.

In his arms, darkness seemed sheltering instead of sinister, and my shaking gradually stopped. The two of us lay swallowed by fleece and down, the worn cotton of his borrowed t-shirt gathering against my fists like a lifeline.

"Why is your skin so rough?" I whispered, my teeth resting lightly around an earlobe. I ran a hand underneath his t-shirt, up the plane of his abdomen, and found that the skin there matched his warm abrasive face and hands.

He didn't touch me back. Instead, he pillowed his head on his crossed arms and watched me as if memorizing every detail. He smiled, considering my question. My palms traveled slowly up his stomach and chest. I breathed him as I felt the delicious friction that came from dragging my damp flesh across a rough surface. He smelled of an impossible mix of crushed pine needles and citrus.

He touched me then. His thumb across my lower lip, one palm cupping the nape of my neck softly, so softly. Fingertips brushed against my eyelids. "I don't know," he whispered back, amused. We whispered everything, almost, in our blanket sanctuary. "It's just how I was made. I've never questioned it." Warm fingertips traced the v-neck of my shirt, skimming the soft skin there.

I pushed up his t-shirt. "You didn't answer my question." I raked my fingers down his rough stomach.

"What… was the question?" Slitted eyes, like a cat about to strike. His thumbs made soothing circular motions against my thighs.

"Skin…" I murmured. His t-shirt was scrunched up right around his neck, his entire chest bare to me. Every muscle, every hollow, was perfectly shaped, but not with fleshy softness. Ethan was a statue, perfect in a frozen kind of way; his skin was almost monochromatic, except for faint shadows cast by bone and muscle. And warm. I kissed a line of firm, possessive wet marks from his belly button to the hollow of his throat, where I still held his t-shirt in a death grip. "Something about skin," I said between kisses, my lips burning from the twin sensations of heat and rough contact.

"Why are you so soft?" he asked. "So vulnerable?" His words came in gasps, as if he were choking. His fingers had found the nape of my neck, and they held me there, taut and careful.

"'Mm not," I mumbled, unwilling to stop my kisses. When I finally found his mouth, my lips were as sensitive as if I had lost a layer of skin. "I'm not going to break. I promise." Carefully, carefully, as if he was the shiny new human and I, the indestructible one, my fingers inched up my t-shirt. "See?" I asked, pushing his roughened palm across my stomach. He tried to draw his hand away, afraid of my bruises, but I wouldn't let him. "The heat helps," I reassured him, and he relaxed. "You won't hurt me." I delicately wrapped my teeth around his lower lip. "Not here. Not you."

Blue-green fire snapped and flared. In that instant way his kind moved, he lay suddenly above me, his hand on the curve of my spine. I held his face to mine, burning my lips with his, urging him closer as my hands roamed his back, finding not a hint of wings or planes of light, only more warm, rough Ethan. His touch on me was light, still hesitant, brushing my hip, the soft flesh of my belly. I pressed myself against him, wanting to burn brighter, faster, to lose layer after layer of skin against him. *Yes, this*, I thought, and I wanted so badly to pull him out of whatever made him so careful with me.

"We can do this. Be together." Ethan held me tight against him. Tension rolled through him, the taut way he held himself back vibrated against me; fear and wonder and fettered joy flashed in his gaze as his eyes roamed my body. "Whatever lays between us now, Light or Dark, human or… not… we can face it." He hadn't asked a question, but it was more than a statement. A declaration, a pledge; I wasn't sure.

"We can," I echoed, and saw, for the first time, silver in his eyes. I recognized it for what it was: my own eyes, my Nephilim eyes, glowing with the same impossible fierceness as his own, reflected back at me. Warring within him, among the desire and want and fear and certainty, there was an echo of my own blood.

A stirring of the blood, a calling and an answer: "Yes," I said, shirring my fingers through that space where Ethan carried Light on his back, "we can do this." And I kissed him deep, drawing him to me, my softness against his strength. I forgot about Asheroth and angels and Nephilim and even about dying brothers. There was no room for anything but him and us and the fire that traveled from his skin to mine, kindling at our touch, until everything burned away and there was nothing but the slow sweet exploration of each other between us. I think I gasped; perhaps he said my name, and then there were no more words for a long time.

Chapter Seventeen

Troublesome

I want to see your wings," I said softly, tracing one finger down Ethan's spine. He arched against my touch and turned his head to smile at me.

"Hmm." He only opened one eye. "It seems a bit much, even for you, to ask me to open the Realms right here in your bedroom." He rolled on his side, openly laughing at me now. "It would be… dangerous. Trust me."

I grabbed the fuzzy fleece blanket that was the only thing separating us. "Realms? You mean, like Heaven and Hell?"

"Some call them so."

"So when I saw them as…" I frowned in the dark, flat on my back now, thinking. "Planes of Light and Dark? And not as wings, with feathers? That's what you carry on your back, then? Heaven or Hell?"

"Light and Dark is perhaps more apt," he corrected. He rolled me on my side and tucked me into the curve of him, my head just under his chin, my skin pleasantly warmed by the contact between us.

"But how do you fly?" I demanded.

The entire bed shook for several silent minutes until I realized he had buried his head deep within the comforter to silence his laughter. I wormed an elbow backward and tried to jab him in the stomach, but, impossibly, annoyingly fast, he caught it. "You'll hurt yourself, doing that," he admonished.

"I'm serious," I hissed in the darkness.

"I know," he said. The shaking started again, but he managed to choke out an answer. "Caspia, we're not birds. We don't fly. What most people see as wings are more like doors."

"To the Realms?" I asked.

"Yes."

"Is that how you move so fast?"

"Mmm. It's like stepping in and out of a door through which space and time are relative. Most humans perceive it as flight, just as they see the Light we carry as wings."

"Or Darkness," I said in a low voice, remembering.

"Or Darkness," he seconded, and then flipped the edge of the down comforter over me, pulling me right up against him. His warm rough hand rested flat against my stomach as I wiggled backward into the curve of his body. "We only open planes to the Realms when we need them, for movement, perhaps, or if we need to draw strength or call for help. You and Logan saw us as few can, no doubt because of your… heritage." The pause floated between us, expectant and full. "I wish I knew more about it. About whatever long-ago Nephilim ancestor left you mercurial silver eyes and the gift of prophecy, but I don't. I would tell you if I knew. You must trust your instincts when it comes to our kind."

I curled my fingers over his as they rested against my stomach. "Ethan?"

"Hmm?"

I took a deep breath. "Just how much Nephilim blood do I have?"

He stiffened, then relaxed and locked his lips against the nape of my neck. "I truly don't know. Enough to make you noticeable to others of my kind. Enough to let you do things other humans cannot."

I sighed. "Just enough to make me troublesome, then."

He laughed. His smile curved against my neck. "Sleep, Caspia. It's been a long day."

"A long, sucky day," I agreed. "From hell. Literally. But I have…" A heavy, unnatural, but not unpleasant tiredness descended suddenly on me. "Questions. Hey! Are you making me…" My brain felt foggy and slow. "Tired?"

Light kisses sent shivers down my spine. Ethan held me tighter. "Sleep, Caspia. You and yours are safe tonight, and in the morning, I'll bring you coffee."

"You fight dirty," I murmured.

As sleep claimed me, soft and peaceful, I thought I heard Ethan whisper, "You have no idea."

"You are heartless, terrible, and cruel," I said from underneath my mound of mismatched, but perfectly comfortable blankets.

"I'm sorry, I didn't quite catch that," said a serenely cheerful voice. "You're mumbling underneath a pile of covers."

"Give. Me. The. Coffee." I threw the blankets off my head and glared for emphasis. Even Ethan, who could punch through walls without blinking, looked startled at my feral pre-coffee snarl. "Now," I added, as the aroma of The Coffee Shop's fifty percent Costa Rican blend wreathed its way around my room.

"No," he told me firmly when I ducked back under my blankets. "No fewer than three people in the space of fifteen minutes told me this was the only way to get you out of bed."

"Then they, too, will die." I lifted just enough blanket to watch him out of one eye. He must have showered while I slept; his brown hair was wet and messier than usual. He wore more of my brother's clothes, dark brown cords this time, and a black t-shirt that fit him much more snugly than it ever had Logan. I bit my lip. No matter how attractive he was, he was holding my coffee prisoner. I wasn't giving in. Yet.

He scanned the blankets for my face. The sunlight hit glints of gold in his hair and lit his eyes, and, even though I'd done nothing but grouch at him, he looked genuinely happy. I almost, almost, relented. But then he slipped two insulated mega cups of my third favorite coffee in the world onto my dresser, miles from my reach, and said sternly, "It's for your own good, Caspia. You're already late for class. Now, get up, please."

Class.

The word registered dimly, like an alarm going off in a distant part of the house that I didn't quite want to pay attention to yet. My bed was so comfortable, so warm. If only I could convince Ethan to bring me the coffee. I could forget all about getting up and going to class…

I exploded out of my nest of blankets like I'd been shot. "Holy crap!" I yelled, startling Ethan for the second time that morning. "I'm late for class!"

"Yes, I told you…" he began.

I vaulted over the side of the bed and lunged for one of the coffees. Ethan dodged out of my way with angelic quickness. He stood watching me from behind my reading chair with narrowed eyes and gradually tightening fists.

"It's Drawing II," I tried to explain, gulping coffee down so fast I barely even tasted it, let alone registered the searing burn down my throat. Halfway through the cup, I came up for air, gasping. "Dr. Christian," I added, as if this explained everything, which, to me and any other student at Andreas Academy, it did. Dr. Christian was the most acclaimed faculty member at Andreas. He'd taught at several prestigious colleges before settling in Whitfield some years back. He was still partial owner of a prestigious New York gallery, and he was responsible for an impressive, groundbreaking body of work in his own right. I had no idea what possessed him to come to a school like Andreas, but he was a major reason for my attendance there. Unfortunately, his brilliance was matched only by his temperamental outbursts and strict classroom policies. I was late, my last assignment had been stolen before being assaulted by Dark angelic kidnappers, and I was going to have to draw left-handed. I was toast, and muttered as much. Ethan only stood there, his eyes getting narrower and his body language fiercer as he crossed his arms and leaned back against my bookshelf.

"You seem upset," Ethan observed quietly.

"Understatement of the century," I fired back. "But you wanted me out of bed, right? Take this cup. And can you get me the other one? I need more caffeine. This is very, very bad. I'm already late; he's going to crucify me. Bad enough I won't be able to draw." In the darkened depths of my closet, I pulled on mismatched underwear. I snagged the first shirt my fingers touched and slipped it over my head. I scooped up jeans, socks, and ankle boots. I didn't even have time to deal with lacing up my shoes. I went to dump everything on my bed and ran smack into Ethan's solid chest. The collision knocked all the breath out of me, tripping me and sending my armload of clothing flying. "Bloody hell!" I yelled, frustration peaking.

I should have known by now. I should have expected it. But his hand on the curve of my spine, steadying me, still surprised me even as it paused time and righted my world. Anchored now, snug in the carved curve of his arm, the heat and steadiness of him washed over me as he watched me with a kind of confused, animal wariness that made me forget, for a moment, to breathe.

"Coffee?" he asked, pressing the second of the cups he'd brought into my dangling hand.

"Thank you." My words came out a little breathy, like I'd just learned to breathe. I risked a quick glance at the bed; just as I'd thought, my haphazard pile of clothes lay gathered at the bottom, folded into a neat stack by the man presently keeping me from falling. Fast, so fast. For the first time that morning, the full impact of who and what he was, what we'd done, hit me, taking me low and cold beneath my ribs. "Ethan." I closed my mouth and felt it curve, all on its own, into a tiny promise of a smile. "I… oh, God. I forgot to say good morning."

He looked steadily back at me and I found I couldn't name all the emotions I saw in his unguarded eyes. I wondered if he could, either. Vulnerable and wary, amused and… something else. Fierce? Possessive? No one else had ever looked at me that way, not ever in my whole life. And this was his first morning in our apartment, and he had brought me not one coffee but two, and I had responded to his gentle reminder about school by totally freaking out on him. I ached to do it over, our first morning together, to fill it with love and playfulness and joy.

"Well, then." Ethan didn't loosen his hold on the curve of my spine. "It seems a rather dangerous event, this waking up business. Perhaps it's just as well that you forgot the good morning bit," he teased, but with an edge.

"Not so much," I tried again, inching the cup of coffee out from between us. "It doesn't have to be." Suddenly, unaccountably shy, I found myself unable to look anywhere but at the hollow of his throat. I kissed it impulsively. He went perfectly, preternaturally still, his hand warm on the curve of my spine. "I'm very new at this," I admitted. I swear his body temperature rose when he smiled; I couldn't see his face, but he absolutely radiated warmth at my words. "Let me try again." I kissed him once more on the throat, longer this time, and let my lips linger there. "Good morning, Ethan," I said against his skin. "Thank you for the coffee."

He didn't say anything. He scooped my chin up in the palm of his hand and kissed me, firmly and without hesitation as if he sensed the veil of shyness between us and wanted to rip it away. It was all I could do not to drop the coffee; Ethan was, as always, an assault on the senses. Raw skin abraded of its uppermost protective layer; impossible scents that mingled seasons and plants and even places; the lowest light humming, so faint I could hear it or not, as I willed; and everywhere, warmth, even inside, where my lips broke from his tasting faintly sweet and spicy all at once. I pressed back against him, snaking my fingers through his hair, seeking kisses, but his lips were moving, making sounds. "School. Dressed in no time, and I can take you."

"I could just not go," I offered, pressing myself against him. His low rumbling laugh traveled across the front of my body.

"You were frantic, earlier," he reminded me.

"I'll take her," Logan said from my bedroom doorway. I froze, grateful Ethan's back was to the door that connected my room to the living room. Hopefully, Logan wouldn't see I was wearing nothing but a Horse to Water t-shirt and underwear.

"Ethan can get me there really, really fast," I countered, risking a peek at my brother from around Ethan's shoulder.

Logan wore one of my favorite sweat suits. The dark green Adidas hoodie and baggy pants were a good color for him. He even had a matching ball cap, pulled down low to shield his eyes, as always. For my brother, this was his version of dress clothes. He didn't quite smile at me, his eyes fixed on the tip of his sneaker instead. But he twirled the car keys easily in his hands and he seemed relaxed. "Come on, Cas," he coaxed. "You're so late now another ten or fifteen minutes won't matter much. Plus I've got breakfast to go for you." He did smile at me then, his shadowed brown eyes seeking mine over Ethan's sheltering shoulder. If he didn't like what he saw, he didn't show it. Instead, he seemed kind of pleased. "Leftover microwave cheese pizza."

Oooh, a definite peace offering. Logan always tried to get me to eat healthy breakfasts like oatmeal and cereal bars. My eyes widened in shock, but I didn't move from Ethan's sheltering form. I was wearing one of Logan's favorite band's t-shirts and little else. There were limits to any big brother's level of tolerance, and I didn't want to test his, not when he seemed so friendly. "Five minutes," I promised. I wanted to spend some time with him, too. I had some things I needed to say to him. It seemed as if today was my morning for apologies. As he turned to leave, I shouted after him. "Hey! I don't have to work tonight. Are you up for the Winter Festival on the Square? I promised to show Ethan downtown Whitfield last night, but… ell, you know."

He paused for longer than I thought he would, both hands tight against the doorframe. He nodded slowly before turning to smile at us. "Sure thing. I'd love to go. I think it's important that Ethan feels at home here. As much as possible." His voice was husky as he looked at the two of us, me obviously hiding, and at the pile of clothes on my bed. He fixed me with a mock glare. "God knows you need looking after, Caspia. The least you can do for Ethan is take him out."

He left quickly enough that my boot bounced harmlessly off the door frame instead of his face.

Chapter Eighteen

Lost Time

I shrank as far back against the wall as possible, and invoked every deity I knew that Dr. Christian would remain benignly ignorant of my tardy, assignment-less presence. So far, so good. I'd texted Amberlyn from the parking lot, begging her to try and create a distraction. She'd texted back that Dr. Christian hadn't yet taken roll and was very occupied demonstrating a particular crosshatching technique he'd used for some famous drawing of his. She even told me which side of the classroom to slink into in order to avoid notice.

I kept working my way down the list of deities, just in case.

"So you can see," Dr. Christian announced in his booming professor's voice, the one that made every female head and some of the male ones lean forward attentively, "that by arranging the lines just so"—he magnified a portion of a flower petal—"the leaves retain the slightly grainy look of live Calla lilies."

A collective sigh went up from the class. I rolled my eyes. Dr. Christian didn't affect me as he did most of my classmates. I recognized his artistic talent and knew I had a lot to learn from him, but I just didn't feel the need to swoon over his model-perfect looks every time he opened his mouth. In fact, I found his plastic perfection kind of creepy.

Instead, I let my mind wander back to my car ride with Logan. He'd given me a steady, if a bit shaky, one-armed hug as soon as I jumped in the car, which he'd kept running so I'd be warm. He immediately shoved greasy pizza into my hands and another cup of coffee. I wouldn't eat, though; I had something to say, first.

"I'm sorry," we both blurted at the exact same time, then burst out laughing.

"I'm sorry," I insisted through a mouthful of cheese. "I've been whiny and self-centered and a terrible brat. If I could, I'd spank myself."

"I'm sorry," Logan sighed, gunning through a yellow light. "I shouldn't have said all of those things to you last night. I was scared."

"God, me too." I chased cheese with coffee. "I'm still scared. We'd be fools if we weren't." I gave up on the pizza in favor of tanking up on as much coffee as I could before creeping into Dr. Christian's class. "But, Logan, what I really want to apologize for is the way I've been treating you. Or not treating you. For pushing you away. I never meant to hurt you. I've been having trouble dealing."

His long, thin fingers looked positively skeletal as they tightened around the steering wheel. "No. You don't owe me any apologies. I haven't exactly been forthcoming with you, either. I pushed you away because I wanted to shelter you. You're my little sister, and I wanted to protect you." He reached out to tuck one escaped strand of unbrushed hair behind my ear. I'd twisted the rest up into a messy knot at the nape of my neck. As soon as he touched me, I got an odd cold feeling at the base of my shoulder blades.

"What do you mean, Logan? What are you trying to protect me from?"

We'd reached the school in record time. For once, I cursed my brother's daredevil driving. Normally, it delighted me. He sighed and pulled me into another one-sided embrace. "Nothing pressing, Caspia. You just get to class, and we'll have plenty of time to talk more after the Festival on the Square."

I stuck my head back in the half-rolled down window and eyed him dubiously. "Promise?"

He rolled his eyes. "Yes. I promise, oh ye who are about to face hell's wrath for being late to class."

I rolled my eyes right back at him. "You're not mad? About…" I took a deep breath. "Ethan?" I squeaked.

Logan placed both hands very carefully on his lap. He looked me straight in the eye. "I watched Ethan rip out what looked like a demon's heart for you, Caspia. More than one heart, in fact. He saved your life, probably both of our lives, and whatever he is, he's not made of Darkness. But more importantly"—he grinned—"Abigail likes him, and she hates almost everyone, so he must be okay."

"Okay?" a sonorous baritone voice echoed from across the room. I blinked. Tiny dust motes floated peacefully in a slant of sunlight hitting the desks in front of mine.

Desks. Oh, hell.

"I said, are you okay, Miss Chastain?" This time, Dr. Christian's rumbling lecture voice was followed by a chorus of prissy little giggles, like minions worshipping their master. I tried to stuff down twin feelings of disgust and alarm.

"Oh, yes, Dr. Christian. Thanks."

"Excellent. I was afraid we'd lost you back there." His smile was kind, even concerned, but something about it just didn't seem sincere to me. I gave him a small smile back, hoping he would leave me alone. "So, would you be so kind?"

I took several deep, centering breaths, trying to make sense of what he was saying. Every face in the room turned expectantly toward me. I searched desperately for Amberlyn, but she looked back at me with the same horrified expectation many of the other students shared. No help there. Just what in the hell was I supposed to do? I realized I'd been sweating, even though it was cold all the way in the back of the class. "I'm sorry, Dr. Christian, but I'm afraid I don't understand," I finally admitted, waiting for the chorus of giggles that was sure to follow. I wasn't disappointed.

Dr. Christian smiled his tolerant academe's smile and left the podium. He beckoned at me to come forward with a graceful sweep of his pale hand. "I merely requested that you share what you have been so feverishly drawing with the rest of the class, my dear," he drawled softly with the barest hint of an accent I couldn't quite place. "After all, you have been quite absorbed in your work since you slipped in fifteen minutes late." The class, predictably, tittered, but I was beyond caring as the blood drained from my face.

I stared at Dr. Christian across a sea of rapt faces, realizing for the first time that I held a watercolor pencil in my left hand. I touched the surface of my desk with my bandaged right hand quickly, but not before I felt an open drawing pad and an entire box of pastel pencils. Something icy with sharp feral claws, ate its way through the lining of my stomach. I knew without looking I had done it once more. Once again I had used the gifts of my Nephilim blood to draw a prophecy. Dr. Christian's dark blue eyes caught mine and held them. I dared not look down. My drawing hand was injured; with any luck, I'd drawn nothing more than barely recognizable squiggles.

Then Dr. Christian smiled at me, slow and soft and wild, and I knew two things all at once: I was afraid to look at the thing I had drawn because it was prophecy and probably damning. Dr. Christian was going to look at it, too, and there wasn't a thing in the world I could do about it.

I started my slow walk down to his desk like a condemned man on his way to dice with the devil. I pressed the drawing pad close against my chest, cradling it there, both arms wrapped around it. A bizarre need to protect it from this man, and from public exposure in general, swept through me. I thought desperately of fainting, or even just running, but that pair of dark blue eyes compelled me onward as surely as if he held a loaded weapon. "It's probably not very good," I said. "I hurt my wrist, you see." I nodded toward it, unwilling to uncross my arms for even a second.

If Ethan was sculpted stone, this man was living fire, every delicate bone catching the light in such a way as to create shifting pockets of shadow when he moved. Hair so golden it couldn't be called blond framed eyes so deeply blue they almost drowned out the irises. His impossibly finely boned fingers steepled together under his chin. "Yes. I see that. How did you acquire that injury, Caspia?"

"Um." Blue, blue eyes like the lake Logan and I like to swim in. In the summer. When it was hot. The lake would be freezing cold, even then. I blinked. What the hell? What was wrong with me? "Uh, I fell." Keep it simple.

A perfect, arched eyebrow expressed doubt in one expressive motion. "I see." But I could hear the whisper underneath his words, calling me a liar, making me doubt myself, doubt my gift, my instincts. I should just relax and tell him about things, this man with the freezing, soothing eyes.

What the bloody hell? Internal alarms were going off. I swallowed convulsively. "I was just practicing. With my left hand. I can't draw at all, with my left hand. I'm sorry, Dr. Christian."

He smiled and gave a tiny shrug, as if to say, such things happen among friends. Only we weren't friends, of that I was desperately certain. I stood in front of him and it was as if we were in a bubble. There was no sound, no time. He held out his hand for my drawing and I recognized the color of his eyes.

They were the color of fire at the very center, when it burns so hot it's almost white.

I watched my hand hold out my drawing. I watched him take it and lay it carefully on the table between us. I watched as his gaze caught and burned, crackling with that fire I had just recognized. The air even smelled like burning. "Oh my," Dr. Christian said, smoothing out my drawing on his desk. "Oh, my dear Caspia. What talent you have."

In full color, using the sure, graceful strokes of watercolor pencils, I had drawn fighting Nephilim, facing each other across some kind of open space. Two Dark Nephilim had their backs to me. All I could see were two pairs of massive, gaping planes of darkness, and across from them stood Ethan, similarly battered, but glowing nonetheless with some fierce inner light. I frowned and leaned in closer because in my drawing, Ethan had no planes of light on his back. His wings were gone, and he was badly injured.

In the middle of the open space, caught between them all, was me.

I held something tight against my chest. I couldn't tell what it was, except that it was made of light, and shone so brightly I turned my face slightly away from it in the drawing, as if it was too bright to look at directly. I half-knelt, one leg flat on the ground, the other bent as if I was trying to rise with my burden. With my other hand I pointed straight at the sky, toward a line of darkness. My mouth was open as if I was screaming.

"Amazing," Dr. Christian breathed, directly over my shoulder. I did my best to ignore him and tried to absorb every detail of the drawing instead.

I seemed to be wearing a loose dress of some kind. That was good; I didn't own anything like that, so I would recognize it if it showed up in my future. It was also just as likely that I was pulling the line of darkness down toward me. I leaned in even closer; there was a familiar shape to the darkness, if I could just place it. Why couldn't I place it?

"…Qualify you for a scholarship," Dr. Christian said. He put his hand on my shoulder and I jumped, shocked back into the here and now. His hand was as cold as I had imagined his eyes to be. The classroom was empty. Except… was that the ripple of shadows in the corner? As if someone was standing there, hooded and watchful, with dark abscesses flaring from behind? I took a hesitant step in that direction, wondering and hypnotized…

Only to be brought back to the present by Dr. Christian's insistent voice. "Miss Chastain," he huffed, as if he'd been repeating my name so much he was sick of hearing it.

"What?" I said, thoroughly confused. Where had everyone gone?

"Oh, don't be modest, Miss Chastain. Your achievement is truly breathtaking. The committee meets at seven next Thursday. We'll look forward to seeing you then." Dr. Christian smiled at me. He had perfectly even white teeth. A nice smile, I thought absently. He ran his hand up my forearm. I shivered. "Are you quite alright, Miss Chastain? Perhaps you need assistance getting to your next class. You are injured, after all."

The desks were arranged on risers. I stumbled on the very first one, on my way to get my books. I felt sleepy and confused. How had I missed the bell ringing? Why didn't Amberlyn wait for me? His chilly hand caught my forearm instantly. "Oh, I'm fine," I said, and stumbled again. His cold hand settled against the curve of my spine.

"I insist," he said, scooping up my knapsack and purse. He put my drawing pad into my bag, and then draped it over my arm as if I was an invalid and walked me to the classroom door. "And, Miss Chastain? Do try and take care of yourself between now and when the scholarship committee meets. No more clumsy accidents, hmm?"

Wait, I thought. Wait a damn minute. "Scholarship? What about my drawing?"

"Well, you have to meet the rest of the committee, of course." A sharp note crept into his voice then. "I have to keep your drawing to show the rest of the committee. I told you that part already." He said the words carefully, enunciating as if talking to a toddler. "You have to come to my office. You have to come alone. Remember that, Caspia: you have to come alone." His instructions should have alarmed me, but I wanted nothing more than to lie down. I repeated what he'd said so I wouldn't forget. "You can have your drawing back then," he said reassuringly.

Looking into Dr. Christian's chilly blue eyes, I suddenly felt tired and cold, exactly as if I had been swimming for hours in the icy water of the lake with Logan. "In your office," I heard myself repeat. "Alone." I stared at him as he nodded once, satisfied, and spun on the heel of his expensive Italian shoe and marched away.

I barely managed to stagger out of the classroom and onto an empty bench. I leaned back against the wall. I was so tired. I would close my eyes for just a second…

I don't know how long I slept on the bench in the hall. When I woke, my cell phone laid underneath my knapsack. I'd been using it for a pillow. I guess that's how I missed all four calls from home. Confused and apprehensive, I dialed back. "Logan? It's me. Can you come get me?"

"Thank goodness, Cas. We were just about to come looking for you. I thought maybe you were with Amberlyn, but when I called, she said she thought you already left."

I frowned at the phone. "What? Amberlyn ditched me after Dr. Christian totally humiliated me in Drawing II. What do you mean, you've been waiting?"

A short silence. "Sweetie, it's late afternoon already. Your last class ended an hour ago. Amberlyn thought you left for home already, or she would have waited. Are you feeling ok?"

I stared at the phone in my hand, and at the rapidly emptying halls. What the hell had happened to me? Did I just fall asleep on a bench? I blinked rapidly, trying to clear my head. There were memories there, foggy and just beyond my reach, of lost time and a long afternoon. But they slipped away when I tried to reach for them, and I had people waiting for me. Concerned people who loved me. My heart warmed a little at the thought, making it easy to banish my lost afternoon. I would remember later. "Um, no. I guess not. So, can you come get me?"

"I'm on my way."

"I love you, Logan."

"Me too, caterpillar."

"Don't you dare call me that in front of Ethan," I hissed. Male laughter echoed in the background.

"Too late," Logan said smugly. "He heard."

"You. Will. Pay." I growled, low and deadly.

Logan sighed, sounding cheerful and long suffering. "Well, yes. I was planning on it. There is a party on the square tonight, after all. I'm sure you'll find plenty of ways to make me pay. Literally, of course."

Chapter Nineteen

The Orchard

We didn't speak much on the drive home. I knew I must have looked alarmingly bad because Logan didn't even complain once when I played the same song over and over. He hated it when I did that. After our third listening of my current favorite obscure band, I eyed him sideways. "Aren't you even going to mock me? I mean, I appreciate the play time and all, but I kinda miss the insults."

He snorted, but kept his eyes on the road. "You look awful, Cas."

And that was it. I should have guessed much worse was in store.

Ethan stood in shadow at the top of the second landing, his arms crossed, body squared and perfectly still. I couldn't see his expression, but his eyes watched me as I walked slowly up one stair after the other. I actually had to concentrate. My feet felt heavy as if I was wearing rain boots filled with water. About halfway up, I looked up at him. His blue-green eyes were clouded like the surface of a pond in early morning, skimmed over with fog. Logan's slight hand pressed on my shoulder. "We were really worried," he whispered in my ear.

"Oh," I said, as the fog grew thicker over Ethan's eyes. I put one foot in front of the other and wondered what emotion he hid from me. "I'm sorry."

Ethan's arms snapped down to his sides as if he were reaching for a hidden set of pistols. He threw his head back; the tendons of his neck strained, standing out. His nostrils flared. The long stairway up to our apartment was shadowy no longer. Lightening whipped across Ethan's eyes through the screen of fog, and twin planes of Light unfurled behind him where normal people have shadows. His fingers curled into claws. His voice, when he spoke, was underlined with the deep bass of distant thunder.

"Where. Have. You. Been?" he demanded, holding himself completely still.

I tried to answer him. I really did. But so many thoughts fought for dominion over my tongue that what came out was some kind of bastard pidgin dementia. He was beautiful. He was terrifying. He was furious. He would never hurt me. He wasn't Asheroth. He reminded me of Asheroth. I wanted to paint him. I wanted him to go back to being normal and almost human. I wanted to stare at him a while longer. Most of all, I wanted things to make sense.

"I don't know because something happened at school after Dr. Christian humiliated me in front of everyone and it made me really exhausted, but did you know I can draw really well with my left hand, and then I woke up on a bench all tired out for no reason, so I called home and I wish I could paint you just like you are now even though you look like you hate me and why are you so angry at me?" I sat heavily down on the stairs after my last good loud yell. I hadn't taken a breath during my whole demented tirade and was actually quite dizzy. Logan's soft, sweatshirt clad shoulder leaned up against me. He'd taken the step just below mine.

"Come on," he urged, nudging me with his tennis shoe. "Let's go up. He's just worried."

"Nuh-uh." I swept my eyes sideways at Ethan. "I didn't do anything wrong." His light was blinding. Someone would notice soon. But perhaps, Whitfield being what it was, that didn't matter.

I knew Ethan moved fast. I had seen, or rather, seen the evidence of it, plenty of times before. But this was different. All at once, I was surrounded by Light. Light, and Ethan's arms.

"Logan," he said. I couldn't see my brother anywhere. His Light was too bright. "Please wait for us inside your apartment. The wards are strong there; you'll be safe. I must take your sister somewhere for a moment."

"What the hell?" I pulled away from him, but he held me tight around the waist, raking me with the fury of his eyes.

"Exactly," he said, pulling me so close against him I had no choice but to mold myself to the shape of his body. I thought of how warm he was, and how well we fit; the top of my head rested perfectly against the curve of his neck. Then I remembered he was mad at me, and had no right to be, and tried to pull away from him again, but there was nothing else except him to hold on to, nothing but him and Light in a freefall void that was like the top of a rollercoaster, forever on pause, never coming down the track. I clutched him tighter and tried not to be sick.

It lasted forever and it lasted for exactly one breath. It was horrible and it was wonderful. It made me want to laugh and throw up, all at the same time, and when Ethan finally let me go, gently disengaging my fingernails from his shirt, the Light faded around us and all I could see was him.

He looked a little less angry. But only a little.

"Do you want to tell me what just happened, Ethan?" I glanced around to give me an excuse to look anywhere but at his mad, accusing face.

"Funny. I meant to ask you the exact same thing," he said, his voice practically thrumming with tension. I spun around so that he could see nothing except my back, taking great care to stiffen my spine even though I felt dizzy and sick, and folded my arms across my chest. That would teach him not to drag me away from my brother at invisible speeds to strangely beautiful places that looked like…

When I saw where we were, I forgot to breathe.

We were standing in the back end of the Parson's apple orchard, except we weren't. It looked just like it, only much, much better. Brighter. Shinier. Radiant. Unreal. The trees hadn't lost their leaves at all. In fact, every leaf on every branch was the perfect deep emerald green of summer. Fruit hung heavy and round from the branches. All colors, from the apples to the blades of grass, seemed dusted with a coat of pulsing lacquer, as if every inanimate thing breathed with color and light. My skin felt stripped down to its rawest layer, bloody tissue laid bare to soft warm breezes and the impossibly enticing smells of an orchard in full ripe summer until my poor weak senses screamed at the overload.

I did what I could. I closed my eyes and thought of home.

All the kids in Whitfield knew the Parsons. They ran the largest farm in town, or rather on its outskirts. They had the largest stall at the monthly farmer's market on the square. They operated the seasonal pumpkin patch and the area's only commercial orchard. It was huge, and, as kids, we all knew where the weak spot in the wooden fence was. At the very edge of the back forty, obligingly screened by a rather scraggly clump of trees, kids from Whitfield had been sneaking into the Parson's orchard for as long as there had been a town. Sometimes we got caught and sometimes we didn't. Oddly enough, at least in my case, that almost always depended on my intentions. Good intentions went unnoticed. Bad ones aroused immediate alarm. Escaping with friends for a bit of peace and quiet and harmless gossip went undiscovered, as did the occasional kissing session with a boy or two I really liked when I got older. I sucked in a surprised breath. I had always thought I just had ill luck. But of course, knowing what I now knew about myself and about Whitfield, I realized it probably had to do with my own nature, or the town's, or both.

I blushed crimson, conscious of Ethan at my back, remembering one memorable occasion when I had been caught, right after junior prom, with a group of friends who'd been planning to start the celebrations with getting drunk and ending them with each couple neatly separated from the rest of the group. Old man Parsons had come himself that time, shotgun in hand, interrupting what would have been a really stupid move on my part. The boy I was dating at the time turned out to be a creep; he stalked me for weeks afterward until Logan beat him bloody.

So many signs. How many had I ignored? And at what cost?

"This isn't really the orchard, is it?" I kept my back to Ethan, not so much because I was angry anymore, but because I was both afraid and fascinated by the shifting, but familiar landscape in front of me. My head was full of embarrassing memories and strange new fears, and the apples on the trees around me glittered a deep blood red.

The color of beating hearts. The color of Asheroth's jacket. I closed my eyes again when my senses began to scream.

"You're frightened." I felt him in front of me instantly, a cloud of cool mist in the middle of too much sensation. His hands on my face were cool, as well, and that frightened me almost more than anything. Never before had Ethan felt cool to my skin. I hugged myself tighter and kept my eyes closed, summoning more memories.

"It's too much. Too much sensation. Pleasure." My lips twisted on the word. "We should go to the real orchard instead. I can show you the tree I fell out of when I was nine. I broke my ankle. Logan carried me home on his back." I felt soft warm earth beneath my knees, exactly like sinking into firm foam. "Why did you bring me here?"

"It's the one place I know you are safe, and even still, I tried to pick a place both familiar to you, and remote enough to evade unwanted attention," he said. Familiar cool leather slid around my shoulders, covering me, cooling the fire across and inside much of my skin. "Believe me, I didn't want to bring you here, Caspia. It's a risk, bringing you to the Realms; even to ones of the Light, and even though you bear Nephilim blood. But you came to me with the unmistakable touch of Darkness on you." He had me by the shoulders, shaking me, voice insistent, relentless. "Look at me! Who was it? Who is it that hunts you? Why do you, and you alone, carry the stench of evil on you?"

Incredulous, I tried to shove him away. I only succeeded in pushing myself flat on my back, confronting an endless indigo sky, completely cloud free. "Evil?" I repeated. I was dimly aware of rage building somewhere inside, but I was too shocked to access it right away. "Did you just apply the words stench and evil to me in the same sentence, you nosy, interfering, soul-stealing angel?" I rolled over into a crouch, conscious for maybe the first time ever of what people meant when they said someone's eyes blazed. Mine heated with a fire, and I was pretty sure that meant they had turned that quicksilver color Asheroth claimed was a sign of my Nephilim heritage. "You arrogant bastard. I have no idea. Are you saying I have some kind of Dark evil in me, and Logan doesn't? That should make you happy, right? That means you're doing your job, right? Since you're only supposed to guard him?"

He flinched. "Caspia." No matter where or how I moved, there he was, relentlessly in front of me. Damn him and his reflexes. "This is important. You must listen."

"Like hell." I jumped up from my crouch, from his calm blue-green eyes, and stalked off into the orchard, heading toward what would be the wooden fence in Whitfield.

He let me get three steps before I walked right into my brother's black t-shirt that looked so much better on him anyway. "You are not in Whitfield, Caspia. You could wander forever here, and lose yourself. You must listen."

"Talk fast," I ground out through gritted teeth. I clenched my fists and looked at the toes of my boots; the Realms of Light, as Ethan chose to call them, were nauseatingly beautiful.

"I wasn't looking for you, exactly, that first night in Whitfield. I had come to guard your brother, and was curious to see you, of course. But we can sense others of our kind, and from the moment I crossed your threshold, I knew you, your brother, or both of you had attracted one of the darkest of our kind. I tracked this… scent… to the witch's shop, where I encountered you."

That got my attention. I snapped my eyes to his beautiful tinted ones, and was startled to see a steady reflection of silver burning there. Silver. In Ethan's eyes. I smiled a little in spite of myself. I liked seeing silver in his eyes, knowing I put it there. "Asheroth," I said, simply, filing away the information that Mrs. Alice was a witch for later. "He had a pack of my hand painted cards. He could only have gotten them there."

But Ethan shook his head. "No. Not Asheroth. I thought it must be him when he attacked and took you. I thought he must have tried to lure you to him. And when I defeated him, I thought the threat was over. But there is something else that hunts you still. Something worse. It clung to you when you returned today, late and confused. Something had you, this afternoon. You must tell me, Caspia."

"Something worse than Asheroth?"

He nodded. "There are different kinds of Falling; some of us turn to Darkness in our despair and isolation, or out of madness. But then, there are those who Fall from outright Rebellion. Those Rebel Nephilim are the Darkest of all. Some would name them Demons. That is what I sensed when you returned."

I felt as if I had been punched in the stomach. "Demons," I repeated, as if confirming the existence of aliens. He merely watched me. "You're telling me you brought me here, knowing a demon is after me, something worse than Asheroth or his buddies, and you left Logan alone?"

"Warded," he corrected, reaching for me again. "Your apartment is warded. And it seems to be you the demon wants, not your brother."

"Oh, well, that's a relief," I said calmly. Too calmly. If Ethan had known me for just a bit longer, he would never have mistaken my tone for anything other than thinly veiled panic and sarcasm. He would never have relaxed his grip on my forearms.

"What happened today? Can you remember?" he asked, low and serious, while the hysteria climbed to a fever pitch inside me.

"I don't remember," I answered truthfully. The lights were awfully bright. I squinted at Ethan's back. Did I see the planes of light that were his wings, or were things just that bright here in the Realms? "I was late for Dr. Christian's class. And of course, he completely humiliated me for it. I went to the library with Amberlyn, then my last class. I… I remember feeling sleepy, and napping on a bench. I called home. That's it."

Light enveloped me, pulsing, a heartbeat between us, and I knew Ethan had covered me with his wings. He kissed me, but it was more than that, it was like he gave me breath when I had none. In his arms, cool instead of warm in this strange place, I felt like a dying patient on life support, and what felt like a thick grimy soap bubble popped around a particularly startling memory. I struggled against him.

"Remember something?"

"My drawing," I gasped. "In class today! I drew you, and Dark Nephilim I didn't recognize, fighting, with me in between. Only you didn't have wings. You looked terrible, too."

His eyes narrowed like a hungry cat's. "And you? How did you look?"

"I was calling something, or maybe yelling. And doing something with my hands. I can't believe I forgot something that important. I wonder if that drawing's gone, too. Why can't I remember? Oh, bloody hell!" In my agitation, I had pushed myself out of the circle of his arms, clenching and unclenching my fists at my side. Furious, I wondered who or what was stalking me and why. I wondered how Ethan was supposed to guard both my brother and me. I breathed in and out, clenching and relaxing my fists.

"In this drawing you were doing something with your hands?" Ethan asked. I looked up to see him standing several feet away in the shade of a too-bright apple tree, watching me with a look I couldn't quite decipher. He nodded once, sharply, down. "Like that?" I had been pacing the perfect ground with its emerald blades of grass in a tight circle. Tracers of shadows floated from my hands exactly like misty breath from my mouth on a cold night. Except this was in bright light, the brightest possible probably, and smoky darkness slipped gracefully from my fingers as I clenched and unclenched my palms in agitation.

I stared at my open palms. "Um, no. Not like that," I admitted, turning my hands over and over in wonder. "What the hell was that?"

"The other reason I brought you here." His smile was predatory and showed too much teeth as he prowled toward me from the trees, slowly. "What if something was coming for you, Caspia? A demon? Do you know what they can do to a human? Especially a weak, sick one like Logan?" I swallowed nervously as he came closer. He didn't look like my Ethan. He looked hungry. He looked feral. I backed away. "Think of a thousand angry Asheroths, and let them loose on your brother." My blood pressure spiked as soon as he invoked my tormentor's name. When he latched it onto my brother's name, I began to get angry. "Think of how Asheroth hurt you." Ethan sneered. "He would snap Logan like a twig. A demon will do much worse. Your brother will be in so much pain he'll no longer even know he has a sister named Caspia, let alone care what the demon does to her." I stopped moving entirely. I was having trouble breathing. Ethan laughed, short and cruel. "Logan would even help do whatever the demon wanted to you, Caspia. And that's before the demon took his soul into the Darkest Realms where the torture would continue forever. That's what's hunting you, what you've led to your bro—"

Ethan never finished his sentence. I whirled on him, pushing against him. "That's enough, you bastard. Take me back. Now." Except that when my palms slammed against his chest, light pulsed outward in a brilliant, blinding burst. He fell, exactly as if I'd shoved him. Hard. Which I had. Except that I'd never managed to move Ethan one single inch unless he let me. And from the stunned look on his face as he lay flat on his back at my feet, he very much had not moved willingly.

A look of pure wonder passed quickly over his face. He locked it down so fast I wasn't completely sure I'd seen it. He shook his head slowly, sadly, at the pure indigo sky. "It's probably too late," he said. "At least you're safe here. Let the demon have him. Save yourself…"

"You complete and utter bastard," I hissed. I kicked him and tried to stifle my yelp of pain; I might have knocked him down with some strange pulse of light, but he still had the mass of a granite statue. "I can't believe I trusted you. Maybe even loved you! Jackass! I'll find my own way back." I turned sharply on my heel and stalked away, toward what would have been the main entrance to the orchard had we really been in Whitfield. I tried not to limp as I thought through possible plans. Could I find another angel? Hitch a ride back? How did these things work?

I hit a solid wall of granite and black t-shirt. "Caspia," it said in a quiet, even reasonable, voice. A light touch grazed my hand, which I had been making into fists quite unconsciously. "Look."

I did.

What had been trails of shadow before were now jagged rips of darkness piercing through the too-bright beauty of the place Ethan had brought me. I stared. Jagged edges. There were sharp, jagged edges of darkness streaming from my palms when I moved them back and forth. "It looks like…" I let my hands drop. "It looks like the darkness Asheroth carried on his back. His… wings. Or whatever."

"Only because you're upset," Ethan said. Suddenly, I didn't care that he had made me so mad, had said such awful things. I understood why, now. "You used Light, too, although shadows will be your greatest weapon." He made a small sound that could have been a laugh. My forehead, pressed against his chest, felt the rumble of it. "I'm sorry for upsetting you, but I had to see if you had other Nephilim abilities, and try to wake them, if you did. I wouldn't have you powerless, or dependent solely on me. You have Light and Dark inside you, Caspia, like all humans. You are neither wholly one nor the other." He caught both my hands in his. "You are a creature of choice."

"And you?"

He was silent. With my forehead against his chest, I measured time in breaths instead of heartbeats. Mine were deep and slow. "I made my choice when first I saw you, and before: the Light, and you."

"Asheroth says you can't have both."

"Asheroth is quite mad."

"Logan isn't really demon food right now?"

He held me tight. It felt so good. God help me, it felt so good. "No, you are the only demon bait I know."

I snorted. "That sounds kind of sexy. Demon bait. I think I like it."

"You would," he said, his voice low and gritty. "I do not. I much prefer the 'even loved you' part."

"Um." I cleared my throat. "You realize the words 'utter bastard' came first, don't you?"

He ignored me. "Even though Logan is safe in a well warded apartment, he is also my charge, and don't we have a festival of some kind to attend?"

"Yes!" I brightened instantly. "I'll show you the Town Square, all four sides of it, you can tell me who is and isn't human, and Logan can buy us stuff because he said he would."

He stiffened slightly. "My kind doesn't carry money."

"I kind of assumed. When you borrowed clothes. Which look way better on you, anyway. I did kind of wonder, though, if you decided to stay…"

He cut me off sharply. "When I stay, I'll get a job. Like everyone else." He smiled into my hair; I knew the shape of his lips against my skin by now, as they twisted against the crown of my head. "I can't wait to be human with you."

"But you can't. I mean, you aren't. Human, I mean," I protested, some small part of me wondering how we had gone from fighting to entwined so very quickly. A larger part of me told the smaller part of me to shut the hell up.

"We do the best we can," he whispered, so softly I barely heard. It was enough. Enough barriers loomed between us: a demon stalker, my brother's tenuous hold on life, his eternal banishment for my sake, me being the cause of his Fall. But for now, his arms and enwrapping Light around us, we were going to the Winter Festival on Whitfield's Old Town Square. I would dress up and hold his hand and Logan's too, and all would be right with the world. "…love you, too…" I heard as the dizzying nothingness of the space and time between here and there compressed and stretched. Familiar nausea warned me of travel even as I closed my eyes tight and clung.

Forewarned, I didn't even stumble this time when Ethan opened his arms and released me into our living room. I ran straight for my closet, kicking off my boots and stripping off my t-shirt quickly. My fingers were on the top button of my jeans, ready to inch them down, when Ethan appeared in my doorway with a face like tightly leashed violence and a hastily scrawled note. Logan's writing.

"What?" I managed to ask, frozen with my fingers at my waist.

"He left already. With Amberlyn. When I asked him to wait." Ethan sounded like frozen thunder.

"Uhh." *I'm kind of getting dressed here*, I thought at him, but telepathy didn't seem to be one of his abilities. "You said the demon wasn't after him. Let me get dressed and we'll go catch up." I indicated my shirtless state. "Or you could go on without me."

Eyes narrowed and lips pinched, he didn't look pleased. "You have two minutes."

"No way!" Men! "I need ten."

"You don't need ten." His smile wasn't entirely pleasant. "I'm very fast. I could dress you."

I stood up straight in nothing but my bra and jeans and put my hands on my hips. I narrowed my eyes. "I don't know if I can make myself mad enough to burn you or stun you or whatever the hell I did before, but if you push me on this I swear I will try. If you intend to stay here and play human here's lesson number one: No one can make a woman hurry up and get dressed. No one. Not God, not the president, and certainly not you. I need ten minutes, but I will try to hurry." I took a deep, calming breath that had the added bonus of focusing Ethan's attention below my neck. "And here's rule number two, just so you know: no matter how much time is involved in the preparation, always tell a woman she looks nice when she's through. Always. Or else next time, she'll take longer."

I kicked a pile of clothes out of the way and slammed the door in his face.

CHAPTER TWENTY

HALF DARK

I wanted to look nice for him. It was as simple as that, a desire as old as time. Looking back, I wonder if that was one of those crossroads moments. If I had just let Ethan speed dress me, or just stumbled into any old pair of jeans and whatever spare hoodie happened to be hanging on the hook by the door, would those few extra minutes have changed anything?

Did fate or whimsy guide me that night? I wondered still.

I closed my eyes and slipped my hand into the deepest recesses of my closet where my dresses lived, relying on my heightened sense of touch to choose what I would wear for Ethan. Since meeting him, everything tactile had become so much more pleasurable. I thought of his porous skin, like a living statue's, and wondered if he experienced the world in the same way. Were my senses heightened because of some deeply slumbering thing in my blood, called to waking? Was the Nephilim in me waking up? Was that why his presence caused such sensory overload? Or was it Ethan himself?

In the double darkness of closed eyes and a darkened closet I touched velvet; cotton so loosely woven it was almost sheer; stiff smooth satin; fine wale corduroy; denim worn sand-smooth with age and washing. And then I had it. My fingers closed on heavy satin, and I smiled at the memory of it. I didn't need light to see it. I remembered.

A heavy, nearly ankle length silver satin wrap skirt. The ribbons were long enough to tie around the waist several times and still dangle into the generous folds of the skirt. Next to it hung a matching shirt with a scooped neckline and three-quarter length sleeves that belled slightly. I had worn it only once before, at my high school graduation. Logan and Mr. Mason had come, since my parents couldn't. I stood in front of the fountain in Blind Springs Park and twirled for the camera, the skirt flowing around me like a Spanish dancer's, catching the multi-hued lights within its folds like a prism. Logan was tall and strong and misty-eyed, seeing me all grown up. It was the first time anyone ever told me my eyes looked silver in the lights of the fountain.

Ethan was the first to tell me my eyes actually were silver.

In the end, I liked the contradiction that stared back at me from my full-length mirror. Neck to knee silver satin covered with a slightly battered black leather jacket that was beginning to feel like a second skin. Silver ballet flats peeked out from beneath the hem of my skirt. I didn't have time to do anything to my hair except brush it and slap on some lip-gloss. "I like it," I told my reflection. "Ladylike. Sexy." I bounced a bit on the balls of my feet and fisted my hands in my jacket pockets. "Trouble, but with style."

"Ten minutes," Ethan said softly from my doorway. I spun, my skirt whirling like a circle of light around me.

I flushed because he had seen me talking to a mirror. "That really was pretty fast, considering," I said defensively.

When next I blinked, his hand was on my hip, between his jacket and the heavy satin of my skirt. "You look very nice," he said softly, so softly, into my ear. "I say that because I want to, not because you told me to." He slipped a tear-shaped crystal pendant on a black velvet ribbon around my neck.

"Where did you get this?" I traced the facets of the crystal absently, twisting to see it hanging around my neck in the mirror.

"From the same source who told me you and Amberlyn routinely take one and a half hours getting ready for dates on weekends." He frowned. "You must tell me about these dates of yours, Caspia. I'm not sure I like it."

"You should check your sources," I said dryly, slipping my arms around his waist. "I haven't been out on a date since Logan got sick. And who knows where my mother kept her jewelry?"

He brightened slightly. "Ah. Of course. Cats have an odd sense of time."

I took several full, deep breaths to make sure he wasn't teasing.

He wasn't.

"Cats," I repeated.

He nodded, completely serious. "Abigail," he said as explanation. "She also said I should dress up a bit." He'd slipped into one of Logan's gray cashmere sweaters. I drooped against his chest, reveling in the soft warm solidness of him while I tried to shut off my brain.

"Abigail," I repeated. The familiar weight of his hand cupped the back of my neck. On the streets below us, my friends and neighbors strolled around the square, enjoying the Winter Festival just as they had every single year I could remember. But this year, I knew some of them weren't quite what they seemed. And some of them knew I wasn't quite what I seemed, and neither was the tall strange man who talked to cats and rubbed my back as if I was one, too. I arched against his hand. "I don't know if I can handle this, Ethan."

"You handled mad Dark angels and mysterious demon stalkers, discovering your own Nephilim blood and awakening abilities just fine."

I shook my head against him. "But cats. That's too much, somehow. It's just… wrong. Bad enough they can think and reason. But if they can communicate? Next they'll want things. Special treatment, a voice in government. Where does it end?"

He laughed softly. "I don't think they're interested in trading down." I groaned into his shirt. "Fine, then. No more about cats. Let's go find your brother."

I squared my shoulders and managed to smile. "Yes. My brother."

He tucked my arm over his and kissed the top of my head. "You look beautiful. If we're attacked, you'll be the prettiest fighter around."

"Umm," I said, uneasiness warring with an absurd urge to laugh hysterically. "Thank you. I think."

How to describe Whitfield as dusk crept in from the mountains, and my tiny, little city held its breath as it changed from light to dark? I wrapped my hands around Ethan's forearm and dragged him down the stairs behind me. I had only ever seen him in darkness or daylight, never at that borderline moment when everything around me seemed to hang, suspended, frozen as the sky darkened, but the city sprang to light.

It was never fully dark or light in Whitfield, but always somewhere in between. The park with its year-round fairy lights and businesses open late into the night held the darkness at bay, even as those same storefronts offered shelter and deep awnings as shade against the sun. And, of course, there was always the park with its stately Southern Oaks and pines, creating pockets of cool and damp shadows when the rest of the town hummed with the business of the day. Whitfield never slept, never stopped breathing, and if I tried to explain in some way that made sense, the words tangled on my tongue until I sounded hopelessly naïve.

The warmth of Ethan's skin heated me through his borrowed sweater. I knew he didn't feel that way. He knew what Whitfield was. He had, in fact, known it much longer than me. What I had only intuited as a hometown I loved was something deeper and older. It was a sanctuary for secrets, both Light and Dark, and none of us knew the full extent of them yet. In a way, I was headed out to meet my hometown for the first time ever. Or at least, for the first time as it really was: odd and beautiful and full of secrets of which I could only see the very surface.

I fingered my mother's necklace as I stopped to adjust my skirt. I was worried, as always, about Logan. I imagined him lost in the gathering crowd, pale but smiling, watching for me as I clung to Ethan's arm. He liked Ethan. He liked to see me with someone strong and good, someone who would and did take care of me. I could let it irritate me if I wanted it to. It was possessive and big brotherly of him, but it was also kind of sweet. So there was that. Logan. I sighed. I supposed I would always worry about Logan. Maybe it was just in my nature.

Ethan pulled me up against him. "Okay?" he asked, and I couldn't help but smile up at him. I didn't want to tell him that the whole town would, in its own discreet way, be checking him out. He had pretty much moved in with us, and everyone would want to know who he was. I frowned a little. That was another thing I was worried about. What would the town think of him? Especially knowing, as I now did, that he was far from human, and that some of my lifelong friends and neighbors were supernaturals, too? He caught my frown and matched it with his own, so I erased it from my face quickly and squeezed his hand. It didn't matter what the town thought. It mattered slightly what Logan thought, but the only real opinion that counted was mine.

Mine, and Ethan's. I wanted him to like Whitfield. It shocked me, the force of my wanting. Despite all the strange revelations of the past few days, the way my hometown beat inside me like a centering heart hadn't changed. It was a part of me. As I stood on the threshold of half dark, watching my little town's merchants, citizens, and mysteries spread out across the square and all four of its closed-off streets, a wistful kind of yearning twisted inside me. The old Whitfield was gone, the one I had thought was nothing but a boring, sleepy Southern city from which I must hide my secrets at all costs or live outcast as a freak. Gripping Ethan's fingers loosely, I knew I stood poised to meet the new Whitfield for the first time. Not as a freak, but as a rather boring specimen of an extraordinary population. Ethan tugged on me gently.

"Come on, Caspia. Logan knows we're coming."

I nodded and followed him out into the bustling square. Every shop in Whitfield had doors thrown wide open with all the lights burning. Some had long tables set up along the sidewalk, piled high with their stock. Tall torches blazed against the deepening night, firmly secured against the ground with concrete cinderblocks laid across heavy wrought iron bases. The torches caught the gold highlights in Ethan's brown hair as he wove through the crowds, pulling me along behind him. He seemed so confident, to know exactly where he was going. I, on the other hand, felt strangely shy, casting quick sidelong looks at tables of food and jewelry before looking back at Ethan's squared shoulders. I trotted a little until I was almost flush against his back; he walked quickly, covering twice as much ground as I would if left to my own devices.

"Do you know where he is? It's almost like you have some kind of tracking device on him, or something." I spoke loudly over his shoulder, hoping my words would hit his ear. The square was anything but quiet tonight. "I mean, is he okay? You're going so fast. I really want to show you the Festival. It only happens once a year." I hoped I didn't sound too petulant, but his single-mindedness was starting to both alarm and irritate me.

"You didn't read the note." We suddenly stood facing each other, one of his hands in its familiar place against the curve of my spine in that impossibly fast way of his. People parted around us, barely slowing. Now and then an acquaintance called out a greeting; I smiled and waved back. In my hands I discovered a crumpled white piece of paper with my brother's familiar scrawl. "I showed it to you earlier. When we first got back to your apartment and found your brother gone." His eyes, his voice, the way he held me, as if to shield me against crowds of people whom I'd known my entire life, all seemed to convey disappointment. I shook the note at him, suddenly angry.

"You shoved this note in my face while I was half-dressed minutes after returning me from a surprise trip to some other…" I struggled for a way to describe the Realms in public. "Other place," I finished lamely. "It was really quite shocking. I'm still not over it." One of my regular customers from the coffee shop bumped into us; she murmured apologies, flashed us smiles and looks of frank appraisal, and hurried on. I smiled fiercely back and hissed at Ethan through my teeth, brandishing the note between us. "So he went to dinner. With Amberlyn. What could be safer? We know she's not going to hurt him. She's been in love with him since the seventh grade."

His hold got a little stronger and his eyes a little narrower. "Caspia. I've explained. There are forces of Darkness…"

Right there on Main Street, with crowds of neighbors, co-workers, and acquaintances swirling around us, I shut him up the only way I knew how. I wrapped my arms around his shoulders and kissed him, very publicly and very hard. Whistles and applause broke out in patches around us, some of them very personal, but I did my best to ignore them. "You said I was the target," I whispered, pressing my lips against his ear. Someone called an encouragement in French. Amelie. Two other familiar voices wondered aloud if I would be keeping him; I couldn't place them, but I would, and god help them then. "I'm armored up. You're with me, and I don't plan to lose you. So we'll go find Logan. And then will you please come to the Festival with me?"

When I eased back, I could have sworn he was blushing. But perhaps it was just the torchlight, playing with the shadows beneath his cheekbones. "I think I must. Since you seem to have drawn all attention within several hundred feet directly to us."

I smiled, feeling the warm flush of embarrassment and joy spreading up my neck and face. "Several hundred feet is just the starting point. By the time we crash Logan and Amberlyn's dinner date, the entire Festival will have heard that you carried me off into the bushes and that the wedding's next Saturday." He blanched, and I added quickly, "Kidding! Really. But if you do want..." I stepped neatly out of the circle of his arms and began walking quickly toward the city's only Italian restaurant. I took a deep breath as his fingers twined lightly with mine. "That is, if you plan to... to stay... with me, or us, I mean, here in Whitfield..." he squeezed my fingers, and I suddenly found it easier to breathe. "Then you really should meet the town." I gestured to the lighted park, the brightly lit stores spilling onto the streets with people and merchandise, the tables of vendors, and knots of people gathered here and there. "This is the perfect time. Love me, love my town," I tried to joke.

"I want to stay." His voice was so soft I could have pretended to imagine it. "With you. You know that."

Our twined fingers suddenly felt like knotted ribbons. "I know that. And for now, I know it doesn't complicate things. Your... mission." The tangled mess that was our linked hands tightened convulsively as one or the both of us clutched tightly. "But... after." After your mission. After you bring my brother's soul safely to the realms of Light. I couldn't say it out loud. I spent several long minutes willing the breath back into my lungs so I could say what I needed to. "What then? If you stay with me then, you'll have turned your back on your purpose, Ethan. You'll have truly Fallen, no turning back."

"Such dark thoughts for a Winter's Festival," he said gently. We stood outside Whitfield's best and only Italian Restaurant, looking in through the glass to white linen tables where Logan sat with Amberlyn, having a swordfight with breadsticks and laughing like little kids. Ethan's lips formed words along my jaw line, just beneath my ear, making me shiver as I leaned into him. "I will stay. If you will have me. If you will not, it does not matter. I joined the ranks of the Fallen the first time I found you crying in an herb shop."

I watched as Logan leaned in close to Amberlyn, her spiral copper curls skimming the shoulder of what he laughingly called his dress sweats. Her hand convulsed around the breadstick. His pale slim fingers stilled them, curling over tanned skin and breadstick alike. Waiters in long white linen aprons carried steaming platters of food around them. People drank dark red wine, talking and laughing over meals pungent with garlic, basil, and tomato sauce. I knew strong odors tended to make my brother nauseated, but he didn't seem to care about that now. His whole world had narrowed to no one but my best friend. He brushed back the curtain of her hair with his free hand and pulled her close. She didn't put up much resistance; she'd spent the years since seventh grade in love with my brother, to varying degrees of seriousness. Her golden green eyes focused on him like the last flicker of light in a dark world. I couldn't see his expression, but the set of his shoulders, the planes and angles of his hands spoke volumes. I knew without speaking or wholly seeing, in that way siblings have, that he held something all at once priceless and fragile. He held Amberlyn the way he hovered over me when I'd been hospitalized with meningitis. He pulled her to him the way he'd gathered a wet and limp Abigail to the bare skin underneath his shirt, sheltering her from the dark wet night when she'd been run over and we were afraid she wouldn't make it to the vet. He curved around Amberlyn as he did the things he loved that might leave him soon, the fragile things hovering close to death. Only I knew that he was afraid he'd be leaving her soon, not the other way around.

A soft chill like ice and mint brushed my neck as I watched them kiss through the window of the Italian restaurant.

Ethan pulled me back against him, his hands at my waist. Some distant voice deep inside warned me that I was being a nosy voyeur. "I'm his sister," I hissed at it, watching as Amberlyn melted into the kiss, weaving her caramel fingers around the back of Logan's fragile, pale neck. Copper curls and long smooth arms melted into my brother like sunshine on frozen marble. "That explains why they didn't wait for us," I told Ethan, who had gone completely still against me.

"Should we… interrupt them?" He sounded strangely shy, as if he wasn't comfortable not knowing what to do. I ripped my nosy eyes away from my brother's love life and, with a slick quickness that reminded me of my own slowly waking Nephilim blood, spun in Ethan's arms until my own rested around his neck. I pinned his blue-green eyes with mine and saw wistful longing there. I knew it wasn't just that Ethan wanted to take me to a restaurant. It was that Ethan wished Logan could have more: more time, more dates, more Amberlyn. I dropped my forehead against his throat so the top of my head rested just under his chin.

The winter will take him.

He's the only one who doesn't treat me like a walking corpse.

"No." I groped for the warm, rough fingers I knew were near. The warm, rough fingers I wanted to claim for my own. Could claim for my own, for the rest of my life, if I wanted them. Unlike the two people in the restaurant inside. "If you can bear it, let's let them be. I'll text Logan to meet us at the fountain." Ethan nodded. "Can we give them an hour? I don't think they've even gotten their salads yet. Can you stand that?"

A tiny piece of a smile twitched along the corner of his mouth. "We'll be close enough, I suppose. Is an hour long enough for…" he gestured to the deepening darkness and gathering crowds. "For whatever you have in mind?"

I shrugged, studiously ignoring friends and neighbors as they moved around us. "I don't have anything particular in mind."

"You keep promising to show me your town," he murmured playfully, pulling on a lock of my hair.

"Mmm. I do keep promising something like that." I stared down at my shoes. "It's just…" I kicked the pavement. "I don't feel like I know it anymore. If I ever did." I huffed in frustration. I hated it when I felt a thing and couldn't put it into words. I flexed my fingers, wondering if I could draw it instead. But there wasn't time. "I just… know where things are."

But Ethan nodded as if I'd made perfect sense. As if he understood me even when I didn't. "Well, come on then," he said, smiling. "I smell fresh cookies. Fresh cookies make everything better. And we'll go from there."

No debating that point.

CHAPTER TWENTY-ONE

EXTRAORDINARY CIRCUMSTANCES

I balled my fists, shoving them deep into my jacket pockets. It had taken long enough, but it felt good to have identified the source of my vague discomfort. Whitfield itself. My town was a stranger. I cast a sideways glance around through strands of my dark hair. Everything looked the same, but I knew it wasn't.

My hometown was a refuge for supernatural forces, and had been since before I was born. Some of my neighbors, and I had no idea who or how many, had the same kind of freakish abilities I had been born with. Or worse.

Some of them weren't even human.

I'd always felt like such a freak. Like there was no one else like me in the whole world.

"You're not alone." Ethan nudged my toe. I glared at him, wondering for the hundredth time if he didn't have telepathy or something.

"Are you going to be sweet and reassuring and follow that up with a 'You've got me, sweetheart,' or do you mean in general?" I asked sarcastically. I refused to be easily cheered up.

He had the grace to look confused. "Both?"

We'd begun to wander aimlessly, following our noses. Storefronts gleamed beside me. Ethan placed himself street side; my grandmother would have approved. She insisted a true gentleman placed himself between a lady and any traffic. There wasn't any traffic, but I gave him silent points anyway. We stopped in front of Pepper's Bakery. "I didn't have to grow up feeling so alone, you know? Not when there were others like me." A young mother stood right in front of the glass display case inside the store, refereeing her two offspring as they argued over their choice of cookies.

"But there are no others like you," Ethan countered. "Not here. Believe me, I'd know. Whitfield remains a refuge precisely because it maintains a high degree of secrecy. A need to know policy, if you will."

"But then how do you know there are no others like me?" I argued back.

"We can sense our kind. Your Nephilim blood marks you out as plainly as a gold coin in a pile of silver to me and others of our kind. But other than some rather obvious signs, or outright declarations, Whitfield keeps it supernatural secrets close."

"Obvious signs?" I asked, my interest piqued. "Like what?"

He sighed. "Like, for example, a neighbor who only came out at night, never ate or drank anything, had extremely pale, cold skin, and never aged." He grinned. "Oh, and if you just happened to catch this neighbor drinking blood that would be a dead giveaway. No pun intended."

I rolled my eyes. "But other than guessing or being taken into someone's confidence, there's no real way to sense other's… differences."

"Right."

"But why?"

Ethan sighed again. "Because there are a whole bunch of supernaturals with different magical systems running around. Like different gangs, or something. It's simpler, more peaceful, this way. Everyone agrees to mind their own business, unless things get out of hand."

"You make it sound like the supernatural Wild West."

"That's not a bad analogy," Ethan admitted. "Those who take refuge here agree to certain rules, including minding their own business except in extraordinary circumstances."

"Like being hunted by evil soul-stealing demons?" Warm baking smells blasted me straight in the face as the young mother chased her children out the door. I couldn't help smiling. I saw an answering grin on Ethan's face.

"I love the smell of fresh sugar cookies," he explained, steering me forward with a familiar hand on my back. "Mmm. Imminent danger counts as extraordinary circumstances. So do developing supernatural gifts."

I stopped to finger some beaded necklaces set up on a table outside the brightly lit bead shop two doors down from the bakery. "So really, if the forces of evil weren't determined to have me, I might never have met you at all," I mused, softly enough so that only he could hear me. "Or known about Whitfield. Maybe I should send them a thank you card."

He gripped my hand, squeezing it. I happened to be holding a necklace made of polished rose quartz. The stones pressed uncomfortably against my palm. "Never think that, Caspia," he almost growled, low and throaty, right in my ear. "Evil, real evil, should it ever show itself to you, will wear the most beautiful form you've ever seen and charm you as nothing ever has. It is flawless perfection you must beware of; poor mad Asheroth was but a pale imitation of the kind of evil I fear stalks you now." Suddenly my palm was spread open in his, my fingers flat and trembling like a starfish newly pulled from the water. He fingered the rose quartz necklace. "The lover's stone," he said, pushing it aside slightly to rub the marks it left on my palm. "I would buy it for you, if I could." His smile was both tight and wistful; his eyes avoided mine entirely. "But my kind doesn't exactly carry money around."

"You can." I tossed him my wallet, palm raised against any protest. "Just look at this jacket. Even if it didn't stop weapons and supernatural wrath, there's no way it's worth more than that necklace." Still looking doubtful, I dragged my lower lip out in a tiny pout. "Please?" I whined. "I really want a present. And you can pay me back." I leaned in really close, right next to his ear. "You know. Later."

I didn't clarify what kind of repayment, and he didn't ask. As Ethan disappeared into the bead shop to pay, I spun around on the sidewalk of the square, giddy and slightly less angry at my hometown than I had been earlier. Neither one of us could help what we were. Let it go. The night wind pulled the thought from me and tugged playfully on my hair. Just for tonight. Let it all go, and come play. I felt Ethan behind me again, angel-quick, lowering the necklace over my head. I leaned backward, knowing without asking or being told that his solid bulk would be there to catch mine. I looked out over the square, at the torches and tables of food and bright trinkets scattered here and there, all backlit by the brilliantly lit, multicolored fountain carved with fantastic creatures. A fierce, deep happiness swept through me.

"Like it?" Ethan asked.

"Love it," I corrected, finding his hand by temperature alone. He pulsed warmth in the chill wind. Erik and a few other musicians were setting up in the grass off the cobblestone square in front of the fountain. A wild surge of recklessness throbbed and I was off, racing toward the gathering crowd. "Do you dance?" I laughed into the wind. "Tell me you dance. Oh, Ethan, please."

He laughed back. I felt him behind me, flowing easily as if his feet weren't even touching ground. "For you? I'll make a special effort to go slow, so you can keep up."

And then he spun me, holding me up so my feet really didn't touch the ground, and spun me with his hands under my forearms as if I weighed nothing at all. My silver skirt flared, catching the light so that it alternately glowed and pulsed with the greens and blues and golds and reds of the fountain. There was music: Erik's fast familiar lead followed by at least two other guitars and layered vocals. Not his full band, then. I idly wondered why. Other instruments drew near: a shy percussionist, an indignant-fingered violinist. Erik played something softer, slower, to take their measure; all knew without speech who was architect here. As the walls of sound rearranged themselves around us, Ethan shifted uncertainly on the grass, and I discovered a new thing about him. "You don't know how to dance slow," I told the moon, half-covered by branches like fingers as if it was trying not to see what the mortals were doing.

"No," he admitted, suddenly stiff and graceless in my arms. "I am almost always moving very fast, or not at all."

"Well," I said, after a moment's thought during which the violinist performed a graceful sonic slide around Erik's commanding lead, "Just pretend I'm feeling wobbly." He laughed, and the curve of my spine under the pressure of his palm felt like a lock clicking shut.

Other dancers joined us, warm textured presences brushing occasionally against our orbit. The music sped, faster and faster, Erik riding his new acquisitions hard. I was dizzy, and the moon shone high against velvet dark through trembling tree-fingers. Through it all was Ethan, laughing, always laughing, refusing to put me down or let me rest until I begged and threatened. Even then he spun me in one impossibly fast last circle, collapsing with me on the grass just beyond the music and dancing.

"So," I panted, flat on my back while clouds wove themselves like ribbons across the surface of the sky. "You can dance. If the music's fast enough. Otherwise, you need me." His laugh sounded more like a barking seal than anything else. I told him so, and he rolled right over on top of me, pinning me so that his wild, dark hair and river bright eyes obscured the moon entirely.

"You're not a terrible dancer," he teased, his smile as big as I'd ever seen it. "What you lack in skill you make up for in sweat."

I giggled. I never giggle. "If I didn't know I'd hurt myself, I'd kick you somewhere very painful right now," I told him between un-Caspia-like fits of snickering. "You'd better get off me. The whole town will talk." I erupted in laughter so fierce I could barely breathe, let alone talk coherently. "If they can… stop casting spells and… drinking blood and… howling at the moon… and… stuff…" I held onto my stomach while tears leaked out of my eyes, unable to finish making fun of my neighbors.

Ethan sat near my head, watching me with the strangest expression on his face, as if unsure whether to stop me or join in.

"So her wits have not yet returned," said a familiar, heavily accented voice from somewhere off to my side. "That is too bad. But I suppose she can still wash dishes."

My giggling turned abruptly into choking. Mr. Markov? At the Festival on the Square? How much had he heard? Or perhaps he was here for the dancing. The choking turned right back into giggling as I pictured blind Mr. Markov dancing under the moon.

"Oh, leave the child alone," chided yet another familiar voice I couldn't quite place. Female. "She's in love." The voice sounded rapturous, then sharpened into a chiding tone I knew instantly. "Not that you'd know love if it bit you on your—"

"Mrs. Alice!" I sat up so fast the world temporarily resembled a carousel ride set on "kill." Ethan's hand was there, supporting me, a firm familiar pressure against the small of my back, or I might have fallen flat again. I gave him a grateful smile that probably resembled a drunken leer more than anything else. "Mr. Markov?" I added, astonished to see my blind employer holding tightly to Mrs. Alice's arm, his glass-topped cane loose in his other hand. As far as I knew, the two hated each other. I'd never once heard them say anything good about the other. "What are you two doing here?"

"Well, that's a forward question, my dear." Mrs. Alice sounded smug as she settled herself onto one of the wooden seats that ringed the cobblestone space around the fountain. She sat carefully, brushing her skirt straight as she did so with the same precise neatness with which she measured and labeled herbs in her shop. Mr. Markov, his familiar scowl never changing, held her shawl out to her. By miracle or coincidence he managed to hold it exactly above her arm. Mrs. Alice nodded sharply, in thanks or because she expected such treatment, and swathed her crisp white cotton blouse with a blue cashmere shawl that matched the deep indigo of her long skirt. "That's better," she said with a sigh, leaning back against the wooden slats. "I swear my bones feel the chill more this year than they did at last year's festival."

"Nonsense," Mr. Markov contradicted gruffly. I'd pulled myself into a cross-legged position on the grass next to Ethan. His hold on my back had turned from necessary to merely reassuring. I moved one hand to his lap and squeezed his knee to show him I appreciated it. "It's a little colder this year; that's all. Of course, this is nothing like a full-on Russian winter. This is more like early autumn along the banks of the Volga." I watched as he began the familiar motions of setting up his chess set.

"You're playing chess." I sounded flat and dull even to myself. "With Mrs. Alice."

"Every week," she agreed. "Why so surprised? Don't you think I can hold my own, Caspia dear?" I looked blankly at Ethan for help. He looked blankly back.

"No! Of course not!" I said quickly. "I mean… of course you can. Um. It's just that I've never seen Mr. Markov play anyone else and lose. And you two… well, I thought you…" I slammed my lips together, suddenly very interested in the silver ribbons of my skirt. I couldn't think of a single diplomatic thing to say.

The chessboard gleamed between them. Somehow, impossibly, the glass pieces glowed faintly, as if lit from within. A sudden image superimposed itself on all the others in my head: Mr. Markov, on the night Ethan came for me, the night Asheroth took me, holding a glass piece in his curved hand. What had he said? Black and white don't exist… shades of gray… prefer the lighter spectrum… And yet, the chess piece, made entirely of clear glass, had flashed red in his hand, as if he'd been holding a living flame.

Several long moments of silence later, when laughter, shouts, and music from beyond my immediate circle bled into my reverie, I realized I had spoken aloud. Mr. Markov nodded slowly. He wore a tiny, unfamiliar smile. I could count on one hand the number of times I'd seen the broken husk of the man who employed me smile. "You listen and remember. This is good. So is plain speaking, my Caspia. But you have much on your mind, and many burdens not of your own making, so I will do it for you this one time. You wonder why I meet to play chess with someone who, at every other occasion, treats me as a bitter enemy." He inclined his head graciously toward Mrs. Alice. "No offense meant, Madam." She nodded just as graciously back. "And, to be fair, I often treat her the same way."

"Well, yes," I said, startled. I glanced swiftly sideways at Ethan. What was the protocol here? I knew Mr. Markov was a magician of some kind, and I'd heard the word "witch" applied to Mrs. Alice. None of that surprised me. Little could, since meeting a creature like Asheroth, or walking hand in hand with Ethan daily. But what was the procedure? Was I supposed to know? Could I, should I, bring it up? Did I want to?

Then Ethan's gentle pressure against my back reminded me that there was something I wanted to know, very badly indeed.

"Oh, tell the child," Mrs. Alice said at last, studying the board intently. She leaned forward and touched one finger to the top of her queen's head. All her pieces turned a deep and instant black. I forgot to breathe. Ice froze the breath in the back of my throat, chilling my neck as it held it trapped there.

Beside me, Ethan hissed. He was up and in front of me, one knee to the ground, the other tensed to spring, both arms carefully blocking me.

"Easy," Mr. Markov barked. "My colleague has offered no insult and poses no threat."

"I see you don't prefer the lighter spectrum, yourself," I said to Mrs. Alice, weakly.

She smiled briefly at me and moved a piece, ignoring Ethan, who was positively bristling in front of me. "It's not for everyone," she said. "Will you call off your… gentleman friend? He's being quite rude."

"He's just being protective," I said defensively. Truthfully, I wasn't sure I wanted Ethan to relax. Mr. Markov moved a piece. His pieces remained white, and a tiny part of me felt relieved. How many more surprises lay in store for me about the people and town I thought I knew so well? "Am I right in assuming you're like Mr. Markov, only… darker?" She moved another piece, not responding. "Ethan? Why couldn't you tell?"

"I am best attuned to our kind," he ground out through locked teeth.

"Really?" This was news. "So we could be surrounded by evil, and unless they were Fallen…"

"You must," Mr. Markov snapped, moving a bishop and snatching up one pawn and a rook from Mrs. Alice, "stop thinking in those terms. Good and evil. Black and white. Absolutes." He set the captured pieces down on his side of the board with an angry thunk. He tapped madly at his temple. "Spectrums, Caspia. Continuums. Shades of gray. Take Mrs. Alice here. She is no different from me. We are both practitioners of the same Art. We are both community leaders of the same Art. However, I lead those who follow a… lighter spectrum. My colleague's path is… somewhat darker. Not evil. Merely different. We meet sometimes as all good leaders do: to sort out differences, to air grievances, to share information. I would not consort with evil."

"And neither would I," added Mrs. Alice, somewhat haughtily, as she demolished a line of white glass pieces.

"But what does that even mean?" I wailed. "Light and Dark. Good and evil. They're just words. They mean the same thing."

"No." Mr. Markov's fist came down on the table, shaking the board and all its pieces. "They are actions, Caspia, as well as words. But the actions behind them matter most. Neither Mrs. Alice nor myself would sit here in the very heart of our home and play chess with evil."

"This town is a refuge for all types of supernaturals, of the Light and the Dark, and yes, we do not always get along." She flashed Mr. Markov a smile. "Sometimes, there is outright war amongst us. But what I think you mean as evil? Sacrificing innocents and mortals, for one? Murder? No. What you must learn, Caspia dear"—she moved a pawn—"is that Dark does not mean evil, and Light does not always equal good."

I remembered Ethan's warning from the bakery: Evil, real evil, should it ever show itself to you, will wear the most beautiful form you've ever seen and charm you as nothing ever has.

His angry voice pulled me back. "Then how do you explain the demon taint surrounding your store the night I first came to you? The night I met

Caspia? Even the Dark Realms will not give it sanctuary." Ethan had risen from his crouch and pulled me with him. He still stood in front of me, but he stood to the side of the chess game now.

Mrs. Alice paused mid-move. She replaced her piece on its original square. "Forgive me, Omar. The rules allow, if I don't remove my hand…" He waved her words away as inconsequential. She rubbed the bridge of her nose with her left hand. Light refracted off the rings she wore. Mrs. Alice stared off into nothing for a moment, her eyes going slightly unfocused. "Such a creature is loose in Whitfield?" she asked slowly.

"Such a creature was in your shop," Ethan told her tersely. "Such a creature bought all her tarot cards and tried to lure her to it by using you as its agent. You are the one who gave her the phone number of a stranger who wanted a 'private commission,' aren't you?"

Mrs. Alice had gone as white as Mr. Markov's chess pieces. She looked ill. Mr. Markov reached for her. "Alice," he said reassuringly. "There was already an attack. A mad Fallen angel, lost for a century, or more, now. We thought it was over, but he must not have been the one. We'll check your wards. We'll get both our circles together, if we must, to reinforce them. Caspia's Guardian said himself he is best attuned to his own kind. It is the same for all of us; we often see only our own kind. It isn't another magic user. That has to be the reason why."

She shook her head violently. "That's no excuse. Why didn't I recognize it? Why didn't I know? To endanger an innocent that way… If her Guardian hadn't come along then… who knows what could have happened?"

A bitter uneasiness had begun to skitter down my neck. "She's not an innocent," Ethan said. I blushed scarlet and was about to protest, but Ethan overrode me. "She's known she has Nephilim blood for a while now, and she's had Nephilim-born abilities her whole life."

"Oh," I said, feeling silly and shy at the same time. I was relieved to know my "innocence" meant nothing more than whether I had a touch of the supernatural or not, and was aware of it. I'd genuinely thought the attacking angels in the park had been out just to insult me. "But Ethan's not my Guardian," I said to Mrs. Alice and Mr. Markov. "Ethan's here for Logan." I wanted to be clear about that.

"Then why…" Mr. Markov began. He thought for a minute, and I actually watched his formerly open face close down into inscrutability. I saw the realization hit him: the man beside me was guardian of my brother's death. "Oh. You're that kind of Guardian." He turned his sightless eyes on Ethan with a new kind of wariness. "Then why, pray tell, aren't you with your actual charge?"

"Because both of them asked me not to be," he said softly—so softly the wind stole his words easily away. His neck and shoulders bowed suddenly, as if carrying a weight none of us could see. "And because I have nothing else to give him."

"Logan's on a date," I said, defensively. "With Amberlyn. They're meeting us here. In just a few minutes, actually."

"The demon seems to be targeting Caspia exclusively," Ethan seconded. He looked at me guiltily. "It seemed a shame to interrupt them." He didn't add, when Logan has so little time, but he might as well have. The sentiment hung thickly in the air around us.

Mrs. Alice shook her head and wrapped her cashmere shawl more tightly around her shoulders. With shaking hands, she began to gather her pieces. They turned from black to white as she gathered them together. "If you'll forgive me, Omar. My mind will no longer allow me to concentrate on beating you this evening. It seems there is much to tell my circle."

Mr. Markov collected the pieces and began methodically storing them in their folding box that doubled as a storage. "As do I," he murmured. "You will allow me to walk you home?" Mrs. Alice nodded and rose in one graceful gesture.

I found myself enveloped in an embrace of lavender and cashmere before I realized her intentions. "Don't let this change how you feel about me, or Whitfield," she whispered, her fingers in my hair trembling slightly with age for the first time in my memory. "I'm the same woman I've always been. And everyone in this town will fight for you. You're one of us, Caspia dear." Lips coated lightly with beeswax and honey, her own preparation and a marvel against the chapped harshness of winter, pressed gently against my cheek. "Your mother didn't know what we were. Your gifts passed her by, somehow. But she was dear to me anyway. I think she would be proud, if she could see you now. You're such a strong young woman." Mrs. Alice smiled at me, and, Dark Witch or not, something lightened inside me. Some burden I'd been carrying slipped off of its own accord. I remembered hot chocolates in her store while my mother bought loose tea and spices. I remembered piling pretty stones into little houses and smiling at Logan who wanted badly to throw one at me, but couldn't because both my mother and Mrs. Alice would catch him.

Mrs. Alice, who brewed special teas when we had colds as children; who bandaged my arm when I'd burned it the night I'd met Ethan; who insisted on drinking my coffee out of fine china; she couldn't be evil. My mother loved and trusted her. So had Gran. She was proof positive that Dark and Evil weren't the same thing.

I had just turned to Ethan, at peace with my decision, when the screaming started far across the square.

I felt it like a punch in the stomach, and I knew.

CHAPTER TWENTY-TWO

TRUTHS LAID BARE

I had one terrible second to look Ethan full in the eyes, to see the horrible certainty stamped there, before grabbing him by the front of my brother's borrowed sweater. My hands trailed shadows as I fisted them. "Take me," I demanded. I didn't shout. My voice surprised me with its low, deadly hiss. "Use your wings if you must. I don't care who sees. But do it. Now."

I was a feral thing, snarling against him, against the rising screams and breaking glass across the square. I had just enough time to see his eyes flare an intense silver as my own terror spiked and reflected back at me, drowning out the pale blue-green tint of his own eyes completely, before light flared at his back and we were gone.

A brief moment of disorientation, of nausea that should have brought me to my knees, but didn't. Grief did that, all by itself.

Funny how we'd spent all our time worrying about Dark angels and the insidious spread of cancer, yet in the end, something as routine as a traffic accident struck the final blow. Later I would read the report. Later I would close my eyes and see the scene of the accident: the way one car had swerved to avoid another, and lost control of the vehicle. I would read about how the driver of the second vehicle had driven into a lamp post, putting himself in the hospital in an effort to avoid hitting pedestrians. I would hear the word "hero" applied to my brother with only the barest hint of a snarl because Logan had pushed Amberlyn out of the way. If he hadn't, she'd have been pinned between the oncoming car and a wrought-iron lamp post reinforced with concrete and steel posts. She'd have been crushed. She'd be dead.

Instead, my brother got her out of the way.

How had he managed it? Long-buried Nephilim blood must have come up boiling because no cancer patient should have been able to move so fast or shove a healthy young woman, even a small one like Amberlyn, eight feet clear of the wreck. Yet he did. Amberlyn recalled only motion and sound and the final jarring impact of pavement well clear of the wreck.

I wondered if I would ever stop hating her.

Lying in a pool of his own blood, flat on his back across the hood of a car, eyes glassy and staring up at the sky, my brother Logan stretched immobile and white. Shattered glass glittered across his body like cheap carnival jewelry. The shoulder and arm nearest what remained of the windshield were oddly angled. One leg lay twisted back and under. But the rest of him seemed grotesquely peaceful as if he had just chosen a particularly dangerous and uncomfortable place to watch the sky. He didn't blink. His chest neither rose nor fell.

Nothing in the whole world existed but my brother: not sound, not the driver of the car, not the flashing ambulance lights, not Amberlyn, not even Ethan. I'm sure someone must have tried to stop me, but I don't remember it. I don't remember anyone touching me or restraining me at all. Maybe they didn't. Perhaps Ethan brought me right up to the wreckage and kept them all away. Maybe they saw something in my face, in both our faces, Ethan's and mine, worse than death. Later, I would wonder how I managed to get past law enforcement and EMTs to perch directly on the car hood next to my brother's inert form, but right then, I was safe inside my bubble with Logan.

"Hey, Logan," I said softly. I found myself looking directly down at him, brushing glass off his forehead. He'd lost his ball cap. He wouldn't like that, all these people seeing his bald head. His glassy eyes held no recognition. "It's ok," I said, sliding up next to him. "You're going to be cold," I told him, placing one flat palm, light as a single sheet of paper in a strong wind, over his heart. "We can't have that." Tears had started. I made no move to stop them. Something subhuman had taken over; the wrecked body underneath my palm was the only thing linking me to the person who had been Caspia. "You can't leave yet," I insisted. "Not like this."

Someone else was inside the bubble with me. Or something. A being made almost entirely of Light. I looked, disbelieving, as Ethan held out his hand to me. "Let me take him," he said, softly, as if talking to a child. The tears were coming harder now, so I had to squint to see him clearly. "Cas. Please. Let me take him." Ethan stretched to grasp Logan's hand, the one attached to his grotesquely twisted shoulder.

Take him? Take him where?

I tried to speak. I discovered a new thing, then; tears don't just happen in the eyes. They collect in the throat, where they can choke and drown. "Resting," I finally managed, almost dying on the word. "He's just resting." I didn't move my flattened palm. It hovered above my brother's unmoving chest. Glass ground into the backs of my thighs, slicing through the silver of my skirt. I did not, dared not move.

"Caspia," Ethan said again. Light pulsed at his back, strong and steady as ever. "Let me take him. He's…" Ethan tore his eyes from me to look, long and hard, at my brother's wrecked body. "He's in agony, Cas. Let me give him rest."

Rest?

"No." I rubbed my face against my free forearm. "He's not dead yet. It's not supposed to happen like this." I looked at Ethan. "You know that. It's not right." This last, in a whisper.

"I don't know that," he countered, releasing Logan entirely. He moved closer to me, crawling up the hood of the car until he faced us both on his knees. "I only know it's my job to see him safely home. To the Realms, Caspia. Where he won't feel any pain. Where your family waits for him. Where it's beautiful. You know it is. It's another reason I took you there, if only to the edges. It's not allowed, but I wanted you to see. Don't you want that for him?"

His voice was soft and warm and all enveloping. He was so careful with me, my Ethan, over my brother's broken body. He was afraid for me, I could tell. This moment could break me, shatter me forever.

He was afraid for us. This moment could break us.

Would break us.

I felt it happening. Half my heart was dying between us, and what could I give him, give anyone, then?

I looked down at my brother again. His blood soaked my silver skirt. "Your… job," I echoed. "And then what? You'll turn your back on the Realms and move in and play house?" My eyes blazed to match my skirt, my hands smeared with blood. "Is that what you want, Ethan? To get this over with so you can hurry up and join the ranks of the Fallen?" I said the word "this" with a brutal emphasis that made me draw my knees up to my chest. "A job—your job—that's what he was the whole time, and you didn't even pay attention to him."

"That's not true." Light enfolded us both. "I'm so, so sorry. Maybe you're right that it wasn't meant to happen this way. Maybe it's not some random accident, and if it's not, I swear to you, we'll find who did this. But he's in agony, Caspia, and I will see him safe." He softened his tone as he steeled himself to gather us both in his arms. "You would want that, too, if you weren't in shock."

Rage, the feral subhuman kind that seared all reason, ran through me in one angry throb. "Get your hands off me," I snarled in a voice even I didn't recognize. "Off both of us." I scrambled backward, laying both hands on my brother's heart. "The Light. You draw power, sometimes. When you…" I trailed off, frustrated. The right words wouldn't come. Fine. I'd show him. Palms out, I tried to focus. "Let me try."

He stood with his head bowed, as if I also held his heart in my hands. "You're going to try to draw power from the Realms. For Logan." It wasn't a question, so I didn't answer. "I should never have taken you. You don't know what you're doing. You'll change everything."

Why did he sound like I was tearing out his heart, instead of giving my brother's back to him?

Sobbing, I pressed down on Logan's chest like I was trying CPR. "I don't know what to do," I admitted. "You only just started to teach me. We had so little time." For once, Ethan looked like the fragile one. I needed him to be strong. I needed him. "Please," I whispered, and then, it was a prayer, of a sort.

"I'll do it," he whispered. "Light save me, I'll do it." Rough warm fingers wrapped around my neck. "It's a gift of your blood, Caspia," Ethan said. Gran's words. "The Light, your drawings… even the Dark. They all come from the same place. But it will take Light to bring your brother back." All I felt was emptiness and cold, bitter fear, until Ethan said, so faint I think I wished it, "Take mine."

Light pulsed against Logan's chest, the same kind I had used to knock Ethan down when he took me to the Realms of Light. It burned through me, taking all my rage with it, out through my hands and into my brother's body where some answering echo in the blood recognized the light and welcomed it.

I fell back against the hood of the car, my palms blistered.

Logan began to breathe.

EMTs swarmed us, crowding around my brother, creating a screen between us with their unfamiliar actions and equipment. Ethan had me around the waist, pulling me backward and out of their way. Only when I was off the car hood did I start to fight him in earnest.

If I had any doubt Ethan was abnormally good, they evaporated right then. He let me hit him. He let me yell at him and claw at his sweater. He let me sob and shriek. In short, I went hysterical on him, and he merely stood there and took it until I ran out of anger and hysterical fear. Even then, he was there to catch me. Eventually, I calmed down enough to realize that Amberlyn was standing beside me, standing statue-like and glassy-eyed, except for a violent trembling that came in occasional spasms.

"It was going to hit me," she finally managed to explain, after many stops and starts. "He pushed me out of the way." Then she burst into hysterical sobbing that didn't stop until I dragged her over to an EMT who seemed more than happy to take charge of her. I didn't want to look at her anymore. Maybe later I would regret it, but for now, I cared about no one except Logan.

No one.

"Would you really have taken him from me?" I asked Ethan, swaying a little with tiredness.

"Yes," he said just as wearily. "And I think you just made a mistake. I'm going to have to take him from you sooner or later. He's dying, slowly and painfully. You've only prolonged his pain."

"Ethan. Everyone is dying. Even me." I felt halfway there already.

His eyes were so solemn. "But I'm not."

We stared at each other, the truth laid bare between us as starkly as possible, backlit by harsh red emergency lights and the mist of frozen breath. Mine. Ethan didn't breathe. He wasn't mortal.

The truth sucked and clawed what little warmth I had left in my body, leaving jagged rips for the chill winter wind to fill. I was shivering, some dimly observant part of me noticed, and I couldn't stop. Nor did I care.

"I'm riding to the hospital with my brother," I told him after what felt like an eternity. A lot of things felt like they took forever, like the amount of time I spent with Ethan and Logan on that car hood. In reality, they'd gone by rather quickly. Funny, what the mind latches onto in a crisis. "And then I'm not sure it's a good idea to be around each other." I sounded flat, uncaring, like I was ordering supplies at work.

"Caspia." My name was a labored whisper. "Do you know what you're saying?"

Pain, raw and unexpected, rushed outward toward every extremity in my body so that I burned like a frostbite victim. Eyes the color of a calm river had become a tidal storm; fists of stone clenched and unclenched against the effort of reaching, of touching. I shied away, scooting backward. "I'm terrified, Ethan," I admitted in a whisper, "that one day I'll hate you for taking my brother. No matter what the reason, no matter how good. One day, I'll hate you." My voice cracked on a sob. I backed away from him where he stood looking at me like a piece of his own personal apocalypse. "And then I'll be dead, and you'll be alone. Like Asheroth. Like the rest of the mad, lost Fallen ones. I can't do that. To either of us."

I barely made it to the ambulance as it left, carrying my brother to Whitfield Central Hospital. I had never felt more alone in my life.

I didn't look back.

"I'm sorry," I said, as politely as I could. I even tried a little smile, but I could tell my face wasn't going to cooperate so I stopped. I gathered what dignity I had left and sat as straight as I could. That wasn't easy in a bloody shredded skirt with one half of my heart hooked up to life support and the other half having just been told to get lost forever. "I don't understand. You must be mistaken. Logan would have told me."

Dr. Ensforth had the grace to look uncomfortable. He flipped some papers for a moment and pretended to study them. In reality, I think he was just preparing himself for a hysterical patient. I didn't blame him, really. If ever there was a patient due for a good fit of hysteria, it was me. I still wore Ethan's leather jacket, but the rest of me was a shredded mess of silver satin and blood. "Well," Dr. Ensforth said at last. "Perhaps Mr. Chastain had someone else he discussed these matters with? Someone outside the family?"

I let an edge of destruction creep into my voice. Not quite a promise of it, but the sure knowledge of someone who'd spent the night in its intimate embrace. "No. I'll repeat myself. Logan would have told me." I tried another smile and wiped my face bare when Dr. Ensforth looked even more alarmed than before. "So there must be some mistake."

He let the clipboard rest lightly on his crossed knee, assessing me. He seemed to come to a decision. "Very well. See for yourself." He placed the clipboard on top of a thick file and passed me the whole mess. "Your brother's instructions are very clear. In the event that his vital signs fall below certain benchmarks, whatever the cause, we are to cease and desist all artificial efforts to sustain and prolong his life as defined by the parameters listed within. It's all right there. I'll be happy to clarify any of the terminology if you wish."

I flipped through the file absently. My eyes had filled with tears as soon as they'd fallen on the clipboard Dr. Ensforth passed me, blurring the words. Only two things stood out, really, but they were the important things: the words "Do Not Resuscitate" and my brother's loopy scrawl of a signature.

Oh God. Logan. Why?

It took me some time to realize I was repeating the question out loud, over and over, and crying, until Dr. Ensforth handed me a box of tissues and another thick file. "It didn't occur to me until a moment ago," he said uncertainly, as if I was a time bomb that might go off at any moment. He frowned at another thick file and also handed it to me. "Did you know the specifics of your brother's last test results?"

"Well, yes. What he told me." I scrubbed my face with scratchy hospital grade tissues. "I always went with Logan for his appointments. But he didn't want me to go with him to this last one. I…" I clenched my fists briefly. It had been the day after I'd met Ethan. I forced my brain to create language even though it didn't want to. "I was under a lot of strain. He wanted me to go to class and have an easy day. I tried to come, but he wouldn't let me." There. I took a deep breath. I hadn't even had to say his name. Ethan. It would get easier, with time. I pretended to scratch my nose and wiped away two traitorous tears.

Dr. Ensforth nodded absently. "What do you know about his diagnosis?"

"Stage two liver cancer. He kept me updated about his treatment. He didn't like me to go with him for the chemotherapy, but I went anyway a lot of the time. I kept his pills organized and made sure he took them on time. Except for that once, I never missed an oncologist's visit." I finished scrubbing my face and tossed the handful of tissues in the wastebasket. I missed. "Why do you ask?"

Dr. Ensforth indicated the file. "I thought it odd that you didn't come to his last appointment. Most patients insist on having their family with them when a terminal diagnosis comes through, but Logan said you had school or something."

My fingers froze in the process of opening the file. "Terminal?" I repeated dully. Suddenly, the DNR order made a sick kind of sense.

Dr. Ensforth continued to study me. "You truly didn't know?"

Fingers still frozen over the file, I just stared. My mind wiped blank. I couldn't think of a single thing to say. Something in my face must have convinced him I really didn't know. He plucked the file from my hand and laid it on the hospital room nightstand. "Is there anyone I can call for you?" he asked, his voice husky with a new, rough sympathy. "A relative? A close friend?"

If I winced on the word "relative," the word "close friend" was like a hot poker through my side. "All our relatives are dead," I told him in a monotone. My brother's cancer was terminal and he'd lied to me about it. "I just told my… someone important…that I never want to see him again."

Dr. Ensforth stood motionless in the hospital room doorway. After a minute, he whipped out a little pad and began writing furiously. "Miss Chastain, I'm going to send someone down to talk to you. I'm going to write you a prescription for some anxiety medication. Temporarily, of course, until we can arrange something long term." I wondered if he meant therapy or commitment. I couldn't bring myself to care about either option just then. "In the meantime, I'll make sure this stays a private room, although it's technically a double. I want you to stay right here in this room with your brother and try to get some sleep. Can you do that?"

"I don't know," I said in a hoarse whisper. Logan looked like a science fiction monster, with tubes and machines that beeped and pulsed and a mask stretched across his face. Soon, those machines would be gone. Soon, Logan himself would be gone, leaving me alone. Alone without even Ethan.

Making a mistake. Prolonging his pain. Ethan had been right. Would he come for him again? Would I see him this time?

I barely heard the thick *snick* of the heavy hospital doors closing. I sat, cross-legged, and watched over my brother before he began to die. Again.

CHAPTER TWENTY-THREE

D.N.R.

I hate the color white and the tickling burn of chemicals in the back of my throat.

What time is it? Where are my clothes? Why am I wearing scrubs?

There are exactly fifty-six white tiles in the wall above my brother's hospital bed.

Who are these people, these strangers who come in and out? Why can't they leave me alone with him? I just want to hold his hand. For a minute longer. I'm his sister. What if he's lost? Or scared?

Look. Look at his hands. Piano player's hands, my mother called them.

Mother.

His hands are so cold.

No, I won't leave.

Get that needle away from me!

Ow! That fucking hurt!

Doesn't matter. He doesn't need those machines. Strong, he's… I'll just… hold his hand, and lay my head down here… with his heart for a pillow…

…it'll be fine, Logan… you'll see…

…be here…

…when you…

…wake.

CHAPTER TWENTY-FOUR

NOT A MIRACLE

I stared at the dead vines that wrapped themselves around the statue more stubbornly than any lover. Even in cold and neglect, they clung tenaciously to their post, snaking around the Virgin Mary statue as if they were the only things holding her together.

Perhaps they were.

Memory told me they were roses. I didn't come to the hospital often, but one of my few vivid memories of the place involved looking down into this wild bit of garden, startled at the rich orange-red hue of flowers that had been indifferently tended, at best. Those roses had been one of the universe's unexpected kindnesses to me, long ago when I badly needed one. Until I'd thrown myself against the glass of my mother's hospital room window, desperate for a glimpse of anything that wasn't death, I hadn't known that particular hue of brilliant orange-red existed. I was still in high school and my mother had been the last of my parents to die. Throughout the entire numbing ordeal, they were the only splash of color I remembered. Ever since, I had tried without success to recapture a color so brilliant it was almost tactile: the downy velvet thickness of a thousand sunsets distilled into one, waiting in a ragged little garden like a present just for me.

Now the last living member of my blood lay dying by slow, painful inches two floors above me and there was nothing in the ragged garden to indicate it still lived, let alone would bloom in the summer. Nothing but the fact that I had seen it happen before and I knew this particular garden was especially tenacious.

I guess it was all a matter of faith.

As the chill wind slithered over me, finding every possible opening in my jacket and every inch of exposed skin, I exchanged my box of brightly colored pastels for a stick of graphite. I had little faith and no imagination today. I would draw only what was in front of me. It was a good policy; I'd adopted it with a lot of things in my life lately. One thing at a time. No looking farther ahead than I had to.

I rubbed my forearms for warmth and tried to count how long I'd been here, in the hospital, spending almost every waking moment at Logan's side. I didn't know. It had been a while. Long enough to make long-term arrangements with school and work. Long enough to ask Mr. Mason to care for Abigail for a while.

But not long enough to forget an absent pair of blue-green eyes and steadying warm hands, rough as stone.

Ethan.

I snapped my focus back to the drawing taking shape under my hands. The vines looked dead, and the statue looked crumbling and a bit moldy in places. I knew better, though. The vines weren't dead. They were just heavy sleepers. It wasn't my best drawing, but I had to stay in practice. Dr. Christian alone, of all my professors, demanded bi-weekly make-up work or threatened to drop me from his class. All my other teachers just told me to check in with them when things "calmed down a bit," as one of them said tactfully. Although Amberlyn joined me in cursing Dr. Christian and all his ancestors, to be truthful, I was grateful for the distractions his weekly workload forced on me. And today, I welcomed any delaying tactic that would keep me from returning to room 213.

A room where my brother, stubborn as ever, had not yet decided to die. Even though they'd removed all so-called artificial forms of life-support, Logan continued to breathe. His heart continued to beat. His brain even registered activity, but not enough, his doctors hastily assured me, to qualify as lucid thought.

Concentrate, Caspia, I ordered myself, staring at the broken, twisted vines with new ferocity. Severe heavy curves for the outline of the stems, touched with a series of straight feathery lines for the broken edges. Or would crosshatching with a pencil be better? How much detail did I want?

My phone vibrated against my hip, buried deep in my jeans pocket. I fell back against the brick courtyard wall, letting my head bang against the hard surface just enough to sting. Everyone who cared about me knew where I was and knew I wasn't exactly in a talkative mood. But I'd managed to drop my graphite somewhere in the scraggly grass, and my sketchbook hung loosely from one hand, so I flung it down on the rough concrete bench with a loud expletive and dug my phone out anyway.

Amberlyn, of course. She'd texted, *Done w/ hmwk at CB. Want company/ coffee? Amelie sez hi.*

Of course I didn't want company. But Amberlyn was the least evil of all possible company, and if she came bearing caffeine, so much the better. I didn't know when or how, and I really didn't care, but some part of me had already begun to forgive her.

She was pretty much the closest thing to family I had left.

And I hadn't forgotten the two of them kissing, my best friend and my brother, tan skin on pale—sunshine on snow—the night of the accident. The circumstances were radically different, but we'd both lost a man we loved that night. Or had started to love. Or something.

Hell and damnation, I couldn't even get it straight in my head. Maybe I was just totally unlovable. Ethan was gone, and I had better get used to a long life of rocking chairs and my new life's companion, Abigail the cat. My thumbs tapped out a quick reply, smearing charcoal dust across my keypad. Right before I could hit "send," an arm clad in blood red leather snaked out and snatched my phone away.

A chillingly familiar voice warned, "Don't. You're in more trouble than you know already. Don't involve an innocent. Especially her."

I froze. I couldn't help it. His was the last voice I ever expected to hear again. I would literally have staggered under the barrage of fear, shock, and panic had I not been so stunned. But somehow, I shoved all those emotions down. I could sort them out later; my worst nightmare was here now. I threw myself against the courtyard wall and brought both hands up in front of me, palms out, in the universal gesture of "stay the hell away."

I hoped it made me look helpless, like a frightened girl cowering against a wall trying to ward off someone more powerful. In reality, I was reaching for the place inside that let me pull shadows when I was really upset. I was also wracking my brain for every single thing Ethan had ever told me about the Fallen, the Nephilim, and Asheroth.

Especially the part about how he was Dark and insane, but not necessarily evil. At least, I hoped that was what Ethan had said. I fervently hoped I remembered the not evil part correctly. Because it was definitely Asheroth who stood across from me now, his diamond-bright eyes wide as a surprised child's. He held his palms out in mimicry or mockery of mine. Black haired, white skinned, mad Asheroth held my cell phone in his hand in the courtyard two floors down from where my brother lay dying and did something tremendously wrong and utterly insane.

He tilted his head and smiled at me, humming tunelessly while he rocked back and forth on his heels. The smile came out wrong and kind of creepy, like a child playing with lipstick for the first time who thinks he's made himself pretty, but instead looks like some kind of demented clown. I did exactly what I would do for such a child: I smiled back, but I could feel my mouth trembling as I did it like a squirming insect just waiting for escape. My teeth locked together against my will and I ground out, "Asheroth. What are you doing here?" Cold marched up my spine. Shadows flickered in lines across my forearms. Experimentally, I spread my fingers wide and flexed them; shadows arced between them like opaque slashes through air. A desperate kind of despair joined the cold marching up my spine when that happened. I didn't want to be able to pull shadows from the Dark Realms. I didn't want to have to. Ethan was supposed to be here, to guard my brother from creatures like Asheroth, so that I didn't have to. I made my smile fiercer to hide the weakness and fear crawling inside of me.

Ethan wasn't here, and Asheroth was. I was all Logan had, and I would be damned if I'd let that psychopath have my brother's soul without a fight.

Maybe literally damned.

The wind blasted through the little courtyard, much colder than I remembered, carrying a few drops of ice-cold rain with it. I hugged myself without thinking, for comfort or warmth or both, and as I did it, thick dark slashes of shadows so black they looked like ink stains followed my hands like tracers.

It's okay, I tried to tell myself. Don't panic. You have armor and shadows. You can fight.

Asheroth's terrible smile slipped when he saw the shadows. "You've been playing with shadows and fire. Very naughty. It certainly complicates things." He struggled to pin his awful smile back in place. "You don't trust me," he said at last. I didn't bother to respond to this less than intelligent observation. His sparkling white eyes narrowed. "So I brought you a present." He reached into his jacket pocket, digging inside as if it were both bottomless and very cluttered. Carefully, as if performing a seldom-rehearsed magic trick, he produced a rather crushed and battered flower. Except for its color, it had seen better days.

Asheroth held it out to me. Arm taut, fingers wrapped with crushing strength around a thorn-studded stem, the action obviously caused him pain. When I realized what it was, I tried to flatten myself against the brick wall even more. I refused to touch it. "Where did you get this?" I rasped at him, against the wind and my own mounting horror. "How did you know?"

Asheroth held a slightly battered version of one of my courtyard roses in all its blooming orange-red glory. The crushed leaves and bruised petals released a sweet, smooth scent that belonged to summer nights and lightning bugs, to bare feet and cricket-song. Among winter-dead vines and decaying statues, Asheroth's offering bordered on desecration. When he realized I wasn't going to take it, his expression changed. His eyes narrowed almost to slits. His muscles relaxed against his bones in a way that made everything about him seem feline and hungry. He prowled closer. "I told you once, Caspia. I keep track of her descendants." He buried his nose in the petals, closing his eyes and inhaling deeply. His voice became very, very soft. "These were her favorite. I planted them here, as she lay dying in this very same hospital. The same hospital where all your relatives have died."

I will not react, I commanded myself, because I knew that's what he wanted from me. I had never before realized how much effort it took to hold myself completely still. Asheroth played with his flower and watched me with his diamond eyes until shadows crackled across my skin, sharp and far colder than the winter wind. He smiled at me as I tried not to shake and watched the shadows break over me like waves.

"They brought you such comfort, before. Even then you looked like her. You stared at them while your mother lay dying like they were the last touch of color in the world. I went back across the sea to get one for you."

"For as long as that," I said to the wind. I didn't know what to think anymore. "You've been watching me for as long as that." Against my wall, I dared not move. Asheroth stood mere inches from me now.

"Longer," he said. He slipped the rose, thorns and all, into my hair where he fussed over its placement for several long, silent moments. "Your Logan, too, although you're vastly more interesting. And by interesting, I mean troublesome. If you believe in Guardian angels, I'm the closest thing you have."

Thorns dug into the delicate skin behind my ear. I told myself that explained the sudden rush of tears. I shook my head wildly, denying it. "Ethan will come," I half hissed, half sobbed. As I said it, I realized I really believed it. "Not for me, but for Logan. He's his real Guardian, not you. And I'll fight you too," I whispered. "I have shadows from the Dark Realms, and Light if I try really hard, and Ethan left me his armor. I probably won't win, but I'll die trying before I'll let you take my brother's soul."

Asheroth's diamond eyes blazed until they burned twin sunspots into my retinas. "He left you in worse danger than when he first saw you, Caspia. With powerful enemies and shadows you can barely control." As he spoke he grew angrier. His voice climbed to a yell and twin voids of darkness began to unfurl on his back. "Did you mean for the shadows to crawl across you like that? We both know the answer is no. What Ethan'i'el showed you is forbidden to human descendants of Nephilim. It makes you very dangerous, to yourself and to the Realms. They will hunt you now, Caspia, both the Light and Dark. If the shadows you summon don't swallow you before you learn control." Between one breath and another he moved from right in my face to the middle of the courtyard, fully formed planes of darkness behind him like hungry broken windows with jagged glass teeth. "He taught you just enough to get you killed," Asheroth spat, disgusted. He clenched and unclenched his fists, a vision of blood-red fury. "And guess what? I can't even kill him for it because he's already as good as dead."

Asheroth's beautiful pale face twisted into a murderous sneer. I looked down to find that he held both my hands in one of his, my wrists spanned easily by his encircling fingers. I realized the unintelligible stream of cursing and pleading came from me, demanding answers in between calling Asheroth all kinds of names. He simply held me until I calmed down enough to form coherent statements. "You mentioned trouble," I pleaded. "Is Ethan in some kind of trouble? Is it because of me? Please. Tell me what you can."

"E'than'i'el expected to be cast out to join the ranks of the Fallen." Asheroth looked grim. "He wanted this. He could be with you then. But that's not what happened. I don't know what went wrong. I have long been banished from the Realms of Light. I know only that he has been sentenced to die instead. I can only assume your shadow stealing was discovered."

"My shadow what? Why?"

Something like sanity flitted across Asheroth's face. "Because you are a weapon now. There was an army once, long ago, of Nephilim offspring. They were powerful enough to threaten the Realms. The war almost destroyed humankind."

"But you've seen for yourself," I protested, feeling sick and dizzy all at once. "I don't know what I'm doing. I'm no threat."

"I know that. Others of our kind do not."

I sank down to the cold, bare ground. Asheroth still had my hands and I didn't care. I actually wanted him to take me. There was nothing left; both the men I cared about were dying. I had nothing now. Nothing. Let some demon Nephilim come for me. I no longer cared.

When the vine-choked Virgin Mary statue shattered under the weight of Asheroth's fists, I realized I had spoken out loud.

"I hope you didn't kill the roses," I heard myself say. The sky started spitting icy rain again. I made no move to keep it off me.

He crouched in the middle of the wreckage, his leather-clad arms pulled tight around his knees. The black void had disappeared and he stared up at the rain-gray sky without blinking. Devoid of cruelty, his face free from lines of pain or insanity, he looked about my own age. If I met him without the forces of Darkness at his back and blood red leather armor, he looked like someone I might actually talk to. Then he turned to look at me with eyes like white Christmas lights, and the brief illusion of normalcy vanished.

"I am so bad at this, Caspia." His whisper was so faint I wondered if I imagined it. "But I am trying. I know what I am. Dangerous and mad and lost. I hurt you. I will do it again, whether I want to or not. I have been lost for too long to come back easily. But there is no one else now. I'm trying, and so must you. Terrible things are coming for you, and your brother too, and you are all I have left of her. You must let me guard you now, in my mad and terrible way." Tears the exact color of his eyes fell into the wreckage at his feet. He didn't brush them away.

"But then you understand," I tried to explain. "You lost someone too. Logan won't be with us much longer. Any day now, the doctors said. And then…"

I found myself at the foot of my brother's hospital bed dangling from Asheroth's fist. He held me several inches off the floor; his fingers twisted into the fabric of my jacket, shaking me like an unruly puppy. "For the last time, Caspia. I said I would guard you both. I do not guard corpses. Use your brain." He let me go abruptly. I caught myself on the bedrail, stomach churning from the abrupt spatial displacement and face burning with anger.

"What the hell is that supposed to mean?" I yelled, rubbing my throat where my jacket, bunched in Asheroth's hand, choked me. Yelling might restore some of my lost dignity. Failing that, it at least made me feel better. But when I whirled to confront him, Asheroth was gone. A hospital intern stood just inside the doorway, staring.

He looked afraid of me; they all did, the interns. I'd punched one of them the day they took Logan off those machines, and then clawed another one when someone stabbed me with a needle full of sedative cocktail. I eyed him speculatively. Had it been him? This one had big dark eyes fringed with lashes wasted on a boy. Too bad I couldn't remember. My memories of that night were… fuzzy. "Dr. Ensforth and Dr. Hildebrand are on their way," he blurted out.

I struggled not to grab him by his white jacket. "Both of them? Where?"

"They're waiting for the rest of Mr. Chastain's treatment team in their offices," he managed to get out before I really did grab him by the white jacket. I ignored his protests and tried to ignore the icy fear crawling up my neck; so many doctors hadn't gathered in Logan's rooms since the night they pulled his tubes.

Please, I caught myself repeating, over and over, deep inside myself. Please. I wanted to ask but was afraid of the answer. Why didn't the idiot intern just tell me? Was he afraid I'd break his neck? Shoot the messenger? I spared a quick glance at his pinched pale face and realized yes, that was probably exactly what he was thinking.

You have to stop this, said a clear, calm voice inside me. The anger, the running, and the hate: it's killing you, and making everyone else miserable, and none of it will bring them back.

I stopped and turned my back on him. The dead little garden with its smashed statue stared at me from the window. "It won't bring either of them back. Not Logan. Not Ethan," I whispered, and leaned my sweaty forehead against the cold glass.

"Miss Chastain? Are you… all right?"

"Just tell me." I wondered if I sounded as tired as I felt. "Tell me what's coming for us. I didn't think I was strong enough, before." I closed my eyes and let the glass carry most of my weight. "But now I don't think it matters."

Silence, for a long moment. And then the poor intern, whom I'd snapped at, grabbed, and probably punched or clawed several days before, took me gently by the shoulders and eased me back from the full-body chill of the winter window. "We all know how hard it's been, and I know you doubt yourself for sticking it out sometimes." My eyes popped open in surprise. "But it's been worth it, Miss Chastain. It's not bad news. Your brother seems to be a little better. His vitals are a bit more stable. The treatment team is trying to understand it. I'm sure they can explain it better than me." He gave me a lopsided smile like a badly wrapped gift. "It's not a miracle, exactly. Just plain old good news."

I whirled on him, right there at the foot of my brother's bed, and caught him up in a tight, smothering hug. "That's miracle enough for one lifetime," I all but whispered. Asheroth's creepy explanation made more sense now; I hadn't trusted it before. I don't guard corpses. Use your brain. But that meant that other dangerous things would be after us now, things even mad Asheroth considered a threat. I shuddered. I would worry about that later. My eyes felt heavy with unshed tears. The intern was actually halfway out the door before I realized he was leaving. "Hey!" I called back. "I don't even know your name."

"It's Dylan," he said, that lopsided smile still plastered on his face. "I'm the one you punched."

I winced. "Ooh. Sorry."

He shrugged, like girls hit him every day. Maybe, in his line of work, they did. "No big deal. You've got one wicked left hook."

"That," I told him, smiling, "is entirely my brother's fault. He taught me." My cheeks felt tight, and I wondered when the last time was that I smiled at anyone like that. "Dylan was my father's name too," I said, softly. "Mine's Caspia."

"I know. Caspia the coffee girl." He looked as if he wanted to say more, but didn't. He left me like that, with his goofy gift of a smile, as I waited to meet my brother's treatment team and hear what their esoteric definitions of "getting better" meant.

Anything that involved the words "Logan" and "not dying," I told myself fervently. That's what getting better meant. Anything at all.

CHAPTER TWENTY-FIVE

LIFE SENTENCE

Not until you tell me what's in it," Logan grumbled from his hospital bed, then sealed his lips together. Tightly.

Even from my mud-colored vinyl cushioned chair in the corner, his entire bearing reminded me of a petulant four-year-old. Amberlyn apparently thought so, too. She sat right on the bed with him, holding a steaming bowl of soup prepared by Mrs. Alice's own hands. "Snitches and snails and puppy dog tails," she taunted, waving a steamy spoonful at him.

Half his mouth twitched, fighting a smile. "I'm pretty sure that's not how it goes."

Mr. Markov and Mrs. Alice exchanged looks of pure exasperation, which was quite a feat, considering one of them was blind. "Things that are good for you," Mr. Markov announced in his thickly accented smoker's growl. He managed to make even a simple statement sound like both a promise and a threat. "Which you will eat without any foolish whiny business. As a man should."

Mrs. Alice snorted.

Amberlyn ducked her head, pretending to study the bowl of soup to hide her smile at their banter. The two had been spending a lot more time together since Logan's accident. They were regular visitors to the hospital, of course. Only Logan and I knew they were working together to find the mysterious collector who'd managed to breach Mrs. Alice's wards and was presumably still a danger. But working together seemed to draw them closer together in other ways, too. Mrs. Alice often took breakfast at the coffee shop, and Mr. Markov always held her arm protectively when they walked together. Which was often.

But then again, maybe there was just some kind of Whitfield wizard war going on I knew nothing about, and they had temporarily joined forces. Would they tell me? Would it be rude to ask? For about the hundredth time this week, I wished for some kind of supernatural rule book. If Ethan was here…

I collapsed in on myself. He wasn't. Deal with it.

"Mushrooms," Amberlyn said. "Shitake, I think."

"Mmm," Logan mumbled, refusing to open his mouth.

My best friend and my brother faced off across a snowy white expanse of hospital sheets. I didn't know who to put my money on; Logan, with his sternly crossed arms, or Amberlyn, with her outrageously cute wrinkled nose. Then she lifted the spoon menacingly. "Your mouth or your lap. Your choice."

He took the bowl from her.

"Mmph," Logan said, through a mouth full of soup.

I wondered if there were any spells on the soup. If so, were they Light or Dark? Was there a Neutral setting? Did I even care? Mrs. Alice looked up suddenly and winked at me. I smiled weakly back.

"Tired, dear?" she asked. I shrugged, deliberately not answering.

Truthfully, I was exhausted. I had actually fallen asleep leaning against the elevator yesterday. While it was moving. Dylan the intern found me and quietly, but firmly herded me back to good old room 213 and threatened to sedate me again if I didn't get some sleep. "I already know you fight dirty," he'd teased. "I have five older sisters and I have no problem hitting girls if it's in self-defense. Or," he shrugged, grinning, "you could just come quietly and get some sleep."

I went quietly with Dylan. I slept. For what felt like five minutes.

"You should go rest, Cas," Logan said quietly. "You know everything's okay here."

He was right. One of the reasons for Mr. Markov and Mrs. Alice's visits had been to place layer after layer of wards on room 213. It was now impervious to attacks of all kinds, and even some casual visits. I'd discovered it kept out at least some types of angels when Asheroth appeared in the threshold one day, furious but unable to enter. He beat his fists against an invisible barrier before resorting to pacing back and forth, giving me dark looks and muttering to himself. Eventually he realized this meant we were both safe and went away. Unfortunately, the wards were so good we also hadn't been able to hear him. Only later did we realize he hadn't been muttering at all. Asheroth's aborted attempt to get into Logan's room had been accompanied by a full force screaming fit. Some of the staff was still scandalized about the strange man with the horrible language who'd come to visit. It might have been funny if I wasn't so exhausted from being terrified all the time.

"Maybe," I conceded. I could call out for Asheroth if I felt threatened between here and home, which was warded even tighter than the hospital. He might come, and he might or might not still be mad about the wards on Logan's room. Either way, I had the shadows. I had Ethan's jacket.

Ethan.

His name finally broke me. Almost two weeks had passed since Asheroth first delivered the news in the garden. I had done a good job not thinking about him. But suddenly his loss hit me like an intense physical pain. I made my hands into fists and dug my nails into the soft flesh of my palms, hard. The sharp bite held the tears back. I wondered how long it would last, this temporary reprieve from my long overdue nervous breakdown.

I shot up out of my chair and practically lunged for my knapsack. I avoided looking at anyone while I dug around for the essentials: keys, wallet, and phone. "Right. So. I'm going to go grab a nap." I slung the bag over one shoulder and hugged Logan tightly, but carefully around his neck. "You be careful," I whispered. "I don't care what you say. It is some kind of miracle. It has to be."

He pulled me even tighter to him. We clung to each other like that for several long moments. "Natural remission," he insisted stubbornly. His words came out thick, coated with the shared but silent understanding between siblings. "The cancer is still there. Just because it's going away on its own, without the drugs and treatment, doesn't mean it's a miracle. Just because the doctors can't explain it doesn't make it a miracle." He meant: I don't want to get my hopes up, or yours, only to have them snatched away.

"My body still has to fight it. It's going to take time and work to make me healthy again, Cas." His dark eyes were serious, so serious, but they were all Logan and no imminent death. The tears started building. I wasn't going to make it out without breaking down.

"But you're not going to die," I whispered against his scratchy cheek. He needed to shave. He needed to shave because he had hair again. He had hair again because he wasn't being pumped full of cancer killing chemicals. I sobbed and rubbed my cheek against his, hoping his rough face would rub mine raw.

He laughed, short and fierce, pushing me away so he could hold me at arm's length. "Caspia." He gave me his wonderful crooked big-brother smile that proclaimed my utter stupidity even as it told the world nobody could pick on me but him. A ragged animal sound got caught in my throat. I really had to get the hell out of room 213 before I lost it and cried like a grown man at his daughter's wedding. "Cas," he repeated. "Of course I'm dying. Everybody is. Death is a life sentence. Didn't you know?" He kept his voice light, teasing me, but the warning traveled between us as surely as if we shared synapses.

A temporary reprieve is all any of us ever have. So don't waste it, dumbass.

"Nap," I mumbled, and ran like the coward I am.

Chapter Twenty-Six

Human

Inside a sterile environment like a hospital, even with occasional forays to gardens and corner markets, things like weather often pass unnoticed. I felt like most of my autumn had been stolen from me. Somehow, the weather had skipped straight to winter. And winter in the Deep South is usually miserable. It rarely snows; instead, we have a kind of dismal gray rain that feels like ice but isn't. Nope. Ice would at least give us a chance of some school closings, or maybe sledding down a hill. Instead, we have a kind of foggy damp chill that settles across the entire landscape and even manages to sink into the bone.

I was completely unprepared for the weather. The rain poured down in a steady icy stream. My hair clung to my face and neck, sending frozen rivulets down my back, soaking me to the skin. My jeans and tennis shoes were completely waterlogged. I had nothing but my indestructible leather jacket and the largest cup of coffee I could find at my work. I wrapped my frozen fingers around it, Amelie's effusive greetings still ringing in my ears, wanting desperately to drink it down to drive the chill from my bones as I sprinted from the Coffee Shop to my apartment. I didn't dare, though. Drinking it would drain precious warmth desperately needed by my frozen fingers. If I couldn't unfreeze my fingers I wouldn't be able to unlock my front door and I would freeze to death in my own stairwell.

I sniffed. Hazelnut. A tiny sip wouldn't rob my fingers of too much warmth.

I ducked into the alley that ran perpendicular to the hardware store and my apartment above it, plastering myself flat against the wall while I drank. Precious caffeinated sunshine made it past my lips, promising life and warmth.

That was when I saw it.

I hated to call it an it, but I couldn't determine its gender, hunched over as it was in a corner of the alley. It didn't move. Homeless people in Whitfield were rare. I had never met any. I clutched my hot coffee and wondered what the protocol was. Call the police? Some kind of charity? But which one?

The huddled figure shivered violently and I silently cursed myself. How long had the person been there in this weather? Maybe I'd better call an ambulance instead. I started toward the person, but checked my steps at the last moment as an ugly thought occurred to me.

What if it was some kind of trap?

My apartment was warded. Logan was safe in a warded hospital room. Yet here was a helpless looking person right outside my door. Where I was completely alone. I inched slowly backward. The huddled figure shivered again, more violently this time. I felt terrible. If this was a trap, it was a really cruel one. "Asheroth," I whispered. Nothing happened. "Asheroth," I hissed, a little more loudly. I didn't know what else to do. My insane Fallen tormentor hadn't given me any guidelines for how to reach him in an emergency. Meanwhile, the possible homeless person slumped forward across its knees, shaking. Was it moaning, too?

Bloody hell.

I waited, getting steadily colder, realizing I would have to ditch the coffee completely if I was attacked and had to pull shadows. I waited some more. When nothing happened, I darted down the alley to the huddled figure in the corner. I could just make out a patch of wet dark hair through arms crossed protectively over its head. It wore a large green and black flannel shirt and jeans. I realized, to my mounting horror, that he was barefoot. He was just too angular to be anything but male. I held out my coffee and prepared to run, wondering if Asheroth would come, and if he would help or hinder.

"I really hope he doesn't show up here. Say his name three times and he might," said the wet lump of humanity through blue-tinged, shaking lips. His skin looked pasty pale. His feet, when I looked more closely, were bruised and scraped, as were his hands. Several nails were torn and blackened. His clothes didn't fit at all. The shirt was huge and missing buttons. The jeans were ripped and looked as if they were much too short. His entire body trembled with the occasional violent quake. He looked worse than terrible, but he lifted his head and tried to smile.

It was a fragile, painful, human smile.

His eyes were the same blue-green glow that walked out of my sketch book weeks and lifetimes ago; that found mine in countless darknesses; that kept me from falling apart more times than I knew. They locked on me now, clear and searing and mine.

"Ethan," I said, his name temporarily sucking all air from the universe.

"Yes," he agreed, smiling hugely, as if he were not simultaneously freezing to death right in front of me.

"But you're… you're supposed to be dead," I said, still staring, as if he were a product of my fevered imagination.

"Yes," he said again, happily. He nodded toward my coffee. I gave it to him. His fingers refused to close around the cup. He shook so badly hot liquid splashed all over his hands. He winced. "I made a trade. My immortality for your brother's natural life span. I wasn't sure they would, at first, but they did it. They made me human. I'm going to die. Isn't it wonderful?"

It will take Light to bring your brother back, he'd said that night. The words were etched forever inside me. Take mine. And I had.

I stared at him. He looked like hell. Logan's words echoed in my head: Death is a life sentence. I stared at Ethan until I remembered I had forgotten to breathe again and that an immortal creature had sacrificed forever for someone I loved.

He was also exhibiting signs of insanity and hypothermia.

That jerked me out of my stupor. "Not yet you're not. Come on." I stripped off my black leather jacket and slipped it around his shoulders. He tried to protest. "Shut up," I snapped. "I'll take it back once we get inside. What the hell happened to you?"

"I was waiting for you. At first it was quite pleasant. Then it became cold and wet. But that only lasted a little while."

"What do you mean?" I asked suspiciously as I struggled to take all his weight. Ethan trembled against my side.

"I feel quite warm, actually. And sleepy."

"Oh hell," I swore. Hypothermia.

"You're mad," Ethan said dreamily. His skin was freezing cold and slick, like a catfish fresh from the river's deepest bottom. I struggled to haul him up the stairs. "I don't understand why. I've solved a number of problems."

"God you're heavy," I panted. I leaned with him against the wall on the second floor landing. He started to slide; I grappled for his arm, slinging it once again across my shoulder. "You have to hang on. Until we get you home." Ethan didn't respond. Head against my shoulder, he seemed to be falling asleep. I debated about calling 911 then and there, but my apartment was only one flight of stairs away. If he needed the emergency room, we could wait for the paramedics in warmth and comfort instead of on the cold stairwell.

When he didn't respond to gentle shaking, I slapped him.

"I thought being human would help me understand you," he complained as we began another climb. "You're clearly angry. You hit me. And yet I did everything you wanted."

I made sure I propped him right up against my front door. If he fell, it would be into a warm apartment. I fumbled for my keys. Cold and shock made my movements wooden. I was having a hard time seeing, too.

I realized why when a trembling wet finger reached for my face. "You're crying," Ethan said, horrified. "Why, Caspia?"

"Because you're dying!" I rammed the key in with a vicious shove.

"You don't want me because I'm a human," he said flatly, cold creeping inside his voice and eyes where before, he had always been light and warmth. "Because I'm going to grow older and die one day. That's why you're crying, and mad."

The door gave way as I twisted the handle; I didn't bother warning him. I didn't know if the wards would accept him anyway. We tumbled backward across the threshold, proving beyond a shadow of a doubt both his benign intentions and his utter mortality. I tried to spare his neck and head by wrapping my arms around them. In the end, I jammed one elbow badly enough to bring even more tears to my eyes, but managed to cushion Ethan's head against the worst of the impact. I lay half sprawled across him, my arms tight around his chest, a leg thrown across his while one hip dug into my inner thigh.

"You idiot," I said at last as warm air streamed over us both and my trembling increased to rival his. "I'm crying because I'm afraid you're dying right now, and I'm mad because you don't have enough sense to come in out of the rain."

He didn't say anything. He just pulled me closer and nudged the door shut with his toe.

What they say is true: the best way to share body heat is skin to skin. With Ethan shaking violently, suffering from hypothermia and countless other small injuries, and me completely terrified, getting warm as fast as possible was truly the only thing on my mind. Practically unable to stand up on his own, Ethan looked as lost as I felt.

I thought it would be easy with him, to strip off the cold clammy things that made us shake and tremble, and cling to each other for warmth. This was Ethan, after all. My Ethan. We'd faced death and madness and despair side by side. We belonged together. I'd stand on the square and declare it to the world. I'd steal all his best t-shirts and refuse to give them back. I'd fight demons and pull shadows for him.

And if any other girl so much as looked at him, I would end her.

We trembled. Our hands shook, reaching for each other, clumsy as things newly made. Something as simple as the act of undressing had become fraught with layers of meaning. Could we do this thing? Not just strip to our shivering skin, but stand before each other truly bare, down to the bone and even soul? He was suddenly, traumatically human, and I was… partly not. How could we navigate this strange new reality?

I burned with shyness, hardly able to look at him. Why this? Why now? Why so strangely shy when there was nothing motivating me beyond the desperate need to warm him? I tried for a button on my shirt, shaking like a junkie in withdrawal. He was hardly doing better; he looked as if putting clothes on had been a struggle, let alone taking them off when his strange new body fought him.

"I don't know how to do this," I finally admitted. "How to be human with you." I had managed the whole row of buttons down my shirt and one boot. The icy air slammed onto my stomach.

He looked worse than pained. He looked as if I'd taken his stars away and left him with the compass instead. And he was still shivering. As I was. His eyes, still the lightest blue-green, roamed my body from head to toe. I wondered what he saw through his newly human eyes. He considered my question for a long time, so long I became afraid of what he would say.

"Then let's not," he said at last.

"Let's not what?" I asked, dragging the word out with dread. Was this the part where he excused himself, decided he was in over his head, wanted to slow things down?

"Let's not be human together." Ethan sighed. His frozen fingers grappled uselessly with the edges of his flannel shirt. I had managed most of my buttons and the other boot. I moved to help him. My shirt gaped open between us, sticking to my arms as I grappled with his clothing. "We'll just be us." His tent-like green and black sodden shirt landed at my feet with a dull thud.

Oh.

Skin. My fingers fluttered toward his abdomen, almost against my will. Smooth and chilled, warming slightly under my touch, his skin felt nothing like a statue's anymore. I skimmed my palm gently, ever so softly, across the planes of his stomach and watched in mute fascination as the muscles retracted slightly under my touch. He could feel me, like I could feel him. He was sensitive now. My face warmed, and I knew I was blushing as I thought through some of the possibilities.

"Just Ethan and Caspia," I agreed in a whisper. Just the two of us, whatever we were and whatever we were becoming, were in it together. Nothing else mattered. Shyness, like buttons, became easier to navigate, now that there were two of us. "Tell me something."

"Mmm?" We were easier with each other now, relearning one another's bodies, our vulnerabilities and strengths. There is a kind of magic in touching. Mothers know, swaddling newborns or holding them close. Anyone who works with animals knows it, too; the best trainers communicate with their hands. Blankets replaced icy wet clothes around us as I grabbed a pile of thick chenille and plush microfiber, wrapping him tightly to me. The warm, dry coverings created a nest where our frozen skin could kindle slowly to warmth.

"My eyes," I murmured. There was nothing graceful about the way we held each other. We were awkward and frozen and feeling our way; Ethan's elbow dug into my ribs and his head trapped my hair. I thought about complaining, but his shaking hadn't stopped. I'm not sure he knew how to control all his movements yet.

"They've been silver since you found me," he told me through chattering teeth. "Like mercury."

I tugged the blankets tighter around him and wondered whether I should have called 911 after all. "My eyes have been flat gray since I lost you," I said quietly. "Like steel." I ran my fingers through his wet hair and down the curve of his neck. Breath, shallow and rapid, warmed my hand. Ethan was breathing. "I'm so sorry." A choking sob I couldn't hold back anymore escaped. "It's my fault. I know it is. You have to tell me what happened. Asheroth told me…"

"Shh," Ethan said, his chilled lips directly against my ear. Cold, but soft. I reached for him, greedy and desperate. But how fragile was my new Ethan? I forced myself to pull back. I didn't want to hurt him. I suddenly didn't know what to do with my arms and hands. Entangled as we were, I just kind of froze.

He laughed at me. "Not so fragile as that," he promised. "And I will tell you what happened. Just not now." He trembled against me, through our blanket wrappings. "Not here. Only the two of us, here."

Suddenly my heart was beating very fast. And so, of course, I had to know.

"Wait!" I practically yelled, startling him into stillness. I pushed him flat on his back. "I want to hear your heartbeat." I seized his hand as I laid my ear against his chest. A slow smile spread across my face, and an answering one curled his lips. "Here," I said, lacing our hands together over his strong human heart. "Didn't you think to check?"

He shook his head, eyes wide with shock and wonder. "I didn't even think," he said. "All I could think about was finding you." He kissed my forehead. "Being with you. And I know I have a lot to learn."

"No, you're doing just fine," I protested, cocooning him in blankets again, pulling his slick skin next to mine. "A whole lot of people never learn to come in out of the rain."

We learned three things together, that first day of Ethan's humanity: skin warms skin, silver eyes light darkness, and our heartbeats measured time together, so that we knew we were no longer alone.

A Taste of...

Angels Edge

2

Darkness in the Blood

PROLOGUE

JACK

If they find you, find a crowd.

My father taught me that. We spent most of our lives on the move. With him, it never really felt like we were running from anything. He always managed to make me feel as if we were on some kind of never-ending adventure, the good guys who were always one step ahead of the bad guys. We were descendents of a bloodline that had once been protectors of our people. But the Nephilim blood had thinned in recent years, and gifts were weak or skipped entire generations. There'd been no serious need for our protection in centuries. Only a few of us remained, even less who knew of our history, or the true nature of our gifts.

We were a people on the brink of extinction, and my father traveled to forget.

I think he also traveled to forget my mother, who died when I was born. "We Nephilim are hard on our women," he would say, with rare bitterness. The truth of it tore at us both. For whatever reason, women with Nephilim blood were rare. If a mortal woman bore a Nephilim child, more often than not, she died.

"But why?" I demanded of my father. "Is it another curse?"

"Perhaps." He sighed. "When a Nephilim loves a mortal, someone always suffers for it." My father didn't like to talk about the past. Our past, especially.

But then, in a little town in upstate New York, the past and our enemies caught up with us all at once.

In New York, Dark angels and the rebel Fallen swarmed our little house in the woods. Dozens of them against the two of us, and even still we might have taken them. But then they brought out our own people to fight against us. Gifted Nephilim descendents; people with gifted angelic blood. Our people, the very people we were supposed to protect, were fighting with the enemy against us.

When he realized, my father just… gave up. His head drooped in prayer or defeat or both. His blades hung slack in his hands. I could literally feel the fight drain out of him.

"Dad," I hissed, my back against his. "What's wrong? Are you hurt? Why'd you stop fighting?"

"They're not interested in fighting us, Jack," he said. I'd never heard him sound so old. "Not really. They will fight if they have to. But they'd rather collect us. Especially you."

"What the hell are you talking about?" *He must be hurt*, I thought wildly. I'd have to fight for both of us. I wove a shield of Shadows around him.

"Jack. Listen. There's not much time." My father pressed Azazel's blade into my hands. Azazel was one of the first to Fall and choose life with a mortal. He loved his bride as only an immortal can, and taught their children weaponry, Shadows, and prophecy. When his beloved died, as mortals must, Azazel made one last special blade. Unlike any other on earth, it had the power to kill angels, Dark and Light alike, cutting through their stone skin like flimsy paper. Only his oldest son knew the secret of its making. Then he used it to cut out his own heart, for he would not walk the earth without his wife beside him. His descendents, my ancestors, have been stuck with it ever since.

That's my bloodline: tragic and deadly, like the blade itself. I didn't want to take the damned thing, but Dad wrapped my wooden fingers around the hilt as he spoke. "There's only been one time Nephilim descendents fought with the Fallen. Only one reason they would fight their own kind. Think, Jack. Remember your history."

I gaped at him for precious seconds. "You mean if they were forced to. Because of another war. Against the Realms? But… how? Why?"

He shook his head impatiently. "Doesn't matter now. War is coming. You have to find the other gifted descendents and warn them. Protect them if you can." He touched the long, curving blade. "Keep this from falling to them."

Do people ever feel ready, when responsibility suddenly passes to them? I didn't. I felt like I was about five years old. "But Dad," I protested. "If they get you…"

He was steel as he shoved me. "They won't get me." No softness at all as he spoke of his likely death. For a while I resented this clipped goodbye. Now I'm grateful. I have no tearful, drawn-out last scenes of my father to weaken me in this place. Love is hard and unforgiving. It's better that way.

"Dad…" I tried again.

"Go. Don't look back. Don't stop."

I didn't.

It was months before they found me again, but eventually, they did find me. We burn brightly, if you know how to see.

Find a crowd. My father's instructions cut across the fear-tinged anger that gripped me as I scanned the run-down building. It was packed with bodies and throbbed with sound. The Nick was one of the oldest, nastiest, best places to hear bands in Birmingham. Rumor had it that blood, sweat, and spilled beer were the only things holding the bricks together. Tonight the building was full beyond capacity; the Dexateens were breaking up, and this was their last show. I wondered if the bouncers would let me in, if the place could possibly hold one more body.

The cold, black abyss of the Fallen opened on the street behind me. They were so near. I brushed the bouncer's arm with the faintest touch of Shadow. I hated compelling mortals, but he had to let me in. There was too much at stake to let myself be captured now.

He didn't even ask for ID. Good. I was underage anyway.

I exchanged the soul-sucking emptiness on the street behind me for the press and heat of screaming, gyrating bodies. Drunken humans fell on me, spilling their beer, yelling song lyrics I didn't recognize in my ears. This was their night, their band's last stand, and I just hoped I hadn't brought something worse than death among them. Two of the Fallen waited on the street outside the club. Would they wait until I left to spring their trap, or would they risk exposure and slaughter by coming after me?

At the bar a pot-bellied guy shoved a beer in my hand. "Anna Lee!" he yelled, pounding me on the back.

"No, Jack," I corrected. So what if he'd called me by a woman's name. I was carrying a lot of knives. It was easy to be forgiving when I could have killed him in the space between breaths.

"Anna Lee-ee," he continued, and I realized it had something to do with the band, with a song.

"Yeah, whatever," I said, taking the beer. "But the name's still Jack."

This revelation startled him. "Dave," he said, pounding on the sweatshirt that covered his gently swollen belly like a sail. His hair was closely cropped, perhaps to hide the fact that he was going bald, so I was a little surprised when his face crumpled like a sad little boy's. It was easy to forget that for most people, life went on. They were completely ignorant of the war between the Light and Dark. "I can't believe it's their last show. I love these guys."

"Yeah," I agreed, although I'd never heard them before. Inside the club, among the press of humanity, I wasn't so worried about being murdered by the Fallen. I could tell the band's reputation was deserved. "Sucks."

"Dexateens rule!" Dave yelled, and crushed me to him in a giant bear hug. I was too stunned to move. He clearly had no idea just how many knives I was carrying underneath my leather jacket. "Dude. Nice jacket. Aren't you hot in here?" Dave yelled above the music.

"Yes," I said, and deliberately turned my back. I couldn't tell him that the only way I'd take this jacket off would be if I was fighting for my life and losing. I needed to slip into the Dreamtime. I needed to find out what went wrong that let two of the Fallen find me. I needed to check on the gifted Nephilim descendents who hadn't been captured.

The bar was as good a place as any, in a venue this chaotic. As the first Nephilim descendent gifted with Dreamwalking in several hundred years, I could step in and out of sleep as quickly as diving into a pool. I propped my head up on my arms and fell into the still dark Dreamtime almost instantly.

Just as quickly, I found her. The little girl slept behind high fences in a wealthy Birmingham suburb, complete with sprawling lawns and all the safety her mortal father's money could buy. In sleep she burned brightly. No fighting capabilities, but then she was still quite young. She was so remarkably gifted with animals that she could sense their spirits and speak with them.

My father's warnings came back to me:

Women with gifted blood are rare.

I'm supposed to protect them above all others.

Young, helpless, and female, this sleeping little girl made the perfect bait. And I'd fallen right into their trap.

In the Dreamtime, Fallen angels surrounded the girl, ready to pounce the second I came near her. Even worse, they'd tracked me here. More had joined the two who waited on the sidewalk. I wouldn't be able to help the girl or my real target: the young woman to the north, the artist who could summon Shadows.

I'd seen her in the Dreamtime, sleeping with an orange cat and a restless young man. Caspia, the last Azalene, besides me.

Of all the Nephilim descendents still free, the young woman was by far the most important. Since my father died… I shut down the thought. It had been a surprise to find another descendent of Azazel's line. She was the only other one of us gifted with Shadows, but she was wildly untrained. If she fell to the Dark Realms, given enough torture and time, she could become their perfect doomsday weapon. I was on my way to her when I realized the little one was in danger. I hadn't seen the trap until it was too late.

The bartender gave me a hard look when I woke, so I stuffed another bill in the jar before sliding into the crowd. Dave the pudgy Dexateens disciple saw me coming and tried to push his way toward me. I ignored him.

I would have to fight the Fallen if they were still waiting. I tried to recall an alley, a parking lot; anyplace I could draw them where there would be few mortals. The packed club would be a disaster of epic proportions. So when I saw them slide through the door in a pool of darkness, unnoticed by the bouncers, I reviewed my very limited options.

Underneath my jacket, I wore nothing but tattoos and blades. The tattoos were weapons, of a sort; the symbols channeled and amplified the Shadows. They're the only things that give mixed bloods an edge in a fight against them. Angels can't bear them; their skin is hard as stone. I inched my jacket open just enough to reveal my ink and Azazel's blade.

Their reaction was gratifying.

"Not here," the one in snakeskin hissed. "You wouldn't dare."

"Don't make me," I said softly.

Something ancient, evil and cold unfurled at my back. A portal opening. My fate reflected in the Fallen one's eyes because even they were afraid of the Dark creature materializing at my back. Only something very ancient and powerful could make the symbols on my skin burn in warning. I knew before I turned that it was too late, much too late for me to help anyone. The trap had closed around me. I could only hope that I would survive in the Dark Realms long enough to find the others and a way out.

Poor drunk Dave made his way through the crowd carrying two beers. A surge of admiration for the man rushed through me, followed quickly by fear. Things were about to get very, very strange if Dave was lucky, deadly if he wasn't. I lunged for him, Nephilim-quick. The blade was out of its sheath and wrapped in my jacket before he dropped the first beer. I shoved the bundle at him before he could drop his second, slicing one of the tattoos on my forearm and smearing blood across his forehead. I whispered instructions in his ear as the crowd around us panicked. The darkness unfurled behind me, the wing-shaped voids. There was so little time, and then I would have to fight. Die, maybe.

"A small town north of here. Whitfield. A family named Chastain. Give it only to them, or someone pledged to their protection. It's more important than your next breath. Say it." Dazed, poor fat drunk Dave repeated everything I said. I hated myself as I pushed him backward into the panicking crowd. I had just placed him under a blood compulsion. He would do whatever I asked him or die trying. It was the best I could do to protect the weapon, to protect the girl.

I turned to face the ancient evil that had trapped me at last. I recognized him, thanks to my father's endless lessons. His empty eyes gave him away. "Belial," I said with a calm I didn't feel. Among the first of the Rebels. One of the most ambitious to Fall. "You have nothing, no one, to threaten me with."

"There are all these people, Jack." He twisted the words into a mocking taunt. "Can you imagine what will happen to them if you don't come with me?" He leaned against the wall with a self-satisfied grin. I didn't have to turn to feel the rising panic. So far, only the people in our immediate vicinity realized anything was wrong. That could change in a heartbeat.

They closed in on me, an ever-tightening ring of Darkness. Belial's blank eyes were fixed on the stage, but I could feel every inch of his attention on me. Armed with nothing but blades and Shadows, I could try and take out a few of the Fallen before panic overtook the crowd. It didn't matter much anymore. Belial had me, and he knew it. No matter what happened here, there was only one choice now: survive the Dark Realms, and get out.

Survive. Escape. Find the girl and fight back.

Unless he found her first.

CHAPTER ONE

CHASING PHANTOMS

I used to break out in a cold sweat when I was terrified.

These days, I break out in Shadows.

I squared my back against one of the sturdy trees of Blind Springs Park and stared up through its branches at the moon. Almost full and only slightly lighter than my quicksilver eyes, it cast just enough light to show the cold darkness snaking between my fingers and creeping up my arms. I closed my eyes and focused on calming my breathing. Dark electric fire crackled across my hands, racing up my arms and arcing across my neck. It felt like a combination of freezing water, marching ants, and someone slithering over my grave.

Once they appeared, only two things got rid of the Shadows: attacking someone or something, or calming down enough that they went away on their own. There was no one in the park but the crickets and me, so the attacking option was out. Lately, it took longer and longer periods of calm to make them go away. I was afraid the day would come when nothing I could do would banish them.

Asheroth had warned me. When Ethan was gone and Logan lay dying, he came to the hospital to warn me. "He taught you just enough to get you killed," the mad Fallen angel raged at me, furious with Ethan for unlocking such a dangerous gift. I hadn't believed my insane self-appointed guardian then.

I did now.

I forced myself to focus on my goal: find Asheroth, get help. Breathe, calm, focus. Find Asheroth and get help for Ethan. Ethan needed help much worse than I did. And Asheroth was the only angel I knew. He had to have answers. There was no one else.

I silently pleaded with the Shadows to stay gone as I stepped carefully away from my tree trunk. I'd been wandering Blind Springs Park for the third night in a row. Each night had been as unsuccessful as the one before. And yet, I couldn't quit hoping that tonight would be when I'd find him. "Caspia Chastain," I hissed as I walked, "when will you learn to be careful what you wish for? The only thing worse than not finding Asheroth might be actually finding him."

I sealed my lips together against the chilly air and crept closer toward the most deserted part of the park. The nearly full moon overhead cast ragged patches of light through the winter bare trees. I was deeply in, now; branches snagged my long tangled hair and snapped against the leather of Ethan's jacket. I could imagine what he'd say if he knew what I was doing.

"Are you crazy, sneaking through Blind Springs Park in the middle of the night? Alone? The same park where the Fallen attacked us just a few months ago? When you know there's still a demon after you? Are you trying to get yourself killed?" my imaginary Ethan raged at me.

Amazing how much Ethan and Logan could sound alike when my welfare was the topic of conversation.

"I'm not trying to get myself killed," I whispered, but I didn't sound convincing, even to myself. I was well aware that what I was doing was far from sane. I knew both Ethan and Logan would do everything they could to stop me. Why else had I snuck out in the middle of the night? "I've tried every other way I can think of to summon him, and nothing's worked." I drew a deep, shaky breath and rocked back on my heels, looking for landmarks. "I need him. We need him. Asheroth. He promised he'd help."

I needed Asheroth because the man I loved had sacrificed his immortality to keep my brother alive. By Ethan's reckoning, his sacrifice had been more than worth it. He got to live a mortal life with me, and Logan was recovering with a kind of speed and strength that amazed his doctors. So much so, in fact, that we'd checked him out against medical advice because we were afraid the doctors might decide to keep him for experiments.

But for Ethan, becoming mortal was turning out to be a painful, ongoing sacrifice. Even now, he slept restlessly, tormented by fever, headaches, and nightmares. His waking hours were a barrage of sensory assault as his body tried to process hundreds of new needs, sensations, and information all at once. His mortal body was strong, but completely alien to him. He had bruises from walking into things, and we had quickly learned not to trust him with anything sharp or breakable. After Ethan's second set of stitches, Logan and I had silently replaced all the dishes with hard plastic and wood.

Worst of all, he could feel the empty space where he'd once carried throbbing, pulsing Light. Like an amputee with phantom limb pains, the emptiness hurt him. He never spoke of it. He thought I didn't know. But the pain in his eyes burned bright, and when he slept his drugged sleep, he cried out for the lost Light that had served as wings. I watched him in the night, hating myself as I massaged his knotted muscles. Three nights ago, I'd finally had enough. I started sneaking out, looking for my mad, self-appointed guardian. I was desperate.

I needed Asheroth to tell me how to help Ethan.

I hoped Asheroth could tell me a way to change him back.

Ethan. Love. I'm so sorry.

It hadn't seemed like such a crazy plan when I'd dreamed it up in the warmth and safety of my apartment. I visualized the small clearing where I'd first met Asheroth months ago. He and two other of the Fallen had attacked Ethan and me. They'd tried to kill each other, and I'd learned about my own Nephilim blood when Asheroth kidnapped me. But none of that mattered now, because Ethan was mortal, and Asheroth had sworn to protect me from an even greater threat, a demon that hunted me.

"Asheroth," I called softly as I had the night before, and the one before that. "Are you there?" The wind picked up momentarily, as if in answer, snapping bare branches against each other and stirring the dead leaves at my feet.

Nothing.

"Hello?" I turned in a slow, tight circle, watching the trees for a flash of red leather. "It's Caspia. If you're there, I need you." A sudden blast of wind hit me from behind, whipping my hair around my face in all kinds of crazy directions. Momentarily blinded, I hugged myself against the chill. "I need help."

Still nothing.

Underneath the curtain of my hair, tears formed. My world was falling apart. I was being consumed by Shadows, Ethan's mortal life was pain-filled and confusing, and I had come to a deserted park for three nights in a row to beg a mad fallen angel for help. I didn't bother to wipe at the tears. At least Logan had found some peace; his recovery was going well, Amberlyn adored him, and he had his old job back.

"Flowers will grow there, in the spring. Silver ones like your eyes."

The voice was hesitant, even shy; it came from behind me. I would have recognized it anywhere. I froze, prey sensing a predator. It was my automatic reaction to him.

"What do you mean?" I finally asked when he didn't elaborate.

"Your tears," he said in the same soft tone as if he'd explained himself fully. Then, with an edge, "Why are you crying?"

There it was. A hint of the unpredictable anger that made him so dangerous. I wrapped my arms around myself and hoped I didn't erupt into Shadows. "I've been looking for you. For three days."

Before I finished speaking, I found myself staring straight into a pair of burning diamond eyes. Rough stone hands gripped me on either side of my ribcage, lifting me so that my feet dangled several inches from the ground and my arms flailed in the night air. I struggled for breath as he crushed me against his leather-clad chest. He stared at me like a fisherman who'd caught a water-breathing mammal. I stared right back: soot black hair, ghost-white skin, and a mad, cutting beauty that would haunt me until I died.

Asheroth.

"What has happened, that you would seek me so, Caspia?" he demanded, the pressure on my ribs increasing with his agitation. His bright eyes narrowed to slits although his voice stayed soft as mist. "You don't appear injured. Are you endangered in some other way?"

"It's… Ethan," I gasped out. My ribs screamed at me. "Please put me down."

"No," he suddenly snarled. He pulled me closer to him until our faces were only inches apart. "Tell me what he's done."

"Nothing," I growled back. As I struggled against his bruising hold, a cold electric darkness pooled in my palms. My fingers flexed automatically. "You're hurting me," I warned.

"You play dangerous games," he said, and dropped me. He regarded me coldly. But his hand lingered on my shoulder, caressing the leather I wore as if to check its integrity.

"I don't mean to. I only want your help." I didn't move from his touch. I was desperate for his help. For anyone's help. But the Shadows were out now, racing across my fingers. Asheroth saw them, and his cold look grew more severe.

"I warned you," he said. The space behind his back, where planes of Darkness served as wings, began to shimmer.

"Yes. You did."

"I could teach you. Someone must teach you before they consume you."

I ignored the electric cold creeping across my hands as best I could. "Yes, but not today. I need help with Ethan. He's hurting. Being mortal… it's agony, Asheroth. I didn't know. I don't think he knew, either." Tears formed as Asheroth gazed at me, still and unreadable. "Watching him… I can't bear knowing he's in that much pain because of me. I came to ask if there was anything to be done, either to make mortality easier on him, or…" I closed the distance until I stood almost nose-to-nose with the Fallen angel. "Or turn him back."

"Make mortality easier on him. Turn him back. E'than'i'el," he echoed flatly. "Not to teach you or train you. Not to keep you safe. He's the reason you creep through the night while evil hunts you."

"Please." I found myself leaning into him, both palms flat against the front of his red leather jacket. Shadows crackled and flared where I touched him. "Please," I repeated, softer this time.

He stared at my hands. "No mortal woman has touched me since she died." He covered my Shadow-pulsing hands with his own cold white ones. In a whisper: "I forget. You're not mortal, and neither was she. Not entirely. But close enough. Enough to be warm." He leaned in so close I was afraid he might kiss me, but then suddenly his hands were manacles around mine, his eyes so bright they burned. "Mortal enough to die."

He clapped one rough hand over my mouth and the other around my waist. Blind Springs Park vanished around us.

I'd forgotten how truly disorienting the abrupt spatial displacement could be. It had been months since I'd traveled this way.

Asheroth held me firmly. I sagged against him as I found myself staring at the front door of my apartment, sick and dizzy. His voice against my ear came fast as bullets and just as merciless. "You must learn to protect yourself, Caspia Chastain. Ethan cannot do it for you anymore. You will not accomplish that by chasing lost Fallen angels in the dark and off the path." He shook me so hard my teeth rattled. "I know you don't see it, but there are dark things roaming Whitfield. Powerful, ancient evils that would love a soft new thing to play with. Those Shadows you wear like cheap jewelry only call to them. You must be careful. If you let E'than'i'el tempt you into dangerous stupidity one more time I will kill him myself. Do you understand?"

When he let go of my mouth, I hissed at him, "If you touch him, I'll end you."

His hold on my waist remained steady. "When you can harm me, I'll worry about you much less." He beat on the door, three booming knocks I was sure would wake the entire apartment.

Asheroth worried about me? Right. "What the hell are you doing?" I hissed again. "You'll wake everybody up!"

"Your dwelling is too well warded for me to enter. Yet another reason why I'd prefer you were inside it this night. And yes, I'm rather counting on waking everyone. I think your brother and the other one should know what you've been up to. They don't, do they?" I pulled uselessly on his arm. Shadows crackled and flared against his jacket. "I rather thought not." He pounded on the door again, even more energetically this time. In fact, he seemed downright cheerful.

Stupid, insane Fallen angel.

The door flew open. Logan stood there wearing ratty sweats with a t-shirt hanging loosely from one arm. He'd tried to put it on and given up on the way. His hair had grown just enough to stick up wildly. Dark stubble covered a long red crease mark down the right side of his face. As he blinked rapidly in the bright hall light, his mouth fell open in surprise. "Cas? What the hell?" But then he took in my wild hair, tear-stained face, and the owner of the red leather-clad arm that held me, and surprise melted quickly into anger. He slowly twined the t-shirt around his fist. "Seriously? What. The. Hell." Logan shook off the last bit of sleep. "Let her go."

I loved my brother. Only he would try to use his dirty laundry as a weapon.

"I don't want her," Asheroth said haughtily, but I swear he sounded amused. "I found her wandering the park. I'm merely returning her to you."

"I am not a lost dog," I growled. I knew better than to hit him, but I was so mad I didn't care. I elbowed Asheroth in the ribs and yelped at the shooting pain that was my immediate reward.

"Then why haven't you released her yet, Asheroth?" Ethan asked coldly, steel lacing his words as Logan angled himself sideways to make room. Ethan's blue-green eyes were fever-sharp, but he held himself steady. "She doesn't appear to want you either."

"She's right here and quite capable of speaking for herself, thanks," I snapped as Shadows continued to pulse harmlessly from my hands against Asheroth's jacket. Logan and Ethan stared; exactly how out-of-control my Shadow-summoning had grown was yet another secret I'd tried to keep. Damn Asheroth, damn him!

"I was waiting for you, E'than'i'el-who-was. You look every bit as terrible as she said you did. I'm so glad. Since you're the reason our Caspia decided it was a good idea to go creeping about in the middle of the night, I thought I'd better see the extent of the damage for myself." He pulled me even tighter against him, pushing out all my air. "You were right, dear," he whispered theatrically as I turned white. "Mortality looks quite painful. How terrible to know he did it because he loves you. Perhaps you were right; maybe this really is your fault," he purred.

Son of a bitch, I thought. I couldn't breathe.

"Son of a bitch," Logan said, and rushed us. His warm human fingers closed over mine. I wanted to tell him no, to warn him about the Shadows, but I couldn't find words. My vision was graying out. Bare seconds after he grabbed my hands, the electric cold between us flared so intensely it seemed to burn, and Logan wasn't holding onto me anymore. I heard a dull thud as his back hit the wall.

Then Ethan was there, cradling my face between his hands. Pale and feverish, he stared straight into my panicked face. "It's going to be fine, Cas," he promised. "Asheroth. End this now. I won't ask again."

"How do you plan to do that, E'than'i'el-no-more? As much as I would enjoy destroying you, I think it might distress her."

Ethan never took his eyes off mine. He spoke two words I didn't know, two words in a language so full of liquid sibilance it was difficult to tell where one word ended and the other began. I didn't think the human tongue could produce such sounds. I knew instinctively I was listening to the language of angels. The effect on Asheroth was electric; he released me immediately, practically throwing me at Ethan with an inhuman snarl.

As Ethan's warm, strong, human arms opened to catch me, I had time to wonder just what two words had such power over mad Fallen angels. I gave myself roughly three seconds to catch my balance before rounding on Asheroth and demanding answers.

There was no sign of him. The hallway was empty except for the three of us. Logan leaned against the wall right next to our apartment door, looking winded and shaky. He waved me off when I started for him. Ethan held me gently by the arm instead. "Caspia," he said before I could ask about Asheroth. His calm, even tone masked a warning. "Did he speak the truth? Have you been wandering the park by yourself, trying to find help? For me?"

I bit my lip. I couldn't look at him. I didn't have to. He tightened his hold and pulled me back against him.

"You," Logan said severely, "are in so much trouble."

"I'm not a child," I announced.

My brother ran a hand through his spiky hair. He shook his head in disgust. "I'm going back to bed." From inside our darkened apartment, he shouted, "You. Trouble. Morning." His door slammed shut.

Ethan didn't say anything. His silence stung.

"I can't stand to see you hurting," I told the empty doorframe. "You don't say anything, but I know you are. And when I think about what you gave up…" I didn't realize I was crying until a warm hand, not my own, brushed my cheek. I half-spun on the ball of one foot until I could tuck my head underneath his chin. "You cry out for your… wings. In your sleep. It's too much. Asheroth only said what I was thinking. It's all my fault."

Cocooned in his arms, the bass of his reply vibrated through my bones. "It was a gift. I was glad to give it. I would do it again."

I let myself rest against his soft t-shirt. "How can you say that?"

"It was a selfish gift. I had a lot to gain. You." He pulled me into the darkened apartment. "Come to bed, Caspia. There's trouble to be in tomorrow."

CASPIA'S STORY CONTINUES IN...

ACKNOWLEDGEMENTS

I'd like to send a massive thanks to:

My students, especially Derrin, Will, and Siobhan. You all kept me motivated and (mostly) in touch.

My writer friends and critique partners-in-crime: Mandy, Alina, Gigi, and other members of the DC workshops; to Ann for her straight talk and encouragement; to the Indies, for kicking butt and taking names, especially Stacey Wallace Benefiel, Jeff Bryan, V.J.Chambers, Lauralynn Elliot, and Kait Nolan; Row80, for being the absolute best writer's group and support network this girl could ask for; to the team at Curiosity Quills: Courtney for her sunny disposition and effortless skill at juggling; Eugene for taking the "whaa?" out of all things technical; the amazing Lisa, without whom this book would not exist in its current form.

Music made my battle with the blank page a little less cataclysmic. To name a few (many of whom look dashing in a bunny hat): Joe Carver of Horse to Water, Glossary, Duquette Johnston/The Gum Creek Killers, The Only Sons, The National, The Moondoggies, Fleet Foxes, Black Rebel Motorcycle Club, Calexico… did I mention Glossary? I did? Imagine that.

To Grace and Max, who take their unconventional childhood in stride most of the time; to Tony for being the sane one (so far); and to Mom for, well, *everything*. You're the smartest, bravest, most kick-ass woman I know.

Lastly:

You have the best smile and the coolest hats. Before you I'd never heard The Beatles. You get it about the ocean. You suspect I actually do believe in magic. You're my best friend, you always believe in me, you still make me laugh, and the desire to smite women who look at you has not faded one bit. Daniel, thank you for everything.

About The Author

Vicki Keire grew up in a 19th Century haunted house in the Deep South full of books, abandoned coal chutes, and plenty of places to get into trouble with her siblings. She spent the last decade teaching writing and literature at a large, football-obsessed university while slipping paranormal fiction in between the pages of her textbooks.

Published works include the bestselling *Angel's Edge* series, which includes *Gifts of the Blood*, *Darkness in the Blood*, and *Blood Redemption*, *The Chronicles of Nowhere* series, and the stand-alone novel *Daughter of Glass*. She is included in the *Dark Tomorrows* anthology with J.L. Bryan and Amanda Hocking, and the *Primetime* anthology with *J.R. Rain* and *Anita Exley*.

When not reading and writing about all things paranormal, she enjoys other people's cooking and keeps vampire hours. She'd rather burn the laundry than fold it, and believes that when an author wins the Newberry, he or she gets a secret lifetime pass to Neverland. She is fond of lost causes and loud music. She currently resides in Central Florida on a lake-front farm full of many furry friends. She loves hearing from readers and can be reached on most social media sites or through her blog, of which she is awfully fond.

THANK YOU FOR READING

http://vickikeire.blogspot.com

Please visit http://curiosityquills.com/reader-survey to share your reading experience with the author of this book!

Darkness in the Blood (Angel's Edge, Book 2), by Vicki Keire

Caspia Chastain is finally coming to terms with the carefully buried secrets of her hometown and bloodline. But someone is kidnapping Nephilim descendents and using them to build an army. An unpredictable new gift threatens to consume her. With it comes a persistent dream: a strange young man with gifted blood who may hold the key to her ancestry.

Ethan has secrets, too. When his past catches up with him, it could tear their relationship and the Realms apart. Soon, Caspia and Ethan must discover if the light and life they've built together can withstand the gathering darkness.

Worlds Burn Through, by Vicki Keire

Chloe Burke has nightmares of a world burned to ash and the strange boy who saves them both. Underneath the dreams lurks a deeply buried reality; Chloe and a handful of others are survivors of a decade old apocalypse that burned their home world to the ground.

Now their ancient enemies hunt them again. To keep their adopted world safe, Chloe must undergo a ritual of blood sacrifice—that is, if her lethal protector, Eliot Gray, can keep her alive to do it. Together they'll uncover even more dangerous secrets buried in the past's deepest, darkest ashes.

The Gathering Darkness, by Lisa Collicutt

They say: "the third time's the charm" and for sixteen-year-old Brooke Day, they had better be right.

She doesn't know it yet but she's been here before—twice in fact. Though, she's never lived past the age of sixteen.

Now in her third lifetime, Brooke must stay alive until the equinox, when she will be gifted with a limited-time use of ancient power. Only then will she be able to defeat the evil that has plagued her for centuries.

Wilde's Fire, by Krystal Wade

Katriona Wilde has never wondered what it would feel like to have everything she's ever known and loved ripped away, but she is about to find out: her entire life has been a lie, and those closest to her have betrayed her. What's worse, she has no control over her new future, full of magic and horrors from which nightmares are made.

Will Kate discover and learn to control who she really is in time to save the ones she loves, or will all be lost?

Broken Forest, by Eliza Tilton

Hopeless he'll never be more than the boy who didn't save his brother, 17-year-old Avikar accepts his life as the family stable boy, trying to forget the past.

But when his sister, Jeslyn, is kidnapped, the thought of losing another sibling catapults him on a desperate quest. With his best friend by his side, and using the tracking skills he learned from his father, he discovers Jeslyn has been taken, kidnapped by one Lucino, the young lord of Daath, a mystical place thought only to exist in fables.

And Lucino has plans for Jeslyn…

Curiosity Quills Primetime – a Charity Anthology for No-Kill Shelters

Curiosity Quills Press brings together bestselling authors like **J.R. Rain**, **Tony Healey**, **A.W. Exley**, and many more to create a spine-tingling, mind-blowing, quirky collection of short stories in their first ever, annual Curiosity Quills: Primetime Anthology.

10% of every purchase will go straight to animals in need. The CQ team has selected humane societies on both the East and West coast that spend well and do not stray from their "no-kill" policies.

CPSIA information can be obtained at www.ICGtesting.com
Printed in the USA
LVOW08s1917100714

393763LV00009B/1164/P

9 781620 073599